# Linked Hearts

## Maria Secoy

All Write Well

# Also by Maria

**Romantic Suspense Fiction**

## TAYLOR INDUSTRIES:

Rural romantic suspense with international intrigue
Linked Hearts
Encrypted Hearts
Tracking Hearts
Guarded Hearts
Auditing Hearts
Hacking Hearts

## Twisted Willow:

Small town romantic suspense full of action & adventure
Gloria's Gumption
According to Cora
Beth's Absolution
Letting in Liz

## On-Trail Love Adventure:

Romantic suspense on the Appalachian Trail
Alongside Lucy
Standing by Stephanie
Crossing with Kiara

## Nonfiction

The Truly Successful Author
The Truly Successful Writer

# Dedicated

to Angel.
Your strength, resilience, and ability to laugh in the face of insanity constantly reminds me of the true meaning of life.

# Contents

# Prologue

**August 22, 2002**

I didn't want to be there. The director set the air too cold and the flower odor made me nauseous.

For some stupid reason, I put on pantyhose under my dress. I never wear them. I'm honestly not sure where the pair came from, but I found them in my drawer and pulled them on thoughtlessly. Within an hour, they had twisted around my thighs and pulled on my flesh while I smiled and pretended like I gave a fuck about the people around me.

For the record, I didn't.

I was there for my husband because I was a good wife, even when I hated the bullshit required of me.

Take Katrina Taylor, for example. She worked the room like a fucking princess at a ball thrown in her honor. All five of her kids were perfectly dressed, including eight-year-old Ophelia. Her sons acted like gentlemen as they escorted people into the room, ushering them up to the casket, and offering them seats. She arranged food for the day and ensured everyone had the transportation they needed, too.

If I had the choice, I would scrap this sham and spend the day on the couch watching movies. There's no reason to be here. The dead don't give a shit, and the living are lying.

"You must be getting thirsty. Here, I brought you some water." Katrina's smile was more cloying than the floral scent burning my nose.

"Thank you so much. Everything looks lovely." I glanced in the mirror over her shoulder to ensure my smile matched hers. No one could accuse me of being rude or ungrateful.

"It's such a tragedy. No one should die so senselessly." Her lips pulled down and her brow furrowed, but in a soft, thoughtful way that made me wonder if she's practiced the expression. I certainly practiced my version of that look. Then again, Katrina was perfect enough, maybe she didn't need to practice.

"Hmm, at least the casket is beautiful, and the portrait turned out nice." There's an art to disagreeing without contradicting others. I can't say this was how I expected to use my communications degree, but that's life. We hop on, hold tight, and hope for some thrills and laughter before it ends abruptly.

I did appreciate the water she brought me. I hadn't realized how thirsty I was until I started drinking. It also gave me an excuse to avoid her pitying looks by focusing on my glass. My feet were starting to hurt, but I wouldn't sit down. It wouldn't be proper, and I'm not one to embarrass my husband by showing weakness. Besides, it would likely twist my pantyhose even more. I wondered if nylon could twist tight enough for cells to die. Could they be performing a pseudo liposuction on my inner thigh fat as I stood there?

"Mom, can Joshie and I go play cards in the other room? The funeral guy said it's fine." Katrina's youngest son, Gabe, was the same age as Joshie, though the two boys were almost complete opposites in every other respect. Joshie was a thinker, quiet and peaceful. Gabe was a tornado who leaped and flipped and spiraled his way through life. Maybe it's because Joshie was an only child, while Gabe had three older siblings and a younger sister.

Katrina looked at me before responding but frowned with disapproval when I shrugged. Joshie stood silently behind Gabe.

"I suppose it's fine, but I want your brothers to keep helping people, okay?" Katrina said.

"They will. Thanks!" Gabe assured her before darting away.

I tousled Joshie's hair as he walked past me. He was a good, sweet boy, and his world had been turned upside down. I wasn't sure if he realized how much his life was about to change.

"What are Nathan's plans for the business?" I couldn't resist asking, even though I didn't want to know the answer.

Katrina sipped her own water nervously. It reminded me of the way adults look when children ask where babies come from. She had to know the question would come up, but choosing the correct answer for the situation was challenging and uncomfortable. It made me glad I'd asked.

Don't judge me. You'd likely feel the same if you stood in my shoes.

"Nothing is certain yet, but the venture capitalist is still interested in funding the project, and while we were here yesterday, Josh's old college roommate mentioned to Nathan that he'd be interested in stepping in and supporting the business side of the company."

She flashed a half grin of regret while searching the room for a reason to escape. Fuck that. The conversation was the best part of my day. I wasn't letting it go. Seeing someone so nice, so genuine and honest, squirm with discomfort muted my own feelings.

"Oh? Greg's interested in joining Nathan?" I asked innocently. There's so much Katrina didn't know, but it wasn't my job to teach her. For now, she could continue being naïve and sweet.

"Yes. Of course, I know they're talking about valuation and compensation to buy out Josh's share." Patrick, her oldest child, waved from across the room, offering Katrina the escape she'd been looking for, but she couldn't just walk away.

She turned and placed a gentle hand on my arm. "Can I get you anything else right now?" she asked.

I tried to look appropriately sad as I assured her that I was fine and shooed her away.

I should offer my condolences to the parents crying softly while clinging to each other as they sat in the front row of chairs and stared at the portrait of a middle-aged man who should be planning their funerals. I didn't though. They were both pompous, uppity snobs, and I had no doubt she'd find something to say about my outfit or my hair or my make-up.

There's a group of men wearing Tom Ford and Ralph Lauren suits huddled in another corner. If my mother were here, she'd have nudged me and told me to introduce myself, but she was with my husband while I was there alone. Watching Nathan and Greg join the well-dressed men dispelled any doubts I had about them being the venture capitalist people.

I turned away from them and faced the room's front, where the pecan hickory luxury casket was displayed. The latch closures hid the velvet interior and pleated head panel along with a few secrets. It's better for everyone to mourn the tragedy of a horrific car accident.

## August 17, 2023

*"The astronauts stuck in the broken ISS have been saved thanks to Taylor Industries' newest technology. Their team of artificially intelligent nanobots was able to locate, diagnose, and repair the issues."*

Each time I heard the report, my blood boiled faster. Yes, Russia had threatened war if we let their representatives die up there, but the news was supposed to report the whole truth—not pick and choose who to turn into a hero.

*"That's right, Craig. It's so great to see this kind of technology being developed right here in the US and used to save lives. Without these specially coded nanobots, we're told the astronauts had no way to repair the damage themselves. Could you help us gain a better understanding of what they are? I can't help picturing the little things from Big Hero 6. Should we worry about them taking over the world?" Mindy asked with teasing humor.*

I rolled my eyes. When did it become appropriate for journalists to joke about technology that threatened us all by comparing it to a children's movie? I forced my clenched jaw to relax. Just once, it would be nice to hear someone ask a pertinent question about who was being given power in this country.

I clicked off the TV and dumped my remaining soggy cereal into the trash with disgust. I knew the truth behind the Taylor's success. I knew the horror, backstabbing, and murder upon which their happy little media story was built. I knew because I was one of the survivors.

I kept my silence and made the best of my lot, but after twenty years, maybe it was time for that to change. I just needed access to their records to fill in a few gaps.

Considering my options, I started with a quick online search for Taylor Industries, which didn't produce much. With no social media and a website that looked like it was designed in the dot-com era, I'd have to get more creative. If I could just make that first connection, I'd find a thread to pull that would unravel everything.

# Chapter 1

Zach cradled his phone between his shoulder and ear, his other hand busy petting Fluffy and feeling her expanding abdomen. The crisp mountain air was still mostly silent, though a few birds and squirrels were braving the February cold.

"What do you want, Izzy?" Zach barked into the phone, his voice sharp enough to startle the alpacas. He immediately rubbed behind Fluffy's ear as an apology for stressing her out.

"I'm just checking in, seeing how you're doing out there in your little oasis." The shrill mockery in her voice made Zach wonder again how he'd ever thought marrying her was a good idea.

Still, it wasn't in him to be a jerk, so he took a deep breath and replied with a calmness he didn't feel. "I'm fine, Izzy. How about you? Still struggling to make ends meet?" He winced as the passive aggressive question slipped from his lips. It was the worst part of their divorce. Zach was known as the guy who'd give you the shirt off his back. He was nice and kind and thought the best of everyone.

Except Izzy.

He couldn't stop the bitter aggression that rose every time he heard her voice. Zach considered apologizing to her, but in the moment of silence before she responded, he could hear the gears turning in her head. Her next words didn't surprise him.

"Actually, I am. And I was wondering if maybe you could help me out with the mortgage this month. You really left me in a pickle when you just stopped paying your half."

Zach gritted his teeth, resisting the urge to hang up. "I don't have a half. We've been over this. I paid for the house while you stored my stuff there. Once I got all my stuff back, it became your responsibility. That was the deal." And it was a damn good deal. His lawyer had been furious that he hadn't insisted Izzy pay him for half the house, but Zach didn't need the money, nor did he care to fight. She'd been the one living in the house while he'd been deployed. It made sense to let her keep it or sell it or do whatever she wanted.

"I know, but things are tight right now. Just this once?" Her tone turned pleading, but where it used to make him feel needed, now he just felt used and manipulated. Zach tried not to allow his annoyance to come through in his words. "No, Izzy. You need to figure it out on your own. It's time to move on and take care of yourself. Maybe it's time to downsize or find a roommate. You have options, even if you don't like them."

A disgruntled huff came before her response. "You know I don't like strangers in my space."

Zach gripped the fence railing with all his strength as he fought to keep snide words about her willingness to allow their neighbor into her *space* and her bed the second he shipped out. It made it easier to ignore the pull he felt to give her what she needed simply because she was in need, and he could provide. It had taken him way too long to learn the difference between being appreciated and being taken advantage of.

"Take care of yourself, Izzy. I hope things get better for you, but you need to handle your own life."

"Zachary," she dragged his name out like a petulant child. "You'd really leave me homeless?"

"I'm not going over this again, Izzy. I don't have anything more to give you. If you're unhappy with the settlement, you'll need to take it up with your lawyer." Considering it had been three years since they signed the papers, he doubted her lawyers would even answer her calls, but that wasn't his problem.

"Uh, Fine. I hope you have a nice life or whatever, too. Bye."

The line went dead, and Zach leaned against Bertha's long, furry neck, feeling worn out from the conversation. "At least you were upfront about being needy and demanding," he whispered into her fiber as she snuffled his hair. It was time for him to prioritize his own happiness, even though caring for others had always come naturally to him.

His phone rang again, and he didn't bother to look before snapping, "Enough Izzy. You're not getting anything else from me. Stop calling."

"Yikes," Doc Ester's voice came across the line.

"Shit. Sorry, Doc." The vet was the closest person Zach had to a friend out here. She was older, direct, and tougher than most Navy SEALS Zach knew. She was also his best friend's aunt.

"Why does she even have your number?" But she continued before he could answer. "No, wait. I'm guessing she was worried about something or needed someone to talk to about something, and you volunteered."

Damn, Doc Ester knew him too well. He grumbled but didn't come right out and credit her with nailing it on the first try.

"Oh, Zach. When you find the right woman, she's going to be the luckiest girl in the world. You just need to make sure she'll appreciate you."

"Yeah, I hate to point this out, but at forty-three, I think that ship has sailed. That's why I'm raising alpacas, remember? I seem to recall you were the one who told me they're the neediest animals on earth."

"I wasn't wrong about that, but they don't give you everything you need," Doc pointed out.

Zach rolled his eyes. "Yeah, they also don't take everything I have while sleeping with my friend. I highly doubt you called to discuss my ex, so what's up?"

"I was just calling to see if I could swing by tomorrow to check on Fluffy. I can put that chip in your youngest as well."

"His name is Butthole, and I'm not changing it. It suits the jerk." Zach didn't see any reason for a cute, but misleading, name. Butthole was both what he ended up calling the alpaca and a fair warning to anyone trying to work with him.

Doc Ester sighed but didn't argue. "I've got a job out in the highlands that will have me further away than usual for the rest of the week. Do you want me to come by tomorrow? Are you seeing any changes with Fluffy yet?"

"Tomorrow's good. Aside from the way Fluffy's belly gets bigger every day, I think she's doing well. She's been walking around and eating. She's snippier than usual, and I thought she might rip Snowball to shreds when she got too close yesterday, but it's nothing extreme."

"Oh good, remember to watch for her refusing food. She might just pick a spot and settle down like Bertha did, or she might behave completely different." Doc had been there for Zach's first alpaca birth about a year ago. She had no plans to come unless there was an emergency. Instead, she was teaching Zach to handle it himself, which he appreciated. "I can wait to chip Butthole after I get back from the highlands, if that's better for you?"

Suddenly, Zach heard a twig snap and saw the young devil heading into the woods.

"Butthole," he yelled while holding the phone away from his mouth to preserve Doc's hearing. "You stupid animal. Get your ass back here."

Through the phone he heard Doc laughing so hard, he thought she might start crying. As soon as she could form words, she answered her own question. "I'll be out between five and six tomorrow. What are you going to do when you have more like him? Will they all get chips? Will you put up a big light board showing each of their locations?" Doc started laughing again as she spoke.

"Butthole might be my first cria born here, but Fluffy was the same age when I got her. She's always been happy to roam free while sticking close to the barn, and I've talked to several other alpaca farmers. They all agreed that Butthole is one in a million and assured me I won't have the same issues ever again," he said with a frown. Zach couldn't imagine having more than one Butthole. He also didn't like the idea of penning in his animals. Even if the space was huge, it didn't feel right.

Doc must have read his mind about the last part. "And you don't want to take away Bertha's porch privileges just because her son's a jerk. I know, I know. I've heard it all before, Zachary. That just means you'll have to keep hunting down your curious explorer," she pointed out. It was nice someone thought Butthole was hysterical.

Zach was starting to wonder if alpaca meat tasted good. He said as much, and she laughed even harder.

"I'll see you tomorrow, Doc," Zach broke in.

"Alright. Go get your alpaca before it's full dark."

"Yes, ma'am. And thanks, Doc. I appreciate you."

"You're a good man, Zach. Sometimes I wish my niece would have connected with you that way, but mostly I'm glad she had you as a friend."

"Friends and alpacas are all I need at this point in life." It was Zach's mantra since retiring.

"Have a good night."

"You, too." Zach hung up and decided to move the females of his herd into the barn before he went chasing after Butthole.

# Chapter 2

Veronica slammed the drawer of her desk shut before twisting to the other side to check the others. Where had the damned file gone? She knew she'd put it in the top right drawer. That was where she always put her Monday file.

She sighed with relief when she opened the bottom left drawer and spotted the pale blue file folder covered in doodles. She loved that her work only required in-person attendance on Mondays, but that came with no forgiveness for being unprepared. Every Friday, Veronica ended her day by compiling what she needed for her Monday meetings and placing hard copies in the folder. The folder was always stored in the same place so she wouldn't have the stress she was currently experiencing.

Having pulled the folder out, she plopped into her chair and took a moment to breathe. Inhale through the nose. Exhale through the mouth. There was no need for fear. She was probably over stressed and working too hard. That's why she kept losing things. She was not going insane. Bringing some social time and balance to her life would help.

Moving deep into Appalachia to claim her piece of her family's land meant leaving civilization behind, but a ninety-minute drive back to the city wasn't the end of the world. When her old high school classmate, Kurt, had asked her out, she expected they'd be going to the lone diner in town. His suggestion that they make it an adventure and meet in the city after he attended his own meetings worked out well, even if it meant going on a date on a Monday night.

They hadn't been close in high school, but that was almost twenty years ago. Even now, Veronica wasn't sure if this would turn into dating, be a one-night fling, or if they'd end up friends. There had certainly been sparks when they'd bumped into each other in town, but that didn't mean much.

Considering Kurt's work dragged him into the city anyway, and Veronica would be out and about going to her Monday meetings, they'd agreed Monday felt like less pressure than a Friday or Saturday. She hadn't said it aloud, but Veronica also thought it might be easier to convince herself to follow through. Or maybe it would be harder to chicken out.

She took one more deep inhale and a slow exhale. Then her phone rang. Since the screen said the call was coming from HQ, she couldn't ignore it.

"What?" she snapped as the call connected.

"Renner's joining us today. I didn't want it to catch you by surprise." Freddy's warning shocked her.

"You don't–" she stopped herself before accusing him of finding her discomfort entertaining. For once, he was being nice. "Thank you."

"Someday I want to know what happened on your date with him. The man still thinks a second date is going to happen. Do Patrick and I need to kick his ass?" Forgetting her younger brother couldn't see her through the phone, Veronica shook her head.

It had been six months since she'd gone on one ugly date with Brian Renner.

*Veronica flung open the restaurant door and burst inside, slamming into the host podium, which was much closer than she expected.*

*"Oh, sorry!" She took a few gasps of air to regain control of her breathing. "I'm meeting someone, but I'm late. Like really late."*

*The host chuckled before waving for her to follow. "You're meeting Brian? He said you'd likely be late and to show you to the table whenever you arrived. Right this way."*

*"Yes. I'm glad he's still here." Renner came into view as they turned the corner into a more private part of the dining room. Considering this was a date and not work, she should probably think of him as Brian instead of Renner.*

*"Veronica." He stood up to greet her. "I'm glad you made it."*

*She could feel the blush creeping up her cheeks. "I'm so sorry I'm late."*

*"I know you well enough to have expected it. I just arrived about ten minutes ago." His cocky half grin was enough for her*

*embarrassment to fade. Their date had been scheduled for forty minutes earlier. Brian had arrived thirty minutes late because he expected her to mess up. She forced the corners of her mouth back up to a smile, but a pit opened in her stomach. Renner was just like her brothers and her parents and everyone else in her life. He expected her to fail. It hurt.*

*"Right. Good. Uh." What was she supposed to say to that? Part of her wanted to argue that she'd just moved back home and had forgotten how long the drive was, but honestly, his lack of faith annoyed her so much she didn't care to continue with the date.*

*Renner was a nice guy, but she'd never felt any sparks with him. She'd agreed to meet him for dinner, hoping that might change, but the opposite was proving true.*

*"Here, I ordered you a club soda with lime, too. I know it's your favorite," Brian gestured for her to sit beside him. Soft jazz played in the background, and the aroma of garlic and herbs wafted from the kitchen.*

*"Thanks." Club soda with lime was her favorite, but Veronica wasn't impressed. Everyone she worked with knew her preference for seltzer. All she saw in the gesture was another man with no faith in her ability to show up on time and order for herself. Accuracy aside, Veronica wanted a man who believed in her.*

*Once she was seated, Brian turned toward her and asked, "How were your meetings today? Everyone was at HQ, right?"*

*"Yeah. It was another Monday full of meetings. You live here in Middleburg, don't you?" she asked, hoping to steer the conversation toward anything other than work. Sure, she could talk about technology, but she wanted a relationship that gave her a break from work. Since the one serious relationship she'd had*

*ended because the guy got tired of her focus on work, this didn't feel like a promising start to a date.*

*"Yes, I rent a house here. It's a three-bedroom, two-bathroom split level." Brian scrunched his nose before adding, "Nothing ostentatious, but having the extra space for a home office has been wonderful since I get to work remote three days each week."*

*Veronica smiled at him and took a sip of her seltzer water. He was so excited about their meal together, she felt rude for not being more energetic. Her true wish was a relaxed dinner, with easy conversation and no need to put on a show. Considering how the evening was turning out, she pulled the drink menu over and browsed their selection. "I think I might have a glass of wine this evening."*

*"Of course," Brian agreed before launching back into work talk. "Hopefully, I'll get a promotion soon and will be able to buy a nicer place of my own on some land. DS has been talking about adding a new manager position, and I think I have a decent shot at it. What about you? Any dreams of becoming a manager at TI?"*

*Thankfully, their waiter came by right then to ask about appetizers, giving her a chance to order a chardonnay.*

*The second he left, Veronica saw Brian's eyes light up as his mouth opened, prepared to ask another question about work, no doubt. She cut in before he could give voice to it, though. "Have you decided what to order for dinner?"*

*Brian barely glanced at the menu. "I think I'll go with the steak. I've heard TI isn't using security dongles. How does that work? I know you have air gaps in place, but with everyone working remote, how do you share and transfer files? It must be such a pain."*

*"Yeah." Veronica nodded absently, her eyes scanning the room. At a nearby table, a couple laughed and clinked glasses. She envied them their apparent ease and connection. As she turned back to the man sitting beside her, she caught a flash of frustration on his face before he returned to smiling at her. Veronica knew it bothered people when she didn't focus on them, but what did the man expect when he wanted to talk about nothing but work? Not to mention the way he was sitting beside her instead of across from her. Looking at him required straining her neck in a way that just wasn't worth it.*

*Renner laughed at nothing before trying again. "You must get so frustrated with Patrick's old-school security set-up, especially since your background is network security, isn't it?"*

*Again, Veronica stifled the flinch as she wished for a first date filled with pleasant surprises instead of a continuation of her work day with a man who knew enough about her for it to feel creepy. Forcing herself to smile and engage with her date, Veronica explained their storage system and the way they used thumb drives to transfer files. "It's a lot like how DS moves files into the secret lab," she finished.*

*"Oh, that makes sense." Brian was practically bouncing in his seat. "But I bet you have to take inventory of those drives and note who's responsible for them at all times, huh? How much of a hassle is that?"*

*The server arrived with their wine, and Veronica took a generous sip, hoping it might dull the edge of Brian's enthusiasm.*

She glanced at the menu, trying to focus on the delicious-sounding dishes as they were told the specials and asked for their orders.

"I'll have the salmon, please," she said. "With rice pilaf and the seasonal vegetable medley."

The server noted her selection and turned to Brian. "For you, sir?"

"Ribeye steak, medium rare, with mashed potatoes and broccoli," Brian said, then turned back to Veronica.

"I'll put these right in," the server promised while ignoring the way Brian had turned his back.

"Thank you," Veronica offered an apologetic smile.

"So, do you have crazy procedures around the storage drives?" Brian pulled them right back into the earlier conversation while leaning closer to Veronica.

She sighed inwardly. "Some, but it's not too bad. We have the copyright on all the code."

Brian didn't seem to notice her lack of enthusiasm and laughed. "Oh, I won't put too much faith in that. I mean honestly, if DS had your code, there's no way they'd still have you under contract. They'd just make a few small changes, claim it as their own, cut a discount to the government, and with the military's support, TI wouldn't be able to do anything about it."

Hackles rising, the restaurant disappeared from Veronica's awareness. "You're saying DS would steal our code and cut us out?" she asked, her focus completely on Renner for the first time that evening.

Finally, the man sensed he'd said or done something wrong, and his excitement calmed. "What? No. I was just joking. I mean, that kind of thing is true for all government contract companies.

*Why do you think we're all so protective of our stuff? Surely, that's not a surprise for you. I know Patrick's aware of it."*

*Not wanting to make her family or her company appear naïve, Veronica forced herself to grin at him. "Of course, that's the whole reason for our air gap system and thumb drives."*

*With just that, Renner resumed contemplating their work and upcoming projects.*

*Veronica focused on her salmon, savoring the delicate flavors. At least the food was good. Occasionally, she glanced up at Brian and made agreeable noises between bites. Mostly, she wondered how much longer the meal would last.*

*When the plates were cleared and dessert menus offered, Veronica declined, eager to end the evening. Brian looked mildly disappointed but rallied quickly.*

*"Well, this has been great," he said, leaning back in his chair. "We should do it again sometime."*

*Veronica forced a final nod of agreement. "Yeah, maybe." Then she snatched the check from the server and tucked cash inside before handing it right back. No way was she letting Renner pay for this meal, nor was she willing to wait for the server to make it back around to collect payment. "Keep the change," she offered as she stood.*

*"You didn't need to do that." Renner looked like a puppy whose favorite toy had just been destroyed.*

*"I know, and I appreciate it. I do need to get going, though. I've got a long drive back home."*

*"Right, of course. Next time we'll meet closer to your place. Maybe we could even make dinner together at your place?" he tried as they made their way out to the parking lot.*

*Keeping her eyes focused on her car, Veronica hummed. "I'll have to check my schedule. I know the next few months are looking pretty busy. Have a great night." She waved and forced herself to keep to a brisk walk instead of sprinting for her car the way she really wanted.*

Freddy pulled Veronica back to the present. "Seriously, Veronica, I'll kick his ass if he, like, touched you or something."

How could she explain that the date was bad but not in any way dangerous or threatening? "No, it's fine. Tell Patrick I'm on my way. And Freddy?" She waited for him to answer.

"Yeah?"

"Thanks." It wasn't something she often said to any of her siblings, but they didn't usually call her with a warning like this.

Freddy's only acknowledgement was a grunt before he ended the call. Veronica allowed her head to flop backward for just a minute. She could finish work, have dinner, and everything would be fine. At least, that's what she told herself before grabbing her folder, her computer, and her master thumb drive and heading toward her front door.

Maybe a date was exactly what she needed to reduce her stress so she could stop losing shit all the damn time. Really, her loneliness and isolation from living way out here was just more proof that it was her own fault for putting stuff in the wrong place. It's not like there was anyone else to mess with it. Besides, who didn't misplace their laptop now and then? Of course, finding it in the spare room instead of its normal place in the living room was a bit disconcerting since she couldn't recall the last time she'd gone into the spare room. Maybe she was sleepwalking?

Veronica pulled her front door shut behind her and then pushed back to check the deadbolt had engaged before heading for her dusty old Jeep. Once inside, she turned her key in the ignition and glanced at the clock. As long as she avoided a logging truck, she'd arrive at HQ just in time for the morning meeting.

Unaware of the drive, she parked in her usual spot with minutes to spare. The home was designed with six bedrooms and four bathrooms, but the game room became a conference room during Veronica's teenage years. Once Patrick left, his room swiftly transitioned into an office, with several other bedrooms following suit as everyone grew up and moved out. Now, the first floor was more office than home, and the second floor held two apartments.

She and Freddy had teased Patrick mercilessly when their dad had gifted him the home to go with his promotion to CEO. Both their parents had been thrilled to move into Patrick's cabin so they could enjoy retirement while their oldest son literally lived at work. It had been Freddy's idea to give Patrick a business sign that said "Headquarters" as a housewarming present, but Veronica had taken the time to find the perfect, extra-gaudy, red neon version that was designed to hang by a business entryway. Those businesses were usually dive bars, but that was what made it perfect.

"Veronica."

The deep voice from behind startled her, but it was only Greg. "Oh, good. If you walk in behind me, Patrick can't argue I'm late."

"Ha, I doubt that will stop him. If he doesn't find some kind of balance in his life, he's going to burn out or die of a heart attack before he turns forty."

"You should tell him to start by leaving me alone," Veronica tried.

Greg patted her shoulder and fell behind her as they climbed the porch stairs. "He wants the best for you. He's just a little dumb about how to show it."

Veronica grumbled about it but didn't argue. Greg was like an uncle to her. He'd been the company's CFO since her dad's founding partner had died in a car accident just as they were starting the business. She opened the door and stepped inside, allowing Greg to follow.

"Finally," Patrick boomed. "I thought you'd learned to show up on time, but apparently not!"

"I am on time." So much for any positivity in her mood. "It's two minutes till, so shut your pie hole and go sit on your throne." Gah, her brother was such a jerk sometimes.

Greg gripped her shoulder again, though it was more firm reprimand than gentle comfort. "Ahem," he cleared his throat to get Patrick's attention. "Am I late also?"

Patrick glared at both of them. "Of course not, Gregory, but you're different."

"Am I?"

With someone on her side, Veronica's whole day started to look brighter.

"You have seniority." Patrick pointed at Greg. Then he shifted his accusations to her. "She has a long record of tardiness."

Veronica leaned forward, prepared to defend herself, but Greg squeezed his grip on her just enough for her to close her mouth before anything came out.

"But she'd not tardy today, nor am I." Since Greg was the same age as their father and had been like a member of the family since before any of them hit their teens, Veronica and all of her siblings respected his counsel. Patrick frowned but accepted his point.

That didn't mean Patrick would stop harassing her, though. "Two minutes, and you better be in your chair," her brother pointed a harsh glare at her before walking away.

Veronica sighed and cruised through the kitchen. She'd hoped having Patrick as CEO would bring upgrades to their security. Instead, he'd tried to upgrade *her* by creating an official, ugly-ass folder with her name on it to record her tardiness, disorganization, and struggle to stay focused. He was determined he'd be the one to teach her how to be a professional. Ten years ago, she'd have appreciated his efforts. Now, well, she'd shifted to trying to love herself the way she was and looked for ways to make up for her deficiencies.

Before joining the team, she grabbed a fresh mug of coffee. Patrick always had Veronica present her weekly report and updates last, so she'd need to stay focused enough to integrate appropriate reports from others into her presentation. It was brutal, but at least Freddy would usually share his notes with her when she spaced out. Early on, she'd begged to present first. Patrick agreed at first, but after two weeks, he officially declared her the final presenter. He told everyone it was because she was the only one who'd put all the pieces together from each presentation to paint a clear picture. Veronica just wasn't sure she believed him. Part of her suspected he just liked torturing her.

# Chapter 3

"**Y**ou stupid, pain in my ass, mule!" Zach glared at the alpaca currently loping off into the forest. "I'm coming to get you, you know!" He shook his fist at the animal before turning his face toward the quickly darkening sky. He reminded himself that his animals were his family now, so he had to love them even when they were jerks. Besides, their fiber brought in good money.

While Butthole was the family's idiot cousin, being a Suri with his rare color made his fiber one of the world's top two percent.

It'd be nice if his mother stepped in on occasion, but Bertha was the oldest of his flock. Apparently, she had reached the point in her life when she had no fucks left to give. Zach knew when he'd purchased her, she'd only birth one or two more crias, but that also meant she was a proven breeder. At times, Zach might admit to a small love for her, too.

Now he needed to get them all into the barn for the night before he traipsed off into the woods after Butthole. As if hearing his thoughts, Snowball strode over and slammed her face into Zach's chest.

"Damn, you hit like a linebacker," Zachary told the animal while rubbing his chest with one hand and pulling a treat from his pocket with the other. "Come on. It's bedtime," he coaxed her toward the barn. Her extra puffy, bright white fiber made her the easiest to spot in the dark, but Snowball liked to be the first to do everything, including retreating to her stall for the night.

"I know, Snowball. You're not a pain in my ass. You beat the shit out of my chest, but it's done with love." He scratched her head as they walked, side-by-side, across the yard.

The others knew the routine and mostly followed behind them. Zachary always gave them treats when they followed him inside, so those with sense were happy to do so. Bertha was the last one in. Sometimes Zach thought she might be checking to ensure everyone else made it safely, but most of the time, he figured she was just lazy and moved at her own pace.

After closing the last gate, Zach gazed longingly at his house before turning toward the woods. As soon as he wrangled Butthole, he'd go home, make himself dinner, put leftovers in the freezer, and lounge on the couch.

Butthole wasn't hard to track since the clumsy oaf left a wide swath of destruction through the underbrush. Still, he'd wandered further than usual, and Zach was starting to worry when he noticed a beam of light sweeping back and forth in the clearing ahead of him.

Someone had just moved into the small, single-story house on the property the previous fall. Most of the mountain was owned by the Taylor family, so Zach figured it was one of them. Everyone in town swung back and forth between hating the Taylors for their wealth and loving them for their generosity and support of the community. Zachary wasn't sure why they'd be out roaming around with a flashlight after dark. But it wasn't his business. Of course, they also could have rented the cabin to a stranger.

He was just about to call out, so whoever it was wouldn't accidentally shoot him, when he noticed a second flashlight beam coming from inside the house. Just then, a motion-sensor light above the carpark illuminated Butthole standing in the clearing like a performer taking to the stage. Zach groaned but didn't move. The hairs on his forearms and the back of his neck stood at attention.

Both flashlight beams froze, and the pieces fell into place. No one used a flashlight inside unless their power was out, and that motion sensor wasn't battery powered. Whoever was here didn't belong.

"Hey, who's there?"

Shit, one of them must have spotted Butthole. Zachary hoped they might mistake him for a deer, but that was doubtful. It was also for the best since Zach wouldn't be able to live with himself if Butthole got shot. The animal might be a pain in his ass, but Butthole was his, and Zach didn't let bad things happen to those he cared about.

Before he could figure out what to do, he heard the cackle of a radio coming to life as the same voice dropped in volume to say, "We're out of time. We need to go now."

Zach clamped his mouth shut and stepped sideways, snapping a twig and drawing attention his way. Hopefully, they'd figure it was just more animals. He stepped behind a large rock outcropping. At least they wouldn't be able to see him.

"Hello? Anyone out there?" the voice called again while waving his beam of light through the forest.

A different voice shouted with annoyance, "Did you really pull me out over a damned animal? What is that thing? Deer don't got long necks like that."

"I don't know what it is, but I think there's another out here somewhere. I heard something."

"Fuck this. Get in the car and let's go. It's cold as shit out here, and she'll be home soon, anyway. We'll try another time."

It took a few minutes of crunching leaves and low bickering before Zachary heard two car doors slam shut. Headlights flickered on, and Zach pulled back tighter behind the rocks when the beams swept across his location. The vehicle turned around. Zach listened for the sounds of tires on gravel to let him know when he could step into the open and retrieve his trouble-making animal.

He stared at the front door and considered his options. His instincts told him to check inside and wait for the mentioned woman, but that would invade her privacy just like they'd done. There were no cars on the property, so it wasn't likely anyone was home or in need of help. He'd come back first thing in the morning.

For now, he'd collect his alpaca and go home. He just needed to find the butthole. With the strangers gone, the animal had wandered back into the trees. Damn, he should have snapped a picture of them, he thought belatedly. Whoever was living here would just have to take his word for it unless they had cameras.

With a huff, he heard the distinct sound of the animal spitting behind him. He was nowhere near close enough to hit him with the mucus, but it did irritate him. Zach suspected that had been the animal's real goal, anyway.

He grabbed the rope he'd slung through his belt and looped it around the long, hairy neck.

"Come on, Butthole. You've had your adventure and dragged me along, too. We're done for today. Let's go home." Zach didn't mind his animals being his primary companions, but he missed having a human partner in his life. He wouldn't let anyone exploit him again, like Izzy did.

He gave his most mischievous alpaca a smack on the ass to encourage him into his stall before closing up the barn and heading inside. This winter was mild, with an annoying lack of snow, but it was still going to drop into the single digits tonight.

While puttering in the kitchen, Zach's mind wandered to the Taylor cabin. It was so far from his audacious expectations, he couldn't put a person in his mental image. At least, he couldn't put any of his imagined Taylor family people into the image. His curiosity had him tossing and turning throughout the night and ripping through his morning chores faster than usual so he could hopefully catch his neighbor before she took off for the day.

# Chapter 4

T humping her head against the back of her driver's seat, Veronica allowed herself five minutes to wallow in frustration. Between her brothers and her failed date, she couldn't help wondering if she were cursed. At least her ninety-minute drive home would give her time to think. She took a deep breath and started her car before pulling from the parking lot.

She knew she had issues. She even had a pretty good idea what they were, but that didn't mean she had solutions. When she was a teen, her mom had agreed to let her try ADHD medication. Veronica thought the little pills would fix her, but they hadn't. Food had never been her top priority. There were too many interesting parts of the world to explore to bother sitting down and chewing. The medication took the hunger cues she already struggled to recognize and made them disappear.

Her ability to disappear into whatever passion project she was obsessed with intensified while on the medication, but it also made her irritable and sometimes almost mean. After two weeks, she'd lost ten pounds, forgotten to go to bed three times, and her mom had to drive her to school after she missed the bus twice. That had been the end of her hope that medicine could fix her.

With her mom, Katrina, supporting her, Veronica had developed tricks to cover her failings. Alarms helped her remember commitments, and colored folders with strict rules about putting things in their place kept her work from completely falling apart. But none of it was enough to cure anything.

Patrick consistently made things more difficult for her, and Freddy enthusiastically supported him. It might sound trite, but her brothers were the worst. She wanted to pack both of them into a crate and ship them to Madagascar. With a little luck, they'd die at the hands of a few crazy ninja penguins.

Since their technology had saved that astronaut, they'd been all over the news and trending on social media, but her brother insisted on ignoring all of it. She didn't give two hoots about their online presence, but without a clear and obvious way to contact them, many people were turning to less friendly approaches. The attempts to access their systems had tripled, and it was making Veronica paranoid. Her brother's refusal to update their procedures made them vulnerable, which was exactly what she was trying to avoid.

When she'd tried to explain, her brother Freddy rolled his eyes and said they'd be sure to consider her suggestion later. Greg had been nicer about it, but still pointed out so much was happening, any major changes would be tough. Patrick hadn't even humored her. He firmly refused to give her time to gather the information she had compiled.

"Listen, Veronica. You're amazing, and we wouldn't have made the advances we have over the last few years without you. I love having you closer, too. I'm not saying you're wrong or that we shouldn't make some changes, but now isn't the time. Let's look at reality. You can't even keep track of the research you did to try to convince me. How are you going to keep up with those updates without letting your work configuring the firewalls slip? Mom's already on my case about how hard you work." He'd said it with a pitiful smile that stung just as much as his point about her inability to keep everything organized.

She'd stewed over the issues with her brothers on her way to meet Kurt for dinner, but the scent of cooking food drew her attention as soon as she pulled into the parking lot. Living in the city had made procuring food easier, but the forest felt like home and reduced distractions. Unfortunately, it meant she sometimes forgot to eat. Today everyone had grabbed plates of food and munched throughout the day. Well, everyone except her. Thinking back, she'd been trying so hard to take notes and be ready for her own presentation at the end of everything, she'd never made it into the kitchen for a plate of anything.

She followed her nose inside, ordered a drink, and drooled over the menu while waiting for Kurt to arrive. But she'd continued to sit alone while her chilled white wine warmed, and her stomach rumbled. Her text asking if everything was alright had gone unanswered, and eventually, the server convinced her to order soup and a small salad. It would be easy to pass off as a starter if Kurt miraculously appeared almost an hour late, and it would appease her appetite enough to quiet down the rumbles from her midsection.

By the time she'd been handed her check with a look of pity, her date was one hour and fifty-eight minutes late.

The sight of her own home pulled Veronica from her contemplation. She had to face facts. She'd been stood up; she was just another mediocre employee at her brother's company; and there was a good chance nothing would ever change.

She slammed the door of her jeep and stomped up the steps to her porch before letting herself inside. Fuck this day and fuck her life. Veronica chucked her messenger bag toward her sofa and stomped down the hall. On the left was her office. It had three monitors, a massive CPU, her ergonomic chair and keyboard, and her favorite scented candle. In there, she felt powerful and in control.

On her right was her bedroom. She'd have to wade through clothes to get to her bed, and now that she thought about it, her sheets were starting to smell funky. She'd meant to wash them over the weekend, but she'd gotten busy doing other stuff.

With a sigh, she turned right to plunge into the chaos and get laundry going. It was when she tripped over a shoe and caught herself by grabbing her dresser that she noticed everything was rearranged. She glanced around with fresh eyes. Her digital clock face was solid black with no numbers illuminated. The plug was lying on the carpet where it had fallen from the wall.

She'd meant to tighten that up a while ago. Looking back at her dresser, she wondered if it had been rearranged or if she'd pushed her jewelry chest to the side in her rush that morning. Despite rarely touching the chest, she may have moved it while searching, but nothing was missing.

As much as her office would soothe her, she knew it would also consume her. She just needed to get through the rest of the evening, and then she could start again tomorrow. She changed her sheets, started laundry, and spent her nightly shower planning how she'd make a to do list first thing in the morning. Veronica was done being a hot mess. It was still early, so she grabbed her Kindle and opened a new book.

The banging needed to stop. Veronica rolled over and onto her Kindle. She must have fallen asleep while reading. Prying it out from beneath her, she checked her clock only to find it was still black. The banging on her front door came again as she grabbed her phone. Two minutes after seven. Who was knocking this early? And why?

"What?" She ripped open the front door without bothering to put on anything over her sleep shorts and tank top. She hadn't touched her hair, either. The way the stranger standing on her front door was staring, wide-eyed, at the aura around her head made it obvious it had dried in an extra-special bedhead arrangement.

"I'm sorry to bother you. I live nearby and just wanted to let you know there were some guys were here last night."

"What?" There were no guys at her house. Hell, most of the guys she knew were her brothers, and they'd been with her at HQ. Well, except for Gabe, but he was overseas and didn't count right then. "Who are you?" She snarled at the stranger on her stoop, noticing the way his dirty blond hair was artfully tousled. It shifted as the wind blew through it, and she knew he hadn't styled it that way. The man just had gorgeous hair above his strong brows and sharply-cut jawline.

"Right. My apologies. I'm Zachary." He held out his hand to shake, and she noticed his forearm. It was rock hard, with defined ridges of muscles and veins. It was the kind of forearm that guaranteed strong fingers that would be able to work magic between her folds.

Veronica rolled her eyes. Her sexual frustration was one more failure to add to her list. Even hook-up apps took one look at her current location and immediately displayed error messages saying there were no matches near her. Part of her had hoped Kurt might help with that last night, but knowing her, she'd gotten the week or day or restaurant wrong, and he thought she'd stood him up. Maybe letting her lady-parts shrivel into dust was nature's way of ensuring she did not pass on her defective genes.

"I can tell this is a bad time." The guy, Zachary, pulled his hand back and turned away.

Veronica hurried to explain, "No, wait. I was rolling my eyes at myself, not you. I'm Veronica." She reached for his hand and reveled in the warm callouses that grazed her skin.

"Nice to meet you, Veronica." Damn, his voice was nice too. It was deep and rumbly.

"Same. What did you mean by guys being here last night?" Then her brain snapped the pieces into place and Veronica scowled. "Why were you here last night? Have you been snooping in my house?"

She should have grabbed her robe before opening the door. Stalkers were not supposed to see a lady in her sleep clothes, and it was cold out. Veronica looked down to confirm her nipples had become unmistakable spikes poking through her thin tank top.

Before Zachary could respond, Veronica held up a finger. "Hang on." Then she shut the door in his face and turned to grab a hoodie and some oversized sweats before stepping into slippers and rejoining him on the porch.

Her mother's voice sounded in her mind cautioning her about strangers and suggesting she have her phone handy so she could call 911. Unfortunately, she'd left that somewhere unknown after checking the time. Patrick joked about duct taping it to her hand. Sometimes she thought that was a brilliant idea. For now, being ravaged by the sexy man on her porch didn't feel like the worst thing that could happen. In fact, it might be kind of nice.

"I needed more clothes," she explained as she pulled the door shut behind her to keep the cold February air from overpowering her baseboard heaters.

"It is cold out," he responded while standing perfectly still with his sleeves pulled up to his elbows and no hint of a shiver.

Veronica raised an eyebrow at him.

"Alpaca sweater under a down vest keeps me warm without getting in the way of my work," he explained. "I raise them myself. The alpacas I mean. Here, feel how soft their fiber is." He held out his elbow so she could feel where his sweater was bunched up.

Sexy man, soft sweater, and he was inviting her to touch him? Discretely, she pinched her thigh to check if she was dreaming before accepting his offer to touch.

"Oh wow." She refrained from stepping closer and rubbing her whole body against his arm. "Where do you get something like that?" she asked. It was a beautiful blend of white, beige, and brown all woven together.

Zachary grinned at her. "From me, of course. I'll bring one by for you. It'll be a bit big, but sometimes they're better that way." He cocked his head in thought for a second before adding, "I'm hoping your calm demeanor means you know the men who were here last night?"

Veronica felt the blood drain from her face and grabbed the doorframe to steady herself. Of course she didn't know anything about men being there last night.

"Woah, easy." Zachary reached out and grabbed her hips to steady her.

"Thank you," she replied before she shook herself and braced to hear more. "No. Who was here?" she prompted. "And why were *you* here?"

Zachary's blush just softened his features, making him even more attractive. "Right. Butthole escaped last night–"

"I'm sorry. Butthole?" she asked.

"He's my youngest alpaca, and he's a butthole, so that's what I named him. Anyway, he's always escaping, but he's not hard to catch." Zachary cocked his head and gave her a lopsided grin before continuing, "Last night, he went further than usual and ended up all the way over here. That's why I was over here."

"So *you* aren't the one stalking me?" Veronica hoped he'd get that she was joking.

Sure enough, he laughed. "Nope. I'm just a man looking for his wayward alpaca."

Veronica couldn't stop herself from chuckling at how normal he made that sound.

"While I was here, I saw a flashlight sweeping across your yard." Zachary's voice deepened with the sincerity of his concern. "Then I noticed there was another one moving around inside. One of them spotted Butthole and heard my steps. He called out to the other that they needed to leave."

"They were in my house?" This was her space. Her home. It was where she worked and slept and showered. There had been strangers here? Inside?

Zachary stepped closer and gently placed a hand on her elbow. "I was going to wait for you to get home last night, but I thought finding a guy standing on your porch, after dark, waiting for you might creep you out." He flinched but kept explaining. "I decided to come back this morning by driving my truck over like a normal person, but now I'm thinking maybe it's too early, and you're still weirded out."

She nodded, but when he stepped back and removed his hand, she stopped him. Even through her hoodie, his warm touch felt good. It was like a solid reassurance that everything would be okay.

"What time did you see them?" she asked.

"It was just before seven. I always put the animals in the barn at sundown, which has been around six recently. I went after Butthole after putting up the others."

Veronica couldn't picture it. What the hell was she supposed to do or know about that information? How was she supposed to be feeling? Maybe once her brain was powered on, this would all make sense.

"I need coffee," she said with a shake of her head. "Come in and join me. Once I'm awake enough to process, I'll probably have more questions for you." And the thought of being alone in her home now felt dangerous, but she didn't want to mention that to him.

"I never turn down coffee, Veronica." Lightning shot through her body when his deep voice rumbled out her name.

"Easy to please, aren't you, Zachary?" she teased.

"Yeah. Just so long as you don't take my money and house before shacking up with my neighbor."

His tone was teasing, but Veronica heard the hurt behind his words. What bitch would do that to a man like him? She'd keep him around for eye candy alone. With soft warm sweaters and a willingness to ensure her safety, Veronica couldn't ask for more.

"I can guarantee you won't need to worry about any of that with me," she assured him.

"Good. In that case, you can call me Zach. I answer to both."

His footsteps matched her rhythm as she made her way into the kitchen. Patrick would have a heart attack if he saw the way she was inviting a stranger in for coffee, but there was something about Zachary that felt right to her. Maybe it was his sweater, but he didn't feel new. He hadn't been offended by the abrupt way she'd disappeared to get dressed, nor did his touch make her flinch. His hands on her hips earlier felt natural, but more than that, they'd made her feel stronger. It was the exact opposite of how she'd felt with Renner. And even though running into Kurt had sparked some arousal, it hadn't come anywhere near the comfort she felt with Zach. Veronica dumped the old coffee and started filling the pot as she asked, "What were the men doing?"

As he explained which part of the house he'd seen the inside flashlight beaming through, Veronica grabbed a filter and pulled the coffee canister from its usual place on the counter beside her sugar. It sounded like one man had been in her office. She was trying to visualize it from his perspective to check her mental map when she looked down into the filter she'd filled with sugar instead of coffee. *What the hell?* The coffee can was always the one closest to the pot. The sugar canister matched, but it stayed between the coffee can and the toaster. Veronica lifted the filter to dump the sugar back into its container with a groan. Maybe the move was messing with her. It had been six months, but that change had forced her to come up with a new order in her life. Maybe she wasn't sticking to her rules the way she should.

# Chapter 5

Veronica had just confidently scooped sugar into her coffee pot, and Zachary wasn't sure what to make of it. Her sigh before correcting it didn't offer any answers and made him wonder how often she had this kind of issue. Was that why she lived so humbly out here alone? Was she the black sheep of the family who was quirkier than most?

Once she'd put the empty filter back in the basket, she flipped off the water to the overflowing carafe, but instead of picking it up and dumping it into the reservoir, Veronica leaned forward on the counter with her head down and her shoulders slumped. She looked... lost? Defeated? Broken? It didn't matter which word a person chose, her body language screamed at Zach to rub her back and murmur words of comfort. That's exactly what he'd do for any of his alpacas, and he used to try it with his ex.

Unfortunately, he'd learned that human women didn't always appreciate being crowded and consoled.

That concern didn't stop him from crossing the kitchen and stepping up close behind her, but it did stop him from touching her without asking first.

"Hey, are you okay?" he asked softly.

Instead of answering, Veronica spun around. Zach was close enough to her that her face landed right in the crook between his neck and chest. If she were a few inches taller, they'd be kissing, which was not an appropriate thought for this moment, Zach chastised himself. That was not what needed to happen. What the hell was he even thinking? He hadn't felt attraction like this since Izzy. He needed to back away and respect Veronica's space. Just because attraction was instantaneous and all or nothing for him, didn't mean she'd feel the same way. In most cases, the opposite was true.

Except Veronica didn't recoil. She leaned into him and thumped her forehead on his chest. "I'm sorry. I think I'm losing it. I swear I always keep the coffee canister closest to the pot, but recently I've been leaving stuff in all kinds of places it doesn't belong."

She started to pull her head back, but Zach didn't want that. Maybe she was as starved for touch and affection as he was. He certainly liked the way it felt to have her leaning against him. Slowly, because he didn't want to startle her, he brought his hands up to her biceps and rubbed her upper arms, trying to find the balance between *We just met,* and *I'm ready to claim you as mine and keep you forever.*

"It could have been the men in your house last night," he pointed out.

Veronica's hands came up to rest on his chest as she pulled her face back far enough to look up and into his eyes. "Yeah, but that only works if they've been here regularly over the last several weeks." Then she snorted in disbelief.

"Hmm, how confident are you that's not the case?" he asked. "Do you have cameras?"

She just stared at him.

"Tell you what. Why don't you pour in the water and get the coffee brewing. Then you can tell me about all the things that have been out of place and when. We'll make a timeline and see if we notice any kind of pattern." He had no idea what he was suggesting, but it was something. He couldn't leave her thinking this was all on her when there were obviously outside forces at work.

"Yeah, okay," she agreed before giving him a quizzical look. "Were you a detective or something?"

"No, I was in the Navy. Their training certainly helps, but I've also gone through several wilderness trainings along with a few search and rescue courses."

When her eyes widened in surprise, he shrugged it off. "I've always liked helping people. Knowing what to do and how to help in a variety of situations makes it easier." He refrained from telling her that he'd once considered law school just so he could go after men who'd hurt a friend of his. Even he knew how extreme that sounded.

An hour later, they'd each had a few cups of coffee and written out every strange thing she could remember, but there was no pattern either of them could spot. It didn't help that they only had timing for when she found something out of place and not when it was put there. Zach was trying to figure out what to suggest next when Veronica's phone rang from the bedroom. She leaped up from the table and ran to grab it. Damn, she was beautiful. Her hair was still flying in all directions, but he liked that she wasn't polished and perfect. If she'd been what he'd expected from a Taylor, with perfect hair and make-up while wearing designer matching pajamas, he'd have mentioned the intruders and run back home. If he hadn't spotted the folder labeled with Taylor Industries on the table in her front hall, he'd have assumed she was just a regular, random person.

Even after everything she'd told him as they sipped coffee, he didn't get the sense that she was anything other than a woman struggling to balance working with her family and doing a job most people assumed belonged to a man.

Speaking of which, the way she'd talked about her former bosses sending her to fetch coffee and speaking to her as if she were a child made him want to hunt them down and feed them to a passel of pigs.

When he'd asked about people who might have something against her, he'd braced himself to hear about her past relationships. Instead, he'd gotten insight into just how big a jackass men could be to a woman in their workplace.

With each new detail she shared, he added to his mental picture of her as a normal, down-to-earth person.

Granted, she was a normal person who spoke about C++, Java, and firewalls the way most people talked about the weather, but he liked how nerdy she was. When he'd asked her to explain about the need for a thumb drive, she'd patiently walked him through the idea of air gaps and explained why it was an antiquated security measure with today's computing power and encryption capabilities.

Zachary was thoroughly impressed by her assertion that the limited space on a thumb drive forced them to lower the encryption security. It was clear she knew what she was talking about, and it sounded like her brother was an idiot for not listening to her and switching to security tokens immediately.

Then his heart had skipped a beat as she grinned with glee and confessed to using her IT powers to translate all of her younger brother's incoming emails into Russian after he'd rewritten some of her code in a way he thought was more efficient. Apparently, her brother failed to consider the future plan to add differing levels of access for different contractors they'd need to collaborate with. Veronica had been pissed about the work she'd needed to repeat, but her passion and skills were obvious.

More than impressed, a surge of pride welled in Zach's chest. This woman could do so much, and yet, he could see exactly how he'd fit into her life. He could see himself cooking for her and listening as she snuggled into him and thought through whatever challenge she was facing. They'd already shared more with each other in a just a couple of hours than he usually shared throughout an entire series of dates with a woman. Maybe without the context of a date, they'd both been able to skip the performative parts of meeting a stranger and be themselves. Whatever the case, Zachary loved the way she relaxed each time he reached out to touch her. He discovered his cheeks hurt from grinning despite the serious nature of some of their conversation.

It was easy to see how she could get so sucked into her work that she'd forget about mundane things like meals and housekeeping. She hadn't said that was an issue, but the way she talked about trying to remember where things were and looking around at her house made it easy for him to guess.

Veronica confirmed it when she'd suggested breakfast, only to realize she was out of bread and eggs and milk. He'd already been admiring the way her eyes crinkled at the corners when she smiled, so he'd seen her resignation as she turned and grabbed a nutrition bar from her pantry. He declined her offer for him to have one as well, but he'd seen the boxes of them stockpiled on her shelves.

Every ounce of his being was screaming at him to make it better for her. He could cook for her, help her find lost things, ensure she got enough sleep, and take care of mundane chores. But he wouldn't. Never again would he allow himself to be used like that.

Still, he could do one thing for her without opening himself up to be taken advantage of. While she was still in the other room, Zach pulled out his phone and flipped to the contact labeled with a single letter B to send a text.

> **Any chance you can pull some info for me?**

He was shocked to see bubbles pop up suggesting an immediate response.

> **Great timing. What needed?**

That was the million-dollar question. Something was obviously going on here, but what? Where did he even start?

> Not sure. Attractive woman connected to Taylor Industries has men breaking in but not taking anything.

This time Veronica's living room clock ticked a few times before response bubbles materialized.

> Any details?

> Veronica Taylor. Two men. Things moved not destroyed. They plan to come back later.

> Pics?

> No

Zach felt horribly guilty about that, but there was nothing to be done now.

> I'll look into things. You have security covered for attractive woman?

Frowning at his phone, he regretted including that detail.

> Yes

He could practically hear the other man laughing, but Zach would not add to it.

Just as he debated what else he could do to help Veronica, she stepped back into the dining area with her phone in her hand.

Her smile was gone, her shoulders had curled forward, and the fun, confident woman he'd enjoyed coffee with had all but disappeared as she told him, "That was work. I need to head into my office and get some stuff done." She gestured back down the hall toward her room full of monitors.

"I should get back to my animals anyway," Zach agreed before carrying his almost empty coffee mug over to the sink. "You'll be working from home all day?" he checked.

"Yeah, and I have to say thank you. I appreciate you letting me know about the men you saw. Maybe I'll get one of my brothers to put in some cameras or something."

"That sounds like a good idea. Would you mind if I swung by later with dinner for both of us?" Damn, he hadn't meant to say that. It was too much.

"You don't have to do that," Veronica tried to assure him, but when she opened her pantry and started to say, "I'll just have…" only to trail off when she realized there was nothing but nutrition bars inside, he couldn't take it back.

"Seriously, it's impossible to cook for just me, and while I can usually freeze leftovers, there are a few meals that I love that don't keep or reheat well. Sharing with you would avoid food waste." He didn't mention how much he enjoyed her company or the way his heart soared at the thought of giving her what she needed to smile and enjoy her life.

Zach wasn't kidding about the issue with too much food, though. He had a couple orange roughie filets he'd been dying to use to make his favorite fish casserole, but he hated reheating fish. If he could bring it over and share it with her, they'd both eat, and the food wouldn't go to waste. It would be a win-win. Which is exactly what he told her before letting her know he'd be back over around seven that evening after he put the animals back in the barn for the night.

"Fine," she agreed. "If you insist, I won't say no. Besides, while I'm not big on most fish, Orange Roughie with rice and veggies and cracker meal fresh from the oven sounds good. I should be done with work by then, too."

"Great. I'll see you this evening," Zach grinned like a fool despite his attempts to contain himself.

When she started to lead him to the door, he waved her off. "I can show myself out. I know you said you needed to get to work."

"Yeah," she agreed with a glance toward her office. Then she turned back to him. "Thank you. Seriously."

"It's my pleasure," he assured her before pulling his vest back on and heading out.

As he got home, Zach pulled out the fish to thaw. Then he spent the day doing the same things he did every Tuesday, starting with cleaning out the alpaca stalls on the left side of the barn.

With his evening plans at the forefront of his mind, Zach whistled his way through his daily chores. As fucked up as he knew it was, having Veronica count on him to provide dinner gave him more purpose than he'd felt recently.

He was spending time handling his youngest alpaca when Doc Ester pulled up his driveway in her truck. Zachary smirked at Butthole as he whispered to the animal, "You can't destroy my mood today. I'm going to have dinner with a beautiful woman tonight, and you can't mess it up. With your new chip, I can find you on my phone any time I want." Regular handling ensured shearing went smoothly, but Zach also found it comforting.

Butthole spit at his feet.

"Hey, watch it, Butthole!" Zach leaped back, but Doc Ester interrupted before he could continue yelling at the beast.

"That animal has your number," Doc Ester laughed as she walked over to join him.

"This isn't what I pictured when you described raising alpacas." He pointed at the innocent-looking older woman who must secretly be a witch. "You should have warned me that they can be jerks."

Doc grabbed a thick pinch of Butthole's hide and stabbed the device depositing the chip under his skin. "Now, what would be the fun in that," she teased. "Besides, I was hoping the challenge would do you good. Amanda always said you were happiest when you were needed."

"What does that mean?"

Doc Ester dropped her tool into her bag and crossed her arms. "Don't play dumb with me. My niece told me all about your mother hen tendencies."

Rolling his eyes, Zachary said, "I do not have mother hen tendencies."

"But you do know what I mean. I seem to recall hearing about a drunken confession that you felt lost and purposeless after your sister died. When was that again?"

Zach groaned. "I feel like once a divorce is finalized, any related event should be banned from conversation—including intel gathered during my bachelor party."

"So you didn't marry a slutty gold-digger to give yourself someone to take care because you need that kind of purpose in your life?" Doc's half-grin, combined with the twinkle in her eye, said she already knew the answer.

"Thanks for coming out to chip Butthole for me, Doc," Zach said. "You can go now."

The woman had the audacity to throw back her head and laugh.

"Oh, Zachary, you are a treasure," she said. "You've been conditioned since childhood to build yourself around someone else's needs and welfare. The minute your parents gave birth to a little girl with down syndrome, they started rewarding you for putting her needs first."

"How would you know?" Doc had made comments like that before. Usually, Zach ignored them, but now he wanted to know.

"It's obvious in the stories you tell, but even more so in the choices you make." She was inspecting him with the same eagle eye she used to diagnose animals. "Zachary, just think about what you did for Amanda and how you watched out for her. That's who you are. You're a protector and a caregiver. Of course, you feel lost without anyone to take advantage of your greatest strengths."

"Exactly. People take advantage of me. I'm not doing that anymore." He'd find his purpose in his animals, even if it meant chasing Butthole around the globe. "You have time to take a look at Fluffy while you're here?"

Doc took pity on him and accepted changing the subject. "Yeah, I'll go check her out, but it sounds like she's doing well."

"She spent some time pacing today. I think she might be picking her birthing spot, but she's still eating."

"Alright then. You want me to come find you when I'm done?"

Zach checked the time. He needed to get cleaned up before dinner. "Uh, if there're any issues, then yes, of course."

"But you've got plans tonight and will be inside ensuring you don't stink like manure?" she finished for him.

His cheeks warmed, and he hoped like hell he wasn't blushing. "Something like that."

"Good for you, Zach. I'll show myself out and send you a text with my follow-up." The sincerity behind her well-wishes reminded him why he'd decided to build his new life near hers.

Wrapping her up in a hug, he thanked her. Then he jogged toward his house to shower.

It was while getting dressed he discovered his conundrum. "Ripped and stained work jeans aren't appropriate, but I can't wear dress pants if this isn't a date," he mumbled to himself. "I don't want to look like a bum, redneck farmer, either." He rifled through his closet for the third time.

A flannel button down would work for a shirt, but he couldn't very well show up in his boxer briefs. He was just about to see if Doc was still around and could help him out when he found a new pair of jeans. Anytime Tractor Supply had a sale, he bought several pairs to pull out when he needed them. They were the perfect balance of not too dressy but still decent.

He packed up the food he'd already prepared and carried it to the passenger seat of his truck. It would be fine there while he ran through the few chores that had to be done in the evening.

# Chapter 6

Veronica saw lights flash across her office window and wondered who'd be visiting in person when she remembered that Zach had promised to return with dinner. Then she looked down and realized she was still wearing her pajamas from that morning. Her hair was in a knotted mess atop her head. She licked across her teeth and was dismayed to realize she hadn't brushed yet either.

> I have to go!

She typed a frantic message to Freddy. They'd been chatting about the latest updates they wanted to recommend after Freddy had found a bug in Wils' code that only appeared when someone hacked in through a hole in Veronica's security programs. She had the hole patched earlier in the day, but

Freddy was saying it wasn't enough. He still wanted them to find a fix for the bug. Veronica had been arguing that it was moot since it only happened when the system was accessed through a side door that she'd effectively nailed shut.

Hot date you forgot about?

No, doofus.

It was a lie. Zachary was very hot, but her brother didn't need to know that. And she had forgotten about their date. Oh shit! Was it a date?

It couldn't be. She did her hair and make-up for dates. Sure, she'd only been on that one lately, and he hadn't bothered to show up, but still. At the very least, she'd fucking showered that day! This could not be a date. Veronica was not prepared for that.

Without waiting for another response from her younger brother, Veronica clicked off her monitor and tried to hop up from her chair just as she heard a knock at the door. Unfortunately, she'd been sitting too long without a break, so her stiff legs failed to untangle from the blanket she'd wrapped around her pajamas instead of bothering to get dressed. Without her feet following her commands she crashed to the floor.

Great.

This was going to be a great fucking date.

She thumped her head against the floor where she'd landed.

"Veronica?" she heard a deep voice yell from her front room. "I heard a crash, so I'm coming in. Are you okay?"

She bolted upright in a rush to assure him she was fine, but Zach appeared in her office doorway before she could untangle herself.

"Kill me now," she pleaded to the universe while covering her face with her hands.

"Looks like it's been a rough day. Your door was unlocked, and the crash had me worried. Are you hurt?" he asked and took his first step toward her.

"Stay back. I smell." Oh fuck. This was bad. "I mean not like bad, but not good. I mean, I'm okay, and don't need help. So just go away." Yep, this was a disaster.

Zach chuckled and rubbed the back of his neck, but he stayed by the door. "I forgot to change my shoes, so I'm still wearing work boots covered in Alpaca spit, if that makes you feel better."

Before Veronica could assure him that it did not, his head snapped up to look at her with wide eyes and a horrified look on his face and blurted out, "And I just walked all across your house with my work boots, which probably have shit on the bottom, so I'm going to retreat to the door and remove them now. I'm so sorry."

Veronica flopped back onto the floor. "Wait. I lost track of time today, so I'm still a mess. Maybe we should try this again another time?" she offered.

Zach took a minute to think before he responded. "Okay, under one condition."

He was setting conditions? What the hell was he hoping for? "Uh?" Veronica wasn't even sure what to ask.

"We'll try for a real dinner date tomorrow night. Tonight, we'll be two stinky neighbors who eat the same food in the same place without judging each other." Then his brows furrowed, and he added, "Unless you already ate tonight or have other plans or something?"

"No, no. I don't have plans," she assured him. It was the improbable lack of judgement that made her hesitate.

"When did you last eat?" Zach asked.

She thought back and remembered pulling a nutrition bar from her cabinet. In her memory, Zach was sitting at her table, so that had to have been this morning. "Huh, I had breakfast today, right?"

"You had a bar. That's not breakfast. What did you have for lunch?"

"I don't think I was hungry. I think that nutrition bar really filled me up this morning." Veronica pulled herself up and off the floor while being careful to keep the blanket wrapped around her. Maybe he wouldn't notice that she was still wearing the same thing as earlier.

He didn't sound like he believed her when he responded, "Right. Not hungry. I'm going to go out on a limb and say maybe you got sucked into work and time just passed without you noticing."

Damn him for being a stupid mind-reader. "How would you know?" she asked.

"My sister used to have the same thing happen when she was playing her video games. I'm betting you're still wearing sleep clothes under that blanket and are worried you smell bad because you haven't done your usual morning routine?"

"At least I don't have shit on my shoes," she grumbled defensively.

"Touché. How about we swap this for one chance for me to come over in all my post-chore grossness without you judging me, and tonight I won't judge you."

Veronica couldn't come up with any better ideas, so she agreed. "Fine. Go take your shoes off and make yourself at home. I'm going to get cleaned up. I'll be out soon."

Zachary grinned at her like he'd won a prize.

"Why do you look so happy about this?" she asked.

"Your hair is awesome." He was fighting to hide his laughter behind his hand, but Veronica could see the twinkle in his eyes and the way his shoulders shook.

"What?!" she shrieked before turning to catch her reflection in the window. "Ohmygosh." It was worse than she'd imagined. Part of the knot had come undone, so she had hair sticking out from her head like Medusa's snakes. She wanted to escape, but she'd have to push past him to get through the door. As she did, he stopped her with a hand on her arm and no hint of amusement or mockery.

"Hey, it's really not that bad. I mean, it is, but it's so bad, it's cute. Like those dogs who are so ugly they're adorable."

"Did you just compare me to an ugly dog?" she checked.

Zach got the same wide-eyed look of horror from earlier. "No. Yes. I mean, not in a bad way? You're adorable. That's what I'm trying to say. I like the way you look, even like this. I think it's nice." Then he stepped back into the living room and away from her. "Sorry. I'll get dinner ready while you..." he waved his hand in her general direction.

Veronica darted over to her bedroom before either of them could embarrass themselves any further. "I'll be out in ten minutes," she called over her shoulder.

This was a nightmare.

By the time she'd pulled on leggings and her favorite long sweater, she'd convinced herself he'd either run screaming into the night or act overly polite until she assured him that he never had to come back again. No way could he want to hang out with her after this mess.

Then she walked into the kitchen and scented heaven. Her stomach rolled over, growled with excitement, and stabbed at her to keep silent until after they'd eaten. They both sat at her little round table, and Zach served them each a heaping plate of rice, fish, and beans.

"This is so good," she mumbled as she chewed.

"It is one of my favorites, but I don't make it often."

Veronica finished the bite in her mouth and took a sip of the wine he'd poured for her.

"I hope you don't mind that I pulled out dishes and poured us both a drink?" he asked.

"No, this is great." She shoveled another bite into her mouth. "All of this is amazing."

"I'm guessing you don't cook?"

Forcing herself to wait until she'd chewed and swallowed gave her time to form a coherent answer. "I am capable of cooking, and I don't mind it when I'm in the mood. But I rarely do it. Cooking feels like one more item on my to do list." She wasn't sure if that made sense, but it was the best she could explain. When she wanted to enjoy food, she could cook and make good food, but it took time, energy, ingredients, and planning that she wasn't willing to expend on a basic body function unless it was a special occasion.

"I can understand, I suppose. I guess my work makes it easy for me to cook every day. Taking care of my animals isn't mentally challenging." He cocked his head to the side and set his forkful back down. "Now that I think about it, I tend to do more of my mental, business, office work on Thursdays, and I never cook on that day. I'm always too tired from doing paperwork."

"What exactly do you do with the animals that's less exhausting than paperwork?"

Veronica felt like that was backwards, but then she'd never run a farm of any kind, so what did she know?

"I wouldn't say it's less tiring. It's just different. The work I do with the animals is very physical. Sure, my body is tired at the end of the day, but my mind isn't. Cooking satisfies something with that."

"Hm," Veronica wanted him to know she was listening and had heard what he said, but she wasn't willing to stop eating to say much more.

"Maybe I should bring dinner over here every day?" Zach asked with a chuckle.

Looking down at her almost empty plate, Veronica realized she'd inhaled most of what he'd given her. She grabbed a napkin to wipe her mouth and pulled her elbows back from the table where she'd been resting them. The man must think she was a heathen. "Sorry. This is amazing, and I was hungrier than I thought. Thank you."

Zach's smile dropped, and he looked down at his plate. "Would it upset you if I brought food over sometimes?"

What was he trying to ask? Was this like that breakfast pickup line where a guy says something about eating together in the morning to get an invitation into bed? Veronica hadn't shaved her legs and was overdue for some lady-scaping, but she'd grabbed her sexiest bra and panty set after her shower. Discussing this over dinner was weird, though.

Or maybe that wasn't what he meant at all? Why was this so hard?

Zach spoke again before she could figure out how to respond. "I'm sorry. I didn't mean to make things uncomfortable. I was thinking about how nice it is to have a conversation with a human instead of staring at a screen or talking to my animals. You seem to appreciate the food, so I thought bringing over an occasional meal might be nice."

Veronica was an asshole. Her brothers had been telling her for years, but she'd always believed she wasn't as bad as they claimed. Now, a nice and attractive man was offering to cook and bring her food, and she was being so obtuse about it, he'd felt the need to apologize. "It's okay. I didn't understand what you were asking. Please ignore my crazy."

Zachary looked up at her with his brow furrowed. "What part of it confused you?" He rushed to continue. "I don't mean that in a snarky way. I'm not saying anything like that. I'm just wondering where I could clarify."

Shaking her head in wonder, Veronica doubted anyone, in the history of ever, had this horrible of a meal with someone they'd just met.

"It was me, not you," she tried to assure him. "I was having this whole inner debate about if you wanted me to invite you to stay the night, which you obviously didn't. I don't know why you would anyway, but it doesn't matter. I was being dumb. If the offer is still there, I'd love to have dinner together sometimes. Maybe I could even cook for you one night, like Thursdays. If I'm doing it for someone else, I don't forget." She frowned and added, "Usually."

Good grief, he must be appalled, but having real food without having to answer a million questions from her mother was too alluring for her not to continue. "I promise my cooking is edible. Some people even say it's good. Except for my chili. I won't make that for you, don't worry. I gave up on that a long time ago."

And now Zach was laughing at her. It was silent, but he was covering his mouth and nose with his napkin as if he were afraid of spitting out his food. The way his shoulders shook hard enough to rattle the chair didn't help.

If this was the last good meal she'd be getting from this man, Veronica was determined to enjoy it. She gave up on conversation, or whatever someone would call their awkward back and forth and refocused on her plate. Ignoring Zach's hiccupping gulps as he tried to get himself under control wasn't easy, but she did her best to keep her expression blank.

Once Zach could breathe and form words, he confessed, "I spent almost thirty minutes trying to pick out pants and a shirt because I couldn't decide if tonight was a date or not. I almost showed up in my funeral pants, but my waistline has expanded since the last time I wore them so they wouldn't button."

"And then you found me in the exact opposite of date-ready condition." The mortification rolled over her.

"No. I'm trying to say we both appear to be struggling with understanding the social situations we're creating for ourselves, so maybe we should just be upfront about it?" He paused for a minute.

Once she'd looked up and made eye contact, Zachary added, "I'd love for this meal to be a casual date where we may end up friends or we may kiss goodnight." The carefully cultivated, mature adult expression on his face looked as real as Monopoly money.

Then he picked up his wine and said, "Either way, I'd love for us to have dinner together sometimes to keep each other company and ensure you eat." The way he followed it with a large gulp from his glass made her think he was trying to be nonchalant about it, and he sounded sincere, despite his awkwardly formal approach.

"So, no sex." Veronica clarified to ensure she understood.

Zach's wine shot from his mouth like a pressure washer turned up too high. The drops added moisture to the remaining food in the casserole dish, seasoned Veronica's plate, and spritzed her face.

She squealed and pushed back from the table laughing but had to admit she liked the unpolished honesty better than the façade, despite the awkwardness and mess. Maybe they were kindred, disastrous spirits after all.

"I'm so sorry," he apologized through her laughter. "You surprised me. I didn't mean to spit on you."

"I have brothers," she shared between her gasps and hiccups of laughter. "They do it on purpose." Forcing herself to take a deep breath and a slow exhale, Veronica dried her eyes and wiped her face. "I should have warned you before I spoke. I do like your idea, though. Both about having dinner together and being clearer about our expectations."

"Is sex an option for our list of expectations?" Zach asked with complete sincerity.

Big girl panties, Veronica! They were both adults. There was nothing wrong with this conversation. "Yes."

Silence.

She was met with silence.

Zach wasn't even blinking anymore.

Maybe she'd broken him?

His jaw was slack, and it looked like a puddle of drool was forming near his bottom lip.

She tried to make it better. "It could be casual, friendly sex. It doesn't have to be romantic or anything."

That got a reaction. The man snarled at her. It was a deep rumble from his chest as he bared his teeth and glared. He did not relax the grit of his teeth as he answered, "If you agree to have sex with me, there will be nothing friendly or casual about it. I don't share, and I don't sleep with women lightly."

"Right. My bad." He thought she was a whore who slept around. Great. This was just great.

"No, not your bad," Zach huffed. Then he stood up and walked around the table toward her with a gravity she'd not seen from him before. Once he was beside her, he squatted down and looked her in the eye. "My former marriage was an epic disaster I never plan to repeat, but I like you and would love to have sex with you. You just need to know that I can't do it casually, and I'm an overbearing asshole. My heart gets involved. I get protective and possessive, so I won't go there and risk you cheating on me. If you invite me into your bed, my acceptance will come with the expectation that we're exclusive. Be sure you're ready for that before you extend that invitation for real."

Holy fuck, his words were like an electric charge delivered straight to her clit. Veronica shifted her hips. She could feel the moisture pooling between her legs, but she also understood what he was saying. And, she would respect it. She might need to buy more batteries, but she would honor his limits. "Okay."

Then he slowly reached for her face without breaking eye contact. When she didn't stop him, he used his thumb to brush a drop of wine from her forehead. She must have missed it with her napkin.

Except, instead of wiping it on his pants, like she would have done, Zach brought his thumb to her lips and offered it to her. It was like a scene from a movie. In fact, maybe this was all a crazy dream. With that in mind, she parted her lips, stretched her tongue forward, and licked the salty wine flavor from his skin.

His answering moan pulled her toward him like a magnet, but before she could lick his lips the way she's licked his thumb, Zachary pulled back.

She was close enough to feel his chest move with his deep inhale. He closed his eyes before saying, "I can't do this. Please don't mistake it for a lack of desire, but I meant what I said earlier."

Veronica had no idea how she was supposed to respond to that. What the hell had his ex-wife done to him?

Zach opened his eyes and stared into hers before dropping his hands from her face and returning to his own chair.

He shoveled the last of his food into his mouth without looking at her.

"I appreciate the dinner," Veronica offered lamely.

He grinned, so it must not have come out as bad as it sounded in her head. "Good. I appreciate the company."

"Friends?" she checked.

"For now, with the potential for more," Zach agreed.

# Chapter 7

Veronica leaned against her front door after exchanging phone numbers and saying goodnight to Zachary. She tried to remember the last time she'd enjoyed a meal with anyone not related to Taylor Industries. Of course, she'd been on dates, but none of those were enjoyable. She couldn't help flinching as she remembered agreeing to dinner with Brian Renner. He was their primary contact at Dynamic Solutions, the company that held the government contract they fell under.

He also lived further from the city than most of his co-workers since the cost of living was so much cheaper. He wasn't nearly as rural as the Taylors, but when Patrick told him Veronica was moving back to Whitetail Mountain, he'd gotten her number and asked her out citing the scarcity of women who were both smart and pretty. She'd been flattered enough to agree to meet him for dinner.

The date started off bad when she arrived forty minutes late and got worse from there. By the end of the meal, she'd practically run away from him.

Patrick had been pissed too, and she could see his point. Their subcontract with Dynamic Solutions was their primary revenue source. They had several other contracts, but none compared to DS. The only good thing to come of it was Patrick's refusal to let her speak with Renner. Everything went through him, which was fine by Veronica. She'd worried Freddy's call warning her that Renner would be at their Monday meeting would change that, but Patrick had seated Renner on the other side of the room and ensured Veronica didn't have to interact with him, despite the way he gave her puppy eyes throughout the entire meeting.

She had to admit, Zachary was probably right to avoid jumping into anything too fast. Her attraction could be inspired more by desperation than real chemistry, and she didn't need to start a feud with her neighbor the way she had her colleague.

Veronica pictured the way Zach's thumb had glided across her forehead. Had her shiver of pleasure been purely from going too long without human contact? Surely that wouldn't be enough to cause the electric spark and giddy joy she felt around him.

Then again, she was concerned about her own mental health, so maybe she shouldn't trust her reactions. Veronica flopped her head back against the door with a thud. She needed someone outside the situation. Veronica grabbed her phone and called her sister.

"This is Ophelia."

"Hey, Phee. Are you aware that you can see who's calling you before you answer?" Veronica's sister might be three years younger, but the entire family swore she was an octogenarian trapped in a millennial body.

"Oh, Veronica, it's good to hear from you. What's going on out there in the woods?"

"I'm losing my shit in the most literal sense of the word, but I do think my mind is slipping. I also met a hot guy who won't sleep with me. And I might have a stalker or two. Wils wants me to restructure the firewall around the bots, and apparently, I like Orange Roughie. How often does a human need sex to avoid going insane?"

Veronica's outburst was met with a breath of silence before Ophelia responded. "Isn't it supposed to be the younger sister calling the older one for advice?"

"Um, have you met our family? We're not normal and generally refuse to do things we're supposed to on principle."

"Fair enough," Phee laughed. "Okay, let's start by splitting this discussion into two parts: work and love. Which should we dissect first? Oh, and I heard about the guy sending flowers to you at HQ. What is up with that?"

"Wait, what? Who sent me flowers? Patrick didn't tell me about that." Had Renner brought her flowers, but Freddy and Patrick made them disappear before she got there? It was something they'd do but given the way Brian stared at her all day, she'd expect him to have said something. Then again, Patrick could have threatened him.

Ophelia huffed before she answered, "Our brothers are idiots. Except for Gabe. He seems to be somewhat human. Some guy named Kurt sent a giant bouquet for you. Mom mentioned it when I talked to her around lunch today."

"Kurt was the guy I was supposed to meet for dinner Monday, but he stood me up," Veronica explained.

"Ohh, so they were apology flowers. You might want to give the man a call. Unless your new man has already laid claim to your heart?" Phee could be a huge gossip, but at least she listened to what Veronica said.

"Arg," she grumbled. "I don't know. I like Zachary. A lot. He feels like home, but he also gives me butterflies. Kurt gave me butterflies, but I feel awkward around him. And, there's the whole thing where he stood me up for our date." Then she remembered that she only found out about the flowers second hand, or was it third or fourth since it was passed from her brother to her mother to her sister? "Why didn't anyone tell *me* about the flowers?"

"Because it's Patrick," Phee pointed out. The man probably forgot about them the minute he saw they weren't for him. "I'm sure he or Mom will mention them at some point. For now, let's discuss your sudden love of fish, and see if we can pick apart why you think you're losing your mind."

This was why she'd called Ophelia. That woman could turn the emotional fallout from an affair into a spreadsheet. She'd be able to help sort through Veronica's spiraling thoughts.

"Zachary made the orange roughie and brought it over for dinner."

"Tell me about him. I've got my notepad ready."

Of course, she'd be taking notes while Veronica talked. Ophelia would end up with a tidy, bullet-point list that she'd organize by priority. At the end of it, the right choice would be obvious. Veronica told her sister about Zachary stopping by and then bringing over dinner. She confessed to the disastrous start to the dinner and the confusing ending.

"Okay, so I understand the confusion between him and your general frustrations, but let's take a different perspective. Remember the guy you dated in college? I think his name was Steve?"

"Yeah, he tried to get me to have sex with his friends." Veronica couldn't forget that disaster no matter how she tried to scrub it from her memory.

"He'd invited you over for a party without mentioning some important details, but when you misunderstood something with Zachary, he stopped to clarify, right?" she asked Veronica.

"Uh, huh."

"So he's not a Steve-level dick. What about Renner? When you didn't enjoy your time with him, he was totally oblivious, right? But it sounds like your new guy paid close attention to both your words and the meaning beneath them."

Veronica hadn't thought about it like that before, but it was scarily accurate.

"It sounds like you and Zach covered some serious conversations, and he got a little growly, but he still spoke with respect, talked to you about everything, and checked in that you were okay with all of it, didn't he?"

"I get your point, Phee. Zach isn't like some of the guys I've dated before, but that doesn't magically mean I won't fuck it up, and it sounds like his last relationship already hurt him enough for a lifetime."

"You didn't mention that. What past relationship?"

"I honestly don't know more than that he was married, and it was bad. He implied she cheated on him, but I might have misunderstood."

"Hmm," Phee made thinking noises while scratching things down on her notepad. "Okay, you need to ask him more about that and confirm that you both agree to talk anytime you get upset to avoid misunderstandings, but it doesn't sound like sex is an immediate concern, and the guy was nice while seeing the real you. It's not like you put on some fake show of perfection for him. I think he's worth exploring something with." Ophelia made it sound so simple.

"But what if it doesn't work out?"

Her sister sighed. "There's an eighty percent chance it won't."

"That's not helpful, Phee!" Veronica stood up to pace the living room. She didn't mean to screech, but she felt so full of energy or anxiety or nerves or dinner that she couldn't contain everything inside herself.

"Imagine everything worked out perfectly. What would life with him look like three years from now?" Ophelia asked with a calmness that made Veronica want to thank her and punch her at the same time.

Before she could respond, her phone chimed with an incoming text from Kurt.

> **Did you get my flowers?**

"Hang on Phee. Kurt's texting me." Then she typed out her reply.

> **No, but I heard they're at Patrick's house.**

> **That's where you work, right?**

"Veronica," Phee's shout was loud enough for Veronica to hear despite having pulled the phone away from her ear. She switched it over to the speaker.

"I'm still here. Kurt's texting about the flowers."

> **Yeah, but we only work in-person on Mondays.**

"What's going on with you two? He had such a huge crush on you in high school, but now he stands you up?" Ophelia asked.

Veronica sighed. "I honestly don't understand it myself. I didn't think he'd ever speak to me again after we went on that date when I was home for the summer after sophomore year of college."

"Oh, I'd forgotten about that!" Phee squealed through the phone. "Did you dump a drink on him or something?"

Rolling her eyes at her sister's memory, Veronica corrected her. "Not at all. He took me to the fair and suggested we ride the scrambler right after getting funnel cakes. It was completely his fault that I puked all over him."

"And now he's sending you flowers?"

> Ah, That's okay. I can send more to your house.

"Apparently," Veronica absentmindedly responded to her sister while trying to tell Kurt he didn't need to send more flowers.

"Huh, but he stood you up," Phee said thoughtfully. "Does that seem weird to you?"

"Phee ninety percent of life seems weird to me." Of course Veronica thought it was weird, but she also thought it was weird that Zach brought her dinner, so she didn't put too much stock in any of it.

"Hm, we'll chat more about that later. Right now, tell me what it might look like if things worked out with the new guy and why you worry you're losing your mind," Ophelia prompted.

Glad to return to the conversation she wanted to have, Veronica launched into her imaginary future with Zach. "Well, he's an alpaca farmer, so we'd still live out here. He'd cook dinner for us most nights, but I'd cook on Thursdays. He'd probably drag me to bed after the news every night, and I doubt he'd ever sleep in. Well, maybe he'd stay in bed to get me naked. He said he was possessive."

"Ronnie, I can hear your smile. You like this guy."

"Don't call me that. We're not kids anymore." Veronica's brothers had given up the nickname after she'd started dick-punching them anytime they used it, but she'd never figured out how to make Phee stop. At least she only used it occasionally and when it was just the two of them.

"Why would you not want to date him?" Ophelia asked.

"I– well, I mean–" Nothing. Veronica had nothing to say in response. Her sister's chuckle said she knew it, too. "Fine. Let's move on to talk about work."

"Veronica, you've been screwing around with computer security stuff since Dad replaced your cheap kiddie diary with Windows '94. When you tried working other places, you were miserable–"

"–because they wouldn't let me stick with the computer stuff I'm good at," Veronica interrupted to defend herself. "They wanted a stupid model to shake some ass while handing out files and making copies."

"I know, and that's part of my point. I'm sure you could find a place that respected you, or at least didn't sexually harass you, but would you really like it better than working for Taylor Industries? Do you really hate working for Patrick?"

"No, but I wish he wouldn't be so mean when I'm late, and I hate presenting last," she whined.

"Have you told him that?"

Oh, the heck with Ophelia and her stupid logic. "He should let me upgrade our systems and start using security tokens so we can store stuff in the cloud."

"I'm going to take that to mean you have not talked to him about it. Also, didn't Mom ban him from asking you to work more than sixty hours a week?"

"I could do the upgrade without working too much."

Her sister sighed so loud, Veronica worried the people in China could hear it. "Based on my notes, you worked so much today, you forgot a hot guy was bringing you dinner and never managed to get dressed or brush your teeth."

Veronica started to interject, but Ophelia knew her too well.

"Nope. Do not argue with me, Ronnie. I'm stating facts. You love your work and enjoy spending eighteen plus hours in front of your computer, but that doesn't make it healthy. Mom and Dad and Patrick are all just trying to help you find some balance in your life. Why do you always fight them on it?"

"You make me sound like I can't take care of myself," Veronica grumbled.

"We both know that's not true. Don't be dramatic. You called me to help you set aside the emotions and consider the situation, so I'm pointing out that what your life is missing is a person who you enjoy hanging out with as much as you enjoy your work. Considering how long you spent talking to Zach and the way you called me instead of returning to your computer after he left, I'd say he has the potential to be that person."

"Damn you, Phee." She was right. About everything.

"Just give him a chance. You said something about you making dinner on Thursdays?" Ophelia prompted.

"Yeah, he does his paperwork that day, and it makes him more tired than working directly with his animals all day, so it's the one day he never cooks."

"See, that's perfect. You used to enjoy cooking when we forced you to do it. I bet once you start sleeping with him, he'll make it worth your while, too."

Now Phee was being the pain-in-the-ass little sister Veronica used to taunt with decapitated Barbies. "If this ends badly, I'm coming to your place to cry, and I expect you to have ice cream ready."

"Will do. Now, what's this about a stalker? And why do you think you're losing your mind?"

Veronica's phone chimed with another text from Kurt, but this one made her gasp.

**I like the Tiger Lilies by your porch.**

"What's wrong?" Phee must have heard her.

"Hang on." Veronica darted to the front window, but there was nothing to see in her yard. No cars but her Jeep; no unexpected lights. "Kurt said he likes my Tiger Lilies," she said to her sister.

"What? How does he see them in the dark? And when did he get there?" Phee sounded as confused as Veronica felt.

"I don't know, but he's not here."

"Oh, you posted those pics on Facebook. Were they blooming then?"

Veronica could practically hear Phee pulling up her Facebook account to check, so she didn't bother responding.

"Yep, he's totally searching you and creeping on your socials," Ophelia said with a giggle. That led them deeper into discussion about Veronica losing track of things more than usual but nothing ever going missing.

By the time they ended the conversation, it was almost eleven. Veronica wanted to grab a cup of coffee and pick up where she left off on the work on her firewall, but her sister's comment about better sleep habits was still swirling through her brain.

Instead, she stood, stretched, and walked over to lock the door before calling it a night. Instead of falling dark once she clicked off the living room light, a pair of headlights illuminated the space. They beamed into her space like an intruder, and Veronica's entire core clenched in fear. Were these the men Zachary had seen? Had they come back?

Ophelia had tried to convince her that she should take the misplaced stuff and Zach's report more seriously, but Veronica couldn't imagine anyone coming all the way out here just to fuck with her. What could they possibly hope to get?

Right then, as the light shifted to create new shadows and illuminate different corners, Veronica wished she wasn't alone. Maybe it was leftover heebie jeebies from Kurt's unexpected comment about the lilies, but the terror took control of her fingers as she texted Zachary without thinking it through.

> **Headlights in my driveway. I'm not expecting anyone. What do I do?**

After hitting send, she considered his farm schedule and realized he was probably asleep. That meant he'd see it in the morning and know she was really losing it. Fuck. Veronica was looking for options to unsend it when her phone lit up with an incoming call from the man himself. Shit. She declined the call in a panic. Well, so much for dating him.

The angle of headlights shifted again and turned away from her window, leaving her in darkness before a hint of red glowed from their taillights as they drove back down her driveway.

Veronica hugged her phone to her chest as tears started rolling down her face. She'd always been scatterbrained, but she was really losing it. She was terrified by a lost car using her driveway to turn around, but she couldn't even leave it at that. No, she'd shared it with the guy she'd just decided to try spending time with. What was Ophelia thinking when she'd argued Veronica could find someone to share her life with? Who would want to deal with her? Even she wanted to escape her own chaos.

She let herself sink back into the couch as she curled up in the fetal position with her phone tucked into her center. She felt the vibration of another call coming in, but she ignored it.

Veronica wasn't sure how long she laid there before the pounding started.

"Veronica, let me in. If you're there, answer the door. I'll break the window to let myself in if I have to! Veronica!"

Zach's voice was easy to identify. "Go away!" she screamed. He didn't need to witness this. She wanted to hide until he forgot what a wreck she was. Tomorrow, she'd figure out what to do, or not do, or whatever. She could always move into HQ with Patrick. That thought added a hysterical laugh into the midst of her sobs.

"I found your spare key, and I'm coming in. Don't shoot me!" she heard Zach yell through the door as she watched the deadbolt twist to unlock.

The next thing she knew, he'd scooped her up onto his lap and was cradling her head against his chest while massaging her scalp.

"Hey, V. It's okay. You're safe. It's okay. Nothing's going to hurt you."

Veronica was pretty sure he'd asked some questions too, but she didn't care to answer them right then. She was so tired, and Zach was so warm and comforting. Once she explained, he'd be gone, and she just wanted a few more minutes before she had to worry about everything again.

Eventually, she ran out of tears and her sniffles dried up.

Zach was still holding her and still rubbing her back. His shirt was wet where she'd snotted, slobbered, and eye-leaked all over him.

"I'm sorry for bothering you. I think I'm done crying on you," she offered softly.

"You're probably dehydrated," he responded.

Veronica let out a deep sigh. "Maybe, but it stopped so you can go or whatever. I didn't even mean for you to come over. I'm so sorry I woke you. I know you probably have to get up early." She tried to pull away from him and climb off his lap, but his arms around her tightened.

"Hold up a minute. I think I've earned a little more than that, don't you?" he asked in little more than a whisper.

Veronica stiffened. "I don't owe anyone anything." She thought he might have muttered a curse under his breath, but she wasn't sure.

"I know, and that's now what I meant. But I'm not letting go or leaving yet, because I need to know that you're safe. You get caught up in your work, and it sounds like losing track of regular life stuff is normal for you. But it's also clear that you are insanely smart, meticulous about things that matter, and competent enough to have made it this far in life. I highly doubt you're crazy, and I do not believe that any of what's happening is in your head. For fuck's sake, Veronica, I saw two guys here with flashlights with my own eyes! You are not making this up, and it's not your imagination. Whatever is going on, your intuition is telling you to be alert. Have you ever panicked over a car turning around in your driveway before?"

Huh, she must have mumbled out some explanation through her tears. "No, but I shouldn't be panicking over it now, either."

"Veronica." Zachary sighed. "It's real. All of it. I refuse to ignore it and risk finding your body once it's too late." His voice was getting louder as he spoke. "You know what? I don't even care if you believe it. I do, and I'm going to make sure you're safe. Fucking hell. I'm not–" He sighed again and shook his head before loosening his arms enough for her to pull back and look into his face.

Once they were eye-to-eye, he continued, "I cannot leave you to whatever happens next. It's not possible. We can work together to figure it out, or you can ignore it while I take care of it. That's your choice, but I'm not letting this go."

The steel in his voice reminded Veronica of the few occasions when she'd pushed her father too far, and he'd drawn a line in the sand and would not budge.

"Why do you care?" she asked.

His eyes flicked as he searched her face before he answered. "As I was lying in bed and rolling back and forth, unable to settle down, I realized that dinner with you was the best evening I've had in years. Years, Veronica." Then he looked up at the ceiling and murmured something that sounded a bit like, *What the fuck am I doing?* "How old are you?" he asked once he looked back at her.

It was not a question she'd anticipated. "Thirty-two."

Zachary huffed an unfunny laugh before he explained, "I'm ten years older than you. I retired from the Navy almost five years ago, and I was married for ten years before that. My land, my farm, this is all my retirement. I've lived my life. I figured I enjoy my animals, keep to myself, and eventually die on my front porch. My will includes an addendum in case my carcass is consumed by wildlife."

"You're not that old." Well, he was older than her, but that didn't mean anything. Forty-two wasn't old.

"I'm too old for the way I feel about you. Even Izzy never made me panic the way I did when I got your text and then you didn't answer my calls."

"That was your wife?" she asked.

"Yeah. We went on a few dates while I was on shore duty, and it started to feel serious. So when I went back on sea duty, I asked her to move with me. I should have objected when she suggested it wouldn't be worth it for her to get a new job. Of course that meant she needed health insurance, so getting married made sense."

"But you didn't love her?"

"In a way I did, but not the kind of love that should inspire marriage."

Veronica wanted to ask about the divorce but having his arms around her felt amazing. She was afraid asking might give him a reason to leave, especially since he probably should leave and get some sleep.

"Hey, just ask. Please. I can see you thinking, and my imagination is starting to run wild." Then he smirked and added, "At least tell me you aren't considering all the ways you could manipulate me into signing over Butthole so you could keep him for yourself."

Laughing the way he'd obviously intended, Veronica decided to ask. It wasn't like she'd been able to hide the rest of her quirks from him.

As soon as she finished her question, he hugged her a little tighter before explaining. "My terminal leave," he stopped when he must have seen the confusion on her face. "We build up time off, especially during a deployment. When our enlistment ends, we use all of that time before separating and officially ending our time in the Navy. In my case, I was on deployment and had eighty-seven days off built up when there were eighty-seven days left on my contract. The Navy sent me home to enjoy my terminal leave before my time officially ended."

"That makes sense."

"Between arranging the timing and the travel required, I didn't know exactly when I'd get back, so I figured I'd surprise Izzy." Zach chuckled. "I did, too. I shocked the hell out of her when I walked in to find her sharing our bed with our neighbor."

"That's bitchy." Veronica was prepared for the cheating, but to do it while he was deployed and with his friend. That was low.

"Yeah, but I should have seen it coming. At one point, she accused me of only wanting her so I'd have someone who needed me and made me feel important. As much as it hurts, she might have had a point."

"I get why you don't want to sleep with me. You'd probably feel the same way trying to deal with me all the time, but I don't understand why you came running over here and won't leave when I'm just like her."

"That's just it. You're not like her at all. She'd have put on a big show with hair and make-up and a nice outfit during dinner only to ask why I didn't bring dessert. She'd have called demanding I come protect her. Heck, she called yesterday asking me for money to cover her mortgage."

Veronica frowned. "Are you two still, like, friends or something?"

"Hell no!" Zach looked appalled. "I'm just too stupid to block her calls, but you know what, I can fix that." He wiggled around to pull his phone from his pocket.

With the way they were sitting, Veronica had a clear view of his screen as he blocked her number from calling or texting him.

"Why now?" she asked.

Zachary shrugged and said, "Why not? It's time. It was probably time a while ago."

"So now what?" she asked. He'd said he wouldn't leave her on her own with all of this, and she didn't want to deal with it by herself. They might as well work together to be friends or whatever.

"Let's start with figuring out who's after you and why," Zach suggested.

Veronica tucked her hair behind her ear and asked the question she hated more than any other. "Do you know who my family is?"

Zachary smiled like he'd won the lottery. "Yes, and no. I know your family owns Taylor Industries, and that it's very successful, but I don't know what the company does, only what you talked about while we had coffee."

She tried to inject some humor into the moment. "Are you saying you know just enough that you don't worry I'll only want you for your money," she teased. "Or do you want me for mine?"

The look of horror on his face had her backpedaling before the final syllable cleared her lips.

"Not that I think you are just here for my money. I mean, you could be, but I don't think that. I meant it as a joke."

# Chapter 8

Zachary didn't miss the truth and vulnerability behind her question. He wanted to shred any asshole who'd tried to use Veronica for her family's money, but he tried to keep his voice even and calm. "I'm not here for your money. I have my own, even after giving Izzy everything she needed to start a fresh life. Has that been a problem for you in the past?"

Veronica studied his face as if checking his sincerity. Then she explained, "I learned to spot and avoid people like that long ago. It really was meant as a joke."

Zachary nodded but didn't speak as he considered pursuing a conversation about the way he believed Veronica deserved to be treated versus getting more information about who might be after her. For now, the latter was more important. "Needing to learn that is shitty, but let's stay focused on your work and come back to that later."

"Of course," Veronica agreed. "None of my work is anything meaningful. I fuck around with firewalls and program them to let some stuff through, but not other stuff. The only time anybody gives a shit about what I do is when an important email fails to get delivered or a phishing email gets through and clogs up everyone's inbox. As a whole, the company does cool stuff, but I'm not smart enough to be involved in any of it."

"Security means protection, so what else do you protect besides email?" Zachary asked without commenting on her self-deprecation... for now.

"Uh, I mean there is other stuff that I build firewalls around."

"Like what? What are you working on right now?" he asked. "Didn't you say something about there being an issue with a firewall that you were trying to fix today?"

Veronica's eyes widened in surprise. Zach wanted to be shocked that she wasn't used to people listening when she spoke, but it fit with everything else he'd learned about her. He gave her time to process and decide what to share.

"Remember that issue on the space station a couple of months ago?" she finally asked.

"Yeah, vaguely. Something broke, and they were all going to die, but then a robot saved them or something."

"Right, so our family business started with using microcomputers and artificial intelligence. My dad was one of the first to apply swarm theory to create semi-autonomous microbots." The intense way Veronica studied his face while she spoke was enchanting, and he loved that she allowed him to confirm his understanding.

"That's where they make little robots that work together like ants or bees, right?" The grin he got in response made him feel taller than the Jolly Green Giant.

"Basically, yes. We were always limited by the need for human commanders or leaders or whatever, though. Think of the bots like soldiers. They needed a human to tell them what to do. It meant they had to execute one set of commands and report back. Then they had to wait for humans to assess the report, make decisions, and issue the next set of commands."

"I can see how that would limit their work, but wouldn't it also prevent them from taking over the world?" As irrational as he knew it was, there was no escaping that fear.

"No. Robots will not be taking over the world. Especially the tiny bots we work with." Veronica chuckled as she reassured him. "Even after all our advancements, if we leave the bots alone for more than about twelve hours, they start attacking and disassembling each other. We've never had a swarm survive more than twenty-four hours without human intervention."

This was where he got stuck. "I believe everything you're saying, but I'm not sure I understand it."

"Have you heard any stories about when AI first became a big thing?"

Zach shook his head, so she explained, "Programmers learned that a bot talking to a bot will devolve into chaos. Neither can make intentional decisions or create an end goal, so the conversation spirals down into nonsense."

"Wasn't some of it racist, too?" There were glimmers of memories about something like that making the news.

"Yes, but it's more than that." Veronica cocked her head to the side and contorted her face into what Zach had to assume was a look of deep thought. "My dad could never get past the need for humans to be involved in every little thing with the bots, but then we had a breakthrough. Well, a couple of breakthroughs," she corrected. "The first was developing nanobots."

"How are those different from microbots?" Zach asked while wondering if he should have grabbed something to take notes while she spoke.

Veronica smiled at him before answering. "Mainly, they're smaller. Nanobots are smaller than a grain of rice, which is technically still micro, but considering we call the pea-sized bots kilobots, and the golf ball-sized ones microbots, we call the tiniest ones nanobots for simplicity."

"Okay, I think I'm following. You have three sizes of tiny robots that work together." Zach was well-aware he was oversimplifying this, but it was his only hope of understanding it on any level.

"Yes-ish. One of the big problems with tiny bots is limited space for programming. Once they get so small, they can only follow the simplest of instructions."

Zachary hummed in thought. "Why not just make them all bigger, then?"

"Because smaller bots can swarm to build other, bigger things. Think about a flock of birds or a school of fish arranging themselves in a certain way. Bots can do the same thing. It means we can send a box of bots to the space station and that one box can become any kind of wrench or tool needed. Even better, they can work together to perform a task. My dad and his old partner figured out how to use friction and electromagnets to get the bots to propel each other. It's deep and complicated, but basically you can tell the bots something like *build a screwdriver and remove that screw*, and they can do it."

It was making more sense now. "Got it. Big bots are smart and little bots are strong."

Veronica blinked. "That's exactly right. I mean, there are more details to consider, but basically." Zach's chest puffed up with pride. This woman was smart, and he was keeping up. At least enough to continue the conversation, anyway.

After rewarding him with a cock-hardening smile, Veronica added, "I never thought to phrase it like that, but I might from now on."

Then she returned to her explanation. "When my brother took over as CEO, we started putting them together to get the best of all worlds. Most people think that was a big deal because the astronauts could have died, but that wasn't what would have happened. They'd have just been stuck a lot longer and maybe had to ration food. The amazing part was that three levels of bots worked together with zero human intervention and completed twenty-three individual repairs. There were a few pieces of debris the bots couldn't figure out what to do about, but they resolved more than ninety percent of the problems the station was experiencing."

Zachary was in trouble. Big trouble. This woman was snatching his heart right from his chest, and he wasn't sure he'd ever get it back. The way her face lit up as she bounced, literally bounced, on the couch while explaining what the bots could do was a level of passion Zachary had dreamed of finding.

He forced back his awe enough to respond. "That's impressive." Impressive enough he'd stayed focused on her face and words despite her bra laying draped across a chair. Her excited bouncing would have given him a wonderful display of her feminine assets, but he'd been enthralled by the rest of her. "How do your firewalls relate to that? Or are you involved in the programming for that project?"

"It's my firewall. Well, it was. My brother found an issue, so we're trying to fix that before anything bad happens."

"And your brother's the CEO?" He knew she'd mentioned that, but he also remembered something about her having several siblings.

"Yes, but that's not the brother that found the issue. Patrick's the CEO. Freddy runs research and design, which also does all our testing. He found that under one specific set of conditions, there's a gap in the firewall. We've never recorded those conditions happening outside of him making them happen in his lab, but it's theoretically possible, so we want to patch the hole. I thought I had the patch, but it turned out part of my code interfered with the bots communicating with each other, so now I have to start over."

"That's what you were working on today." Zachary did remember her talking about that over dinner.

"Yes."

"Who might want to get past the bot's firewall?" he asked. He'd seen for himself that Veronica could hyper-focus and forget about the world around her, but he couldn't picture her losing or misplacing things. If anything, he suspected she'd spent her entire life subconsciously learning to structure her life around her hyper-focus, so she didn't have to think about anything else. Her nutrition bars were a prime example of that. He would bet his pension that she put her keys in the exact same place for at least the last ten years. Someone was intruding on her life and fucking with it. Maybe it was personal. Maybe it was related to her work. It didn't matter to Zachary. He would figure it out and make it stop. He'd keep her safe along the way, too.

"Any of our competitors and maybe some foreign governments." Veronica didn't sound as confident as she had when discussing the technology itself, but her answer aligned with Zach's expectations.

"Tell me about corporate espionage in your industry. How big of an issue is it?" He'd spent enough time in the Navy to know how contractors would bid against each other right before being forced to work together on projects. He knew they all had non-compete clauses and non-disclosure agreements on top of the security clearances and background checks required by the government.

"I don't know." Veronica shrugged. "I guess it's a concern since Patrick's always insisting on air gaps and other archaic and over-the-top measures, but why would they come here?"

"I don't know, but I think we should look into it."

Veronica pulled away from him and hopped up from the couch. "I can go start searching. There are a few people I could ask who might give us a better sense of how that works in theory and some real-world examples of past corporate espionage." She turned toward her office like she was going to work right then.

"Hold up. Veronica, it's after midnight. Sleep first; investigate later."

He loved the way her brow furrowed as she looked at the clock, but he hated the way she ignored her basic needs, like food and sleep.

"I couldn't sleep now, anyway." Her hands were gripping the hem of her t-shirt so hard her knuckles were turning white.

Zachary remembered how upset she'd been when he'd arrived. The headlights had scared the shit out of her, and then she'd berated herself for feeling afraid. She had to be exhausted, but he could see how the thought of lying alone in bed in the dark wouldn't hold any appeal. He wasn't crazy about the idea himself.

"I understand not wanting to sleep, but there's a field of gray between sleeping and working. How about we compromise and turn on a movie while getting comfortable on the couch?" Zachary had a feeling she'd pass out in just a few minutes if he could get her to settle. He just wasn't sure what it would take for her to be that comfortable.

He watched her scuff a toe along the floor as she chewed on her bottom lip and thought about it. She didn't hide or shy away from him, though. Her lip was tooth-free and perfectly steady when she looked up and asked, "Are you going home or staying here?"

"I'm staying here. I'll need to go take care of my animals tomorrow, but they'll be fine until mid-day."

"What movie were you thinking we should watch?" she asked while taking a few steps back toward where he was still sitting on the couch.

He considered saying something like The Notebook, but Zach was pretty sure Veronica was more aware than most people realized. If she could be confident enough to ask if he was staying, he could be honest about what movie he wanted to watch. "I could use a comedy. I want something without the loud explosions and intensity of an action movie, but also light-hearted and superficial. I'm done with deep thinking for the night."

Veronica's smile proved his honesty had been the right choice. "Have you ever seen Without a Paddle?" she asked.

He hadn't, but she promised it fit the bill. She'd turned it on, checked that he didn't mind her using his thigh as a pillow, and drifted into a snoring slumber before the guys had started their hunt for D.B. Cooper.

# Chapter 9

Zachary was having the best dream ever. His dream woman was sliding his cock between her thighs and begging him to fill her up and make her scream. Okay, he might have added the begging, but he hadn't had a dream like this since his first deployment. It only took his shipmates catching him moaning in his sleep once for his subconscious to learn to keep dreams PG. He wasn't in the Navy anymore, though. He could enjoy this dream. Zachary slid his hand down to stroke himself but found something blocking his access.

It was soft and warm, and it moaned.

He glided his hand over the bunched-up fabric waistband and across the smooth skin above it until he felt the dip of a belly button.

The moan was replaced with a soft chuckle followed by a confused hum.

Zach pried open one eyelid enough to confirm that his memory of the night before was real. He was on his side and wedged between the back of the couch and Veronica. Her backside was pressed firmly against his front, and he was horrified to realize he'd been the one sliding his cock between her very real thighs.

Shortly after Veronica had started snoring, he'd set the sleep timer on the tv and adjusted them to both lay down. When she'd texted her fear but not answered his calls, he'd thrown on the same new jeans he'd worn earlier. Veronica had mostly slept through him rearranging them on the couch, but she'd stirred enough to complain about the rough pants being uncomfortable, even through her thin sleep pants.

Which was why his pants were now hanging off the armchair while his morning wood escaped the confines of his boxers and explored the beautiful woman he was curled around.

Zach tried to shift and wiggle to climb out from behind Veronica, but he didn't have any room to work with. His movements were just adding friction to his excited wood and making the situation worse.

"Your dick is huge."

Veronica's sleepy murmur had him freezing in place.

"Sorry," he started.

"Don't be." Her hand squeezed between their bodies and rubbed along his length. There was no pressure, and the angle was awkward, but Zachary's cock didn't care. It was so freaking happy to be tended to, the firework's fuse was in danger of being lit.

Zach slid his hand further up and under Veronica's top to reach her breasts. Despite her small size and almost skinny form, each breast had just enough volume for him to cup it in his palm while brushing his thumb over her nipple.

Instead of the moan he expected, Veronica fell silent and resumed stretching and twisting her fingers to make better contact with his dick.

"Nipple play not your thing?" he asked.

She sighed, "It's fine. I don't mind it."

Zachary's head reared back and slammed into the cushions of the couch. He shifted his weight up so he could roll her onto her back beneath him while he used his arms to hover over her. "Fine is not what we're going for here. Your nipples aren't an erogenous zone for you, and your belly button is ticklish. What does turn you on?" he asked.

She shifted her eyes to avoid connecting with his and didn't answer.

Maybe she didn't know. Maybe she was embarrassed. Maybe it had been long enough she wasn't sure anymore. It didn't matter.

He leaned down to kiss her jaw from her chin back to her ear. Once there, he whispered, "I want to hear every sound, every moan, and every whimper. Don't hold out on me, beautiful."

Zach didn't wait for a response before nipping and licking her earlobe and down her neck. She moaned when his teeth nipped at the skin by her collarbone where her neck connected to her shoulder, so he kept his open-mouth kisses and gentle sucks focused on that area while enjoying the way she tasted and smelled. Her noises encouraged him even more, and the world around them disappeared.

When her hips began thrusting up toward him, and her squirming developed a desperate edge, he couldn't stop his chuckle, "Need something?"

"Move," she demanded immediately. "Fucking, please move. I need more."

His delight at her desire might make him an ass, but he was willing to live with that if it got her to beg for him like that.

He lifted her shirt higher and dipped his head to place a single chaste kiss on each side of her chest before grazing his teeth down the right side of her ribs. Veronica's hips bucked up into him again.

"Move. Lower. I need more." She was shifting and wiggling to try to pull her shirt the rest of the way off while also attempting to rub against him.

"Let me help." Zach pushed up to his knees and sat back on his heels long enough to remove his own t-shirt before reaching forward to grab the hem of hers.

Just as he leaned forward, she lifted up. They collided halfway causing Zachary to lose his balance and pitch forward. Veronica's arms were trapped in her shirt, and Zach couldn't let go fast enough to prevent her from rolling off the couch with him.

But instead of aggravation or hurt, Veronica laughed as she landed on top of him. "I like this better anyway," she said as she flung her shirt across the room. "Now it's my turn."

She followed the same path he'd taken by starting at his chin and working her way back to his ear before traveling down his neck.

Zachary wasn't sure when he'd grabbed her hips with his hands and started grinding her center against him, but damn, did it feel good.

"Oh fuck, yes!" Veronica seemed to be enjoying it as well. "Condom. Please, Zach. Please tell me you have a condom," she begged.

It hit him like a giant bucket of ice water. He didn't have a condom because he didn't do random hookups. Hell, he hadn't slept with a woman in more than a year. They needed to slow down.

But Veronica was humping him with an intensity that could nullify the need for a condom. He could easily come just like this, and the gasps and whimpers that slipped out between Veronica's rapid breaths made him think she wasn't far from orgasm either.

Zach managed to pull back just far enough and just long enough to consider his options when he looked up and noticed the lamp on her side table had two knobs.

His grip on her hips changed from encouraging to stilling.

"What?" she asked as she looked at him with fully blown pupils and rosy, red cheeks. "As much as this makes me feel like a teenager, we can just hump each other into a happy ending."

"Why does your lamp have two knobs?" He didn't think before it flew from his mouth.

"What?" This time she sounded annoyed. Her pupils were shrinking, too.

"I'm sorry. I just..." He wasn't sure how to finish his sentence. "It's important. It's not the right time, but–" That was when it hit him.

He put a finger in front of his lips to signal that she should stay quiet. Then he shifted her off of him as he said, "I don't think we should do this right now. I need to take care of my animals." Then he stood up and pointed at the lamp.

"Right. Yeah. Later, I guess, or whatever." Veronica rolled to her knees before standing up from the floor and wrapping her arms around herself. She hadn't understood what he was trying to tell her.

He walked over and signaled again for her to stay quiet. Then he rubbed her upper arms and leaned in to whisper in her ear, "I think someone planted some kind of surveillance on your lamp. I'm not going anywhere just yet." He brushed his lips across hers while she stared at him. Then he stepped back to the lamp to get a closer look at the extra black doodad.

It was high enough under the shade, he'd have never seen it if he hadn't been lying on the floor looking up. When he touched it, he found it had a magnet holding it to the metal part of the light. He pulled it off and showed it to Veronica silently.

She reached out and plucked it from his palm before casually carrying it into the kitchen, where she dropped it into the sink, turned on the water, and ran the garbage disposal.

Zach stepped up behind her and wrapped his arms around her. "I'm sorry I made you think I was actually going to leave."

"Why did you say it?" She sounded so confused.

"Well, I was kind of thinking we might want to hold on to the device to show the police or maybe see if we could learn more about where it came from before whoever put it there knew we found it."

He felt her skin heat as it turned a shade of pink that would have been adorable if she hadn't stiffened with embarrassment.

"It's okay. We should check the rest of the house. If there's one, there's probably a thousand. We'll save the next one." Zachary liked that she took logical action and didn't want her second-guessing herself.

"I think that's cockroaches, not listening devices," she said as she pulled from his arms.

"Hey, seriously," Zach waited until she turned to face him again. Then he pulled her lip from where she was worrying it between her teeth. "It makes complete sense to destroy it the way you did. I'd have likely done the same thing if I'd found it in my house. I just have a different perspective because no one is invading my space." It was enough for her shoulders to drop as she nodded at him.

"Do you really think there's more?" she asked.

Zach wasn't sure how to answer, but she spoke again before he could.

"Is that why nothing's been stolen? Do you think those guys were here to leave the listening devices?"

"It would explain things," he said.

"I don't like that they've been here," Veronica confessed softly.

"Me either, but we'll figure it out. We should check your office, too," he pointed out.

She nodded. "Why don't you do that while I shower and make coffee."

Did she really trust him in her office? He raised his eyebrows at her, but she just nodded at him and pushed gently on his chest like she wanted him to get on with it.

By the time the coffee had finished brewing, they'd searched the rest of the house. Zach had found another bug stuck to the back of one of her monitors in her office, but he hadn't found anything else. They should probably do a full sweep with a scanner, but knowing roughly how much these devices cost, Zach would be surprised to find more than one per room.

This time she'd looked at him for approval before shoving it down the disposal. He should have asked her to keep it, but seeing the vulnerability on her face, he couldn't do it. If destroying them made her feel better, that's what they'd do.

"Why are they doing this?" Veronica asked as she poured coffee into his mug.

He shook away the thought that the extra-large Tigger mug she'd put in front of him felt like his, despite this only being the second time he'd used it and considered the question. "You said they've been moving stuff around for almost a month?"

"I've been losing stuff for about that long."

He gave her his most disbelieving side-eye. "Really?" he asked.

She sighed and sank into the chair across from him. "No, but it just feels crazy to think people are breaking into my home and moving stuff around and planting listening devices. I've never been in a spy thriller before. This is nuts!"

"Are your brothers having similar issues?" he asked.

"No." She hadn't even paused before answering.

"Have you asked them?"

"No." She didn't pause, but now she was glaring at him.

"A listening device in your office but not your bedroom suggests this is connected to work. If nothing else, it sounds like Patrick might be able to get information about the devices."

Veronica sighed and looked down into her coffee mug. "I shouldn't have run the second one through the garbage disposal. Fuck. He's going to be pissed I don't have anything to show him."

"Will he really doubt you?" What kind of assholes were her family? Fuck that. Zachary would make them see the truth.

"No, but he will want the evidence so he can learn more about it."

Veronica's phone started buzzing and dancing across the table in front of her before Zach could point out there were other ways they could look into things. "It's Freddy," she said as she picked it up and connected the call.

Zach couldn't hear anything from the other end of the conversation, but based on the way Veronica's shoulders crept toward her ears as she made occasional sounds of agreement without ever saying a full word, he could get Freddy was chewing her out about something. He waited for her to interrupt him, but she was letting him rant. It made her look small. And tired. And sad.

He stood and strode around the table before snatching the phone from her hand and putting it on speaker. "This is Zachary, and you need to listen for a minute."

"Excuse me?" the gruff male voice asked.

"I have you on speaker, so Veronica can be a part of the conversation too, but this needs to be a conversation and not just her listening to you say things that make her feel shitty."

"What? I wasn't making her feel shitty. I was giving her a hard time about being late for work again. She's always late for work. She's supposed to be at her computer by eight, but I always have to–"

Zach ended the call.

Veronica's eyes got big, and she reached forward to grab her phone back, but he turned to block her with his body while he clicked the message button for the recently ended call.

> 2 guys broke in & planted mics. Call back to discuss. Politely.

It took a few minutes for the phone to light up with an incoming call, and the screen said Patrick instead of Freddy. "Do you want me to answer?" Zach asked Veronica.

"No, I've got it." She held out her hand.

He gave the phone back, but before letting go he added, "If he starts saying shit like Freddy was, I'm stealing that back. That was bullshit."

She waved him off with one hand while connecting the call with the other. Then she turned on the speakerphone before greeting Patrick with an overly chipper, "Good morning!"

"It's not good if someone broke in, V! When did this happen, and why didn't you call us?"

Before Veronica could respond, Zach snarled, "Be nice or we're hanging up."

"Oh fuck. Are you being held hostage?" Then Patrick raised his voice to a shout. "What do you want? You better not hurt my sister!"

"Patrick, stop. That's Zach, and he didn't kidnap me. I'm not being held hostage. He's the one that found the bugs, and he pointed out that I should tell you and Freddy about it since one was found in my office."

Veronica and Zachary both waited while Patrick murmured threats and curses about thieving fucking assholes. "I'll be there in ten. Text Freddy to meet me there." Then the call ended.

"Are your brothers always that big of jerks?" Zach asked.

"No, they're good guys. Patrick's just busy and usually overwhelmed."

"That sounds like a bullshit excuse. What's Freddy's deal?" He would kick both their asses if he had to, but if Veronica cared about them, he'd rather find a way to make them act like decent brothers. Did they not understand the value and responsibility of having a little sister?

"Freddy's probably the most sensitive person I know. He's always trying to be funny and joke around, but he feels it deeply when he upsets someone. It's not something he likes about himself, which is probably why he called Patrick instead of calling me back. I'm betting he's kicking his own ass right now." Veronica was typing into her phone as she explained. A second later, she held it up and turned it so he could see the screen, starting with her message to Freddy.

> **Patricks on his way & wants u 2 meet us here.**

> **Sorry for b4. C U in 15.**

Zachary mentally tried to smooth his ruffled feathers back down. No one should be anything but nice to Veronica, but these were her brothers, and he needed to respect those relationships.

"If they hurt you, even verbally, I will knock them on their asses," he told her.

Veronica smiled and leaned her forehead against his chest. "As much as I appreciate that, it's not necessary. They do care, and they are nice guys. Sometimes they just act a little stupid."

He grumbled but didn't argue.

"Don't you need to go take care of your alpacas?" Veronica asked.

"No, they'll be fine for a few more hours. If you genuinely want me to leave, I will, but I meant it when I said I'm going to keep you safe. Do you at least have a gun and know how to use it?" He'd just assumed that anyone living alone around here would be armed, but based on Veronica's reactions to everything happening, he was starting to question that.

"No, and what do you mean, *at least*? Guns are the extreme end of things." She planted her hands on her hips and gave him an accusatory stare.

Zach debated jumping right into the gun issue, but she made a fair point. Many people made other choices to protect themselves. "Fair enough. What's your personal protection plan?" he asked.

She shifted her weight from side to side and pulled her hands together to pick at her nails. "Uh, I didn't know I'd need one, so mostly it's just to run and hide, I guess. I mean, I can always kick a guy in the nuts."

*Do not freak out on her*, Zach coached himself while rubbing at his forehead and looking at his feet so she couldn't see his expression.

Once he'd taken enough deep breaths to be done internally losing his shit, he looked back up and asked, "Do you have mace, a whistle, or a taser?"

She squinted her eyes at him like she knew he wouldn't like her answer. "No."

Zachary had prepared himself for that, though. He didn't flinch before asking if she'd taken any self-defense classes.

"Who would expect to need them out here?" Veronica flapped her arms. "I live in the middle of nowhere. There's no one here to assault me."

Keeping his face blank, Zach stepped into her space and cupped her cheek with his right hand. "You're supposed to be safe here, and I'm glad you've always felt that way, but this is a different situation now." He spoke softly and tried to lace care and compassion through his words.

"I don't want this. I don't want any of this. Why is it happening? I'm nothing. Why is anyone bothering me?" She leaned against him, so Zach wrapped his arms around her.

Before he could say anything else, they heard a car pull up the drive. Veronica stiffened.

Zach kissed the top of her head and rubbed her back. "It's probably one of your brothers. I'm going to check while you stay here."

Then he grabbed the pistol he'd placed on the table by her front door the night before and stepped onto the front porch just as the driver got out of the car.

"I'm guessing you must be Zach," the man called out.

"Are you Patrick or Freddy?" He was willing to bet it was Patrick, but Zach was trying to avoid assumptions so he could focus on the facts.

"I'm Patrick, and who are you to be on my sister's porch waving a gun around?"

Seriously? Zachary had the gun pointed at the ground. The safety was on, and he had already checked the terrain and moved to the left side of the porch so he'd be aiming to the right where there was a steep incline that would work as a backstop if he had to fire. He had to remind himself that this was Veronica's brother. "I'm the one who's here validating her feelings, confirming that she's not crazy, and doing my best to keep her safe. You know, the kind of things I'd expect someone who cares about her to do." It might not have been the nicest thing he could say, but he hadn't sworn at the asshat or shared his real feelings about what a shitty brother Patrick was.

"I highly doubt there's any real danger to Veronica specifically. While I have no doubt there's some crazy shit going on, that's been true since news broke about our role in the ISS incident." Patrick dropped his gaze to the ground and rubbed at his brow like Zach had seen officers do when they knew they were cruising into a rough mission.

That didn't mean he was willing to let Patrick get away with being a dick. "So you've had people breaking into your home too?"

The fury that blazed in his eyes when he looked up made Zachary wonder what Patrick had been dealing with, but before he could ask, another car pulled up the gravel drive. "Here comes my brother. Freddy. We're good now. You can go back to wherever it is you usually are."

The flat tone and blank expression didn't reassure Zach. "That's not going to happen. I'll be staying right here until Veronica tells me she wants me to leave."

"Where is she now?" Freddy had parked and was walking toward Zachary slowly, but he didn't look concerned.

"She's inside." Zach knew they weren't the threat, but he couldn't bring himself to relax his stance or his grip on the gun.

Freddy rolled his eyes as he walked right past, opened the front door, and called out, "Ronnie, I'm home!"

His shout was immediately followed by a grunt as he curled into himself and collapsed to the floor.

Zach looked up from his body to find Veronica standing just inside her doorway with a huge scowl on her face.

"Jesus, fuck." Patrick had made it to the steps. "I thought Mom told you to stop doing that. If she doesn't get grandkids because you destroy our ability to reproduce, she'll whoop your ass."

"First, she told him to stop calling me Ronnie, and I've never once hit either of you any other time. Second, Ophelia or I could give them grandkids, too. Third, that was also for being an asshole on the phone this morning."

Freddy let out a squeak from where he was clutching his genitals and writhing on the floor.

"We need to talk about who's been breaking in and what they want from Veronica," Zach reminded everyone.

Veronica's face relaxed as she stepped back and waved them in.

Zach stepped over Freddy and placed his gun back on the table after double-checking the safety was still on.

Patrick followed him and used his feet to nudge Freddy over enough to close the door. "Get over it, Freddy. She had a point about the nickname, and I seem to recall you admitting to being a jerk before."

"Out of curiosity, how many kids are in your family?" Zachary asked.

"There are five of us, and I have no idea how my parents kept us all alive," Patrick answered.

He said it lightly, but there was a wince as he admitted to the challenges his parents must have faced. Maybe Veronica was right about him being stressed, but that didn't give him an excuse for being a jerk.

"I'll get another pot of coffee going," Veronica offered as they moved into the living room.

Once they each had a mug, Zachary explained what he'd seen and prompted Veronica to share everything she'd experienced. Then he'd watched as Patrick shoulders dropped, then his chin dipped, and finally the man's face fell into his hands as Veronica spoke.

When she finished, Zach thought they'd turned a corner, and Patrick would be onboard with doing...something.

Instead, Patrick spoke without uncovering his face. "I've been getting weird phone calls at all hours of the day and night. I hear what you're saying and agree it's not good, but I don't think it's about you. I think this is more fallout from all the publicity."

Zachary didn't give a shit about the cause. In his mind, the end result was the same, and it was a potential danger for Veronica. He spent the next half an hour trying to get him to see that someone invading his sister's home required more of a response than gathering the company legal team to track down former employees and enforce their non-compete clause. Zach stood up when he was too angry to sit still any longer.

"I'm going to walk around outside a bit," he told the Taylors.

Veronica stood as well. "Are you okay? Do you need to leave?"

He pulled together a smile for her, though he wasn't sure how convincing it was. "Yeah, I'm just going to check out your property a bit and then take care of my animals."

"Oh, okay. I guess I'll see you later?" Veronica looked uncertain, and he didn't want that.

"I meant every word I've said, so don't think you're rid of me. I'll be back in time to make dinner." He didn't want her to doubt him, especially not at a time like this, when she was doubting everything else.

Her face lit up with a real smile, and she nodded at him.

Zachary had seen a couple of outbuildings on her property that looked like they were still in decent shape. If they were good enough, he'd bring his animals over so he could just stay here with Veronica. If not, he'd have to either convince her to come back to his place or he'd be back and forth between the two properties constantly. He didn't mind going back and forth, but he hated the idea of constantly feeling like he'd have to leave. Zach might not know much about what was going on, or what the future held, but he did know Veronica was someone special. He wouldn't risk that over an inconvenience. Besides, he had a gun and was trained to use it, while she'd never anticipated her home being anything but safe and happy.

# Chapter 10

The minute the front door shut behind Zachary, Patrick started in on Veronica. "Who is that guy, and why are you letting him into your office?"

"He was checking for more microphones, and he found one, so maybe you should thank him instead of acting like an ass," she snapped back.

"Veronica, I don't think you understand. Since news about the incident on the space station was covered at an international level, we've been fielding constant requests from other countries and other companies all wanting our code. If they get ahold of it, we're sunk. It's our one thing. I'm trying to expand and get us into other stuff, but Dad never intended us to do more than code AI bots, so we don't have any infrastructure for it. We *need* to keep that code proprietary!"

Veronica heard him. She did understand how important it was to their business, but his concerns about Zachary were way off base. "I hardly think the alpaca farmer next door is going to be the one to steal from us," she pointed out.

"But you don't know that, do you?" he countered. "How long has he lived here? I don't remember an alpaca farm from when we were kids. Listen, we'll buy you a home security system or put in cameras for you. I agree you should feel safe in your home, but how can you assume he's safe?"

"He moved in four or five years ago, after retiring from the Navy." Veronica crossed her arms over her chest and glared at her brother. He needed to trust her more.

"Which means he has connections that would make it easy for him to sell anything he finds." Patrick was bent at the waist to bring him down to Veronica's eye-level as he huffed at her.

Before she could clock him upside the head with the TV remote, which was the closest potential weapon, Freddy grabbed Patrick's shoulder and pulled him back a step.

"Both of you need to *stop*." The last word exploded from Freddy's mouth as he shifted his glare between the two of them. "Veronica, do you even have a copy of the code here?"

"Only the firewall. Remember Mr. Paranoid over there refuses to let me have direct access to the code for the bots. That's why I have to send the firewall code to you to test it." She tilted her chin toward Patrick.

"It's not paranoia when it's the company's only asset!" Patrick screamed.

"Maybe if we didn't make it so complicated to combine systems, we'd have time to create other assets," Veronica shot back.

"Enough!" Freddy shouted. "Veronica, go to your office and see if you notice anything moved around. Patrick, grab the laptop I know you brought with you and get set up at the table out here. Instead of fighting about shit that already is, we're going to make a list of specific things they could have accessed. Then we're going to start planning what to do about it."

As the third of five children, Veronica could count on her fingers the number of times Freddy raised his voice and got assertive enough to shut Patrick up. It was enough for her to stomp off toward her office. At least Freddy recognized that putting her and Patrick in the same room right now wouldn't be good for either of them.

Since Freddy had his laptop in the messenger bag he'd carried in with him, they'd all been able to spend the day working at Veronica's house. She'd made a full list of every proprietary bit of code she had on all her hard drives and thumb drives. She inventoried every storage device and piece of hardware in her office. Nothing was missing, and none of what she had would be enough to do anyone any good without collecting other pieces to go with it.

Patrick agreed that there wasn't an imminent threat, but he still spent the rest of the day checking the security on all their systems and sending out companywide reminders about his air gap and data storage policies.

At least it kept him busy enough to let Veronica and Freddy work together on the firewall patch to secure access to control of the bots. Not that there was any real threat there either.

By the time she heard another vehicle pulling up her drive, it was late afternoon. Unlike last night, she wasn't spooked by the sound of tires on gravel. She was too tired to give a damn. While she'd gotten more done with Freddy working beside her to tag-team the project, dealing with her brothers all day was exhausting. It didn't help that she felt like she was hunting down shadows.

Her home had been broken into, but nothing was taken. Her firewall could be breached only by the person who managed the system behind it. Her brother was screaming about international spies and corporate espionage, but Veronica couldn't see any of it. To her, it felt like a personal invasion of her space and her home, but Patrick made it sound like he was being threatened in some way too. Was she being dramatic over something they were all dealing with?

When she stepped onto the porch to greet the new arrival, she saw the same trees, the same yard, and the same trails she'd been seeing for more than a decade. There was no real threat here.

She sighed as Zachary pulled a reusable grocery sack from the back seat of his truck.

"I brought dinner," he called out.

"Oh good. I'm starving. Someone failed to offer us lunch," Freddy said from behind her and cast an accusatory look her way.

"Sorry, man. I didn't know you'd still be here, and I only brought enough for two," Zachary said with a smirk.

He really was the perfect man. He brought her food, made a great pillow, and ran off her brothers just as she was starting to plot their death.

"Seriously?" Freddy grumped.

"Get over it, Fred. He's here for more than just eating food." Patrick had packed up his stuff and didn't even pause on his way to his car. Once he'd put his bag in, he turned back to the porch. "When you show up on Monday," he paused to glance at Freddy before making eye contact with Veronica, "on time, I expect both of you to have reports analyzing all of our digital security along with your detailed response plan should there be a breach."

"Aye, aye, Captain," Freddy responded with a sarcastic solute and snappy click of his heels.

Veronica flipped him the bird but also nodded her agreement and assured him, "I'll be there by eight." Then she offered to take the bag of food from Zach, but he shook his head and dropped a kiss on her temple. "Say goodbye to your brothers and join me at the table," he instructed as he headed past her and into the house.

"Does that mean you're really kicking me out?" Freddy asked.

She considered telling him he could stay and work in her office, but she'd had enough brotherly love for one day. "Yeah, you should head home. You could swing by Mom's on your way. I'm sure she'll feed you."

"Yeah, but that will come with a lecture about my graphic t-shirts, and how it's time for me to grow up, blah, blah, blah." He turned to go collect his stuff, and she followed.

On his way back through the living room, he waved to Zach, "Thanks for feeding her. Maybe suggest a reasonable bedtime for her. Hell, you could probably adopt her into your pack of goats or whatever. Just watch your balls. I swear she should have become a UFC fighter."

Zach nodded and waved back, but his jaw was firmly clenched, and he didn't say anything.

Freddy turned to her and fished something out of his pocket. He held it out, so Veronica extended a hand. As a little blue tablet dropped into her palm, she gave him a questioning look. She didn't do drugs, and Freddy knew that. What the fuck was he giving her? And why?

"It's a Valium. Well, the generic version, but it'll still help you stop jumping at shadows, so you can function like a normal person." Then he headed for his car with a solid slam of her front door.

Before Veronica could turn back toward her kitchen, she felt the heat of Zach behind her. He rested his hands on her shoulders and asked, "Is this okay?" as he started to knead the muscles around her neck.

"More than. It feels amazing." She let her head fall toward her chest and tried to release all her tension from the day.

"Did he really give you a pill and tell you to chill?" Zach asked after a minute of massaging her.

"Yeah."

Zachary's fingers stopped working their magic. "You get that's fucked, right?"

"It's really not." How could she explain so he'd understand? "We spent the day going through everything. It's got to be someone going after Taylor Industries, so no one's after me. There's no real danger. We need to get my parents involved, and we should have a security team or something, but Patrick doesn't want to disappoint Dad."

Zach nudged her shoulders to suggest she turn to face him, but the rage curling his lip and crushing his eyes surprised her. "Someone. Broke. Into. Your. *Home*. That is as dangerous of a threat as you're going to get. You sleep here."

He stepped back and started to pace. "I'm not leaving you alone. I'll stay here if I need to. It would be easier for us to stay at my place, since your barns aren't in good enough shape for me to bring the chickens and alpacas here. But I'll go back and forth. I can set up better security here and change your locks. I'd like to add a bar to your doors as well." Then he stopped pacing and rubbed his temples. Without looking up, he murmured, "Fuck, this would be so much easier at my place." Then he turned to face her and asked, "If I just kidnapped you and dragged you to safety, how much computer stuff would we need to drag along for you to still be able to do what you love?"

"Kidnapping is never the answer," she tried to tell him. The way his eyes shifted to almost solid black as he stalked toward her like a panther approaching its prey was equal parts terrifying and hot as sin.

"Listen to me carefully, Veronica. I have the utmost respect for your autonomy, but if you think there's even a one percent chance that I'll let any harm come to you, you're wrong. If that means I have to drag you back to my place, I'll do it. I don't know what this is." He gestured between the two of them.

"But unlike your brothers, I'm not blind to your intelligence, passion, fear, or the reality of the danger you're in."

She should be upset or offended or something. Her brain was screaming about twenty-first century women being able to take care of themselves. But deep in Veronica's gut, Zach's declaration was a relief. The thought of being alone in her home after dark scared the crap out of her. He'd been right to point out that she had no plan or weapons to defend herself, and while her brothers were probably right about the threat being against the company and not her, she couldn't help thinking about the listening devices she'd run through the garbage disposal. With them destroyed, would whomever come back to plant new ones? Would they try something even worse?

"I appreciate all of that, but you also have to understand Patrick's perspective. He's always been the responsible one. It's why Dad made him CEO. Anytime life doesn't follow his plan, he takes it like his personal failure."

"No doubt," Zach agreed and pursed his lips. "I hope someday he figures it all out, but I don't give a shit about him or his problems. I'm worried about you."

Veronica tried to remember a time when someone hadn't just cared about her, but put her above all others. The guy she'd dated in college ended up proposing to her roommate. Renner was more interested in using her family's code to advance his career. Even Kurt hadn't shown any interest in her until after Taylor Industries was all over the news.

Going home with Zachary and letting him take care of everything sounded amazing, but Veronica was too old for fairy tales. She pinched her fingers to the bridge of her nose.

Why didn't adulting come with a handbook or a manual or something?

"I'm sorry I got so worked up." Zach had stepped into her space and hunched down to her eye level, watching her with his head cocked to the side as he spoke softly.

"It's fine. Let's just eat," she said with resignation. Maybe food would fix things. At least it would fix the hungry feeling she was just starting to notice.

"No lunch again today?" If there had been any hint of condescension or mockery in his tone, Veronica would have... done something. She wasn't sure what since she didn't have mace or self-defense skills or anything else useful. And that just pissed her off more.

"No, I didn't eat lunch today, either," she snapped.

Zach didn't say a word, but he did return to the table and scoop baked macaroni onto her plate before serving some for himself.

Veronica swung through the kitchen to wash her hands before joining him. As she sat down and inhaled the smell of tomatoes, basil, and bacon, she managed to grunt out, "Thank you."

They both ate in silence before she spoke up again. "Is there bacon in here?"

He grinned. "Yep, it's my secret ingredient."

"It's good."

"Thanks. I'm sorry I got loud earlier."

Veronica waved him off with her fork. "It's okay, and I'm sorry for being so short myself. My brothers make everyone scream eventually. You should hear my mother." She was trying to joke, but Zachary didn't laugh.

"She must be a strong woman to have raised five of you."

Veronica couldn't help smiling as she thought about the havoc they'd wreaked. "Gabe was taller and wider than her before he finished middle school, but it never stopped her from taking him to the ground."

"She couldn't do that with Patrick?" Zach asked.

Swallowing quickly to avoid spraying her food across the table as she laughed, Veronica tried to figure out how to explain. "Patrick never needed that. The one time Freddy convinced him to stuff a hollowed-out tree trunk with fireworks, he ran telling on himself to Dad the second Freddy lit the fuse. Mom and Dad didn't even have to punish him. He canceled all his plans for the next two weeks and spent every spare minute clearing trails."

"Sounds like a fun guy," Zachary's dry observation irked Veronica.

"He's my brother. He carried me almost a mile back to the house one time when we were playing in the creek, and I found a leech attached to my calf and freaked out. I refused to walk on that leg. Gabe offered to pull it off, but I was terrified to let anyone touch it. Patrick carried me piggyback all the way home to Mom." Frowning as she remembered how that ended, she decided it was a good story to explain all her siblings. "Mom went to get the first aid kit, but while she was gone, Freddy came running in. Gabe had told him about the leech, and he wanted to know if it was true that salt would kill it. By the time Mom got back, there was blood, salt, and leech ooze everywhere. I was crying, Gabe was doubled up laughing, Patrick was screaming at everyone to clean up the mess, and Freddy had run off to Ophelia's room with what was left of the leech."

Zach had stopped eating while listening to the story. In hindsight, it might not have been the best tale for the dinner table. Veronica watched as Zach opened, closed, and opened his mouth again. "Wow," he eventually said.

"Sorry."

"No, I'm just picturing the chaos. What happened with the leech and Ophelia?"

"Phee's a little different from the rest of us." How could she explain so Zach would understand? "I mean, we're all different. Patrick's perfect; Freddy's fun; Gabe's relaxed on the surface, but more protective than anyone I've ever known; and I'm... me. But all four of us love being outside. We were always covered in mud and sweat, and Mom kept a stash of iron-on patches to fix the rips we tore in our clothes."

"But not your sister?" Zachary asked.

"Nope. She wore dresses and begged for make-up. Anything with the potential to make her dirty was a big, fat, no."

"The leech didn't go over very well, did it?"

Veronica appreciated the way Zach chuckled, but she hadn't told him the rest yet. "Ophelia doesn't have quite the same sense of humor as the rest of us," she tried to warn Zachary about what was coming.

He raised an eyebrow and stifled his laugh. "What did she do?"

"She's the baby of the family, so everyone tried to coddle her and push her around, which she hated. By this time, she was ten. Dad had just given her a pocketknife for the previous Christmas."

"Uh oh," Zachary must see where Veronica was going with this.

"Yeah, she whipped it out and stabbed Freddy right through his bare foot."

"Oh shit!"

"Exactly. My sister is gorgeous, but she's fucking deadly. She trains at a fighting gym and can kick everyone's ass. When she was little, we called it her homicidal switch, because she goes from happy to murderous in the blink of an eye."

"How did your parents survive? I mean my parents just had me and Helen, and we gave them a run for their money. Granted Helen had Down's Syndrome, so there was an extra challenge, but nothing like that." Zach waved his hand toward Veronica as he referred to everything she'd described.

Now it was Veronica's turn to chuckle. "Wait till you meet my mother. You'll understand then."

"She certainly has my respect. Do you want more pasta?" Zach asked.

"No, I'm stuffed. That was really good."

"I'm glad you liked it. I'll pack up the leftovers and clean up the kitchen. Do have a blanket and pillow for the couch by chance?" He grabbed both their plates.

Chewing on the inside of her cheek, Veronica considered her options. She had to admit staying by herself all night was terrifying, but asking Zach to sleep on the couch and run back and forth to his place to take care of his farm felt mean. Inviting herself to his place wouldn't be rude when he'd suggested it, even though putting the words together to do so was awkward.

"Uh, you asked about my computer stuff?" she tried.

Zach set the plates on the kitchen counter and turned back to her grinning like a kid in a candy store. "Does that mean you're letting me kidnap you?"

"I'll need to pack up an extra monitor, and I'm hoping you have a table or desk where I can set up my stuff, but I'll come with you to your place so you don't have to trek back and forth. It has to be easier than moving all your animals. Plus, I kind of want to meet Butthead."

"Butthole," Zach corrected with a smile.

Veronica picked up their glasses and took them to the kitchen while asking, "Do you name all your animals? And is it just alpacas? I thought you said something about chickens, too."

Zach proceeded to tell her all about Bertha and Fluffy. The thought of seeing a baby alpaca be born excited Veronica, though she wasn't sure about how messy and gross the ordeal sounded.

"They don't usually need much from me," Zachary assured her. "Occasionally, a leg will be in the wrong place or something else will cause the labor to stall. I'll step in then, and it gets very gross, very fast, but that all disappears when you see the newborn stumble to their feet for the first time."

"And the chicken?" Veronica prompted. "Do you breed them, too?"

Zachary laughed. "Yes, and no. Every two or three years I keep one rooster to fertilize the eggs so I can raise the next generation of the flock, but roosters are such mean fuckers. I don't keep them around any longer than absolutely necessary."

"Don't they also protect the hens, and like, I don't know, keep out the foxes or whatever?"

"That's what the alpacas are for," Zach explained with a conspiratorial wink. "The two species live well together. The chickens help keep the alpacas healthy by eating pests that bother the alpacas and snails that can give them worms. For their part, the alpacas spit at any predators that get too close to the chickens."

"Wait, so you keep them all in the same pen or whatever?" Veronica was having trouble picturing this.

"I don't generally keep them penned up at all, but they do roam around the property together. I swear before Fluffy got knocked up, she spent half her day chasing a few of them around as if they were playing tag. The chickens don't mind it either. They're happy to follow their alpaca buddies. Hell, most of them will catch a ride on an alpaca back now and then. Well, except for Butthole. He refuses to let any of the chickens ride him. In fact, sometimes they chase him around." Zach's brow furrowed in thought.

Then he added, "They probably do a lot to keep Butthole in check for me. There's not much he's afraid of, so having a group of chickens who scare the shit out of him is probably one of the biggest reasons he only wanders off after I've put them in the coop for the night."

Veronica's mental image had her choking on her laughter.

Zachary didn't ask her any more about her work or the family business, for which she was grateful. As soon as they'd cleared the table, he nudged her toward her bedroom. "Why don't you go pack? I'll take care of clean-up and dishes. Then we can head over to my place."

"Okay. Um, I'm going to need help, I think." Veronica was trying to picture how she could transport her set-up efficiently while ensuring she had what she needed. There was no way she could leave her desktop behind, and she did have a smaller monitor to go with it. Of course, she'd bring her laptop, so technically that would give her two monitors. She'd just miss the huge fifty-five-inch on the wall that let her pull up two windows and sit far enough back for her eyes and shoulders to be comfortable.

"Veronica," Zachery's smooth voice calling her name brought her back from her mental wanderings. "Can you share whatever worries just ran through your mind?"

She sighed but told him about her conundrum. Taking the monitor off the wall felt like too much work, but not having it felt uncomfortable—literally.

"I have a new TV. My old one died last fall, so I took advantage of Black Friday deals and picked up a nice 4K one. I think it's forty-five or forty-eight inches instead of your fifty-five-inch one, but it has Bluetooth, internet, and HDMI ports. It sits on my entertainment center, too. We can move it to your workspace pretty easily."

Veronica was relieved. She could work with that, and it would make transporting everything easier. "Great."

Zach smiled at her like she'd given him a gift instead of allowing someone to take over the use of his TV. "Good. Go pack, but don't try to take anything out. I'll help carry it all, so we make fewer trips."

She couldn't argue with that. After a quick nod of agreement, she turned for her office. Contrary to what she believed his expectations to be, she didn't care about the clothes she brought and had no worries about forgetting toiletries. Veronica's biggest concern was her work. She and Freddy had made enough progress during the day for her to have a good idea what else needed to be updated for the firewall to protect access to the bots without interfering with their internal communications.

# Chapter 11

Zachary had gone to bed shortly after helping Veronica unload her Jeep and get settled with her stuff. He'd shown her to the guest room, but she'd plopped onto the couch and said she wanted to work for a bit. Early morning chores and lack of sleep the night before left him too tired to argue with her about needing sleep to stay healthy.

He didn't know when Veronica had eventually fallen asleep, but the fact that she was curled up on his couch instead of in the spare room he'd offered her led him to believe it had probably been very late. Her leggings and t-shirt didn't look anything like the pajamas she'd answered the door in the other morning, but they looked comfortable enough for him to be uncertain if they were regular clothes or if she'd changed into them before crashing.

Either way, he tiptoed to the kitchen to get coffee brewing. He'd go handle his first round of morning chores, and then come in to make breakfast.

Releasing the animals from the barn, checking the water troughs, and feeding them didn't take long. Life would be easier if he had a corral for them. He surveyed the land for the seven thousandth time and came to the same conclusion as always. The terrain, stream, and cabin placement made it impossible for him to give them enough space while fencing around them.

Maybe he needed to reconsider selling Butthole. He'd planned to keep him for breeding since he was Zach's only Suri. Despite the way his coat stuck out at crazy angles, making him look appropriately deranged, his wool was some of the softest and most uniquely colored of any alpaca. Even Doc Ester suggested he spin the light rose gray wool himself and sell the yarn directly for a slightly higher price than most alpaca wool.

But, if he didn't have to worry about Butthole running off, he wouldn't need a pen. Then again, who knew what Fluffy's cria would be like. It could make Butthole look compliant, and Butthole was his first male cria. He'd be ready to mate before too long, and then Zachary wouldn't need to pay for breeding. Eventually, he'd need to expand the gene pool, but every female he'd used to start his flock had come from a different lineage, and he'd intentionally selected a different macho to breed each of his girls. Having Bertha, his oldest female, give birth to the only male worked out perfectly. Butthole could mate any of the other females, including any other offspring from this current generation.

Perhaps the jerk could read Zachary's thoughts, because he was sweet as pie that morning. Veronica was still snoring softly when Zach returned to the cabin for his coffee and breakfast. Instead of eggs that would cool quickly, he decided to whip up pancakes and bacon. It was heavier than he liked, but he wanted Veronica to have a strong start to her day.

The bacon worked its magic and wafted under Veronica's nose with enough strength for her to stretch and yawn just as Zachary was flipping the last pancake of the batch. He'd already set the table with butter, syrup, applesauce, and utensils. Filling plates in the kitchen wasn't a big deal and would save space, since his table was only designed to seat two.

"This smells amazing," Veronica commented as she walked into the kitchen after using the restroom. "Do you cook like this every morning?"

He chuckled. He'd do it for her if she wanted, but that might be a bit intense for this early in their relationship, so he shared a more honest answer. "I usually make eggs. Sometimes I make them with toast or on a sandwich. Other times, I pair them with sausage or bacon. Occasionally, I'll make biscuits and gravy or something decadent, like pancakes."

"I guess working outside doing physical stuff means you need more fuel in the morning, huh?"

"I don't know about that. I have to imagine your brain works better when you're eating well, too."

Veronica just shrugged, and he wondered if she knew what it was like to spend a day working with a healthy breakfast fueling her system.

"Here." He handed her a plate. "Take what you want. I've got toppings and utensils on the table already. I'll pour your coffee and take it over while you load up your plate."

Veronica accepted the plate and peered at the food like she wasn't sure how to start. Knowing she might need time to get comfortable, Zachary left her to it and walked over to get her coffee. He'd already seen she preferred to drink it black, so that was easy. She followed him to the table, but as she sat, he couldn't help noticing she'd only taken one pancake and two pieces of bacon. While his pancakes were fluffy, he kept them the size of his palm. He considered six to be a normal serving and had expected her to grab at least three or four. Still, he didn't say anything.

He grabbed his own plate and joined her at the table. They both ate quietly for a bit, but Veronica had finished off her food long before he was done.

"Where did you learn to combine applesauce and syrup on your pancakes?" she asked while watching him eat.

"Go grab more food, and I'll tell you about it," he offered.

"Oh, I'm okay. I don't tend to eat much in the morning."

"And you tend to forget lunch, which I'm more likely to ignore if I know you had a good breakfast. Stop now if you're truly full, but know I'll be pestering you to join me for lunch in a few hours if you that's all you eat."

He purposely looked down at his plate while she considered it.

"Is the applesauce mixed with syrup any good?" she asked.

"Yep, you should try it."

That was all it took, and she was grabbing two more pancakes from the kitchen. "Is there a ratio that's best?" she asked.

"Everyone has their own ideas about that. I like fifty-fifty, personally, but my sister always went with something closer to eighty percent syrup and twenty percent applesauce. That ends up tasting more like apple-flavored syrup, but it's good in its own way."

Veronica nodded and carefully scooped two spoonsful of applesauce onto her pancakes before turning the syrup upside down of the same spoon to measure out two spoonsful of maple sweetness. "Your sister taught you to mix them?" She reminded him of his earlier promise.

"Oh no. That was all my mother. Dad had a sweet tooth longer than a vampire's canine, and she always worried about our sugar intake. Making us mix the two cut down on how much syrup he'd use and was good for the rest of us, too." Then he waited to see her reaction to her first bite.

Her brow pulled down as she closed her mouth around her fork. She tilted her head to the side as she started chewing, but her eyes soon widened with delight. "Wow. That really is delicious. It cuts the sweetness just enough, and the apple flavor is amazing with the pancakes and the bacon."

Zach grinned back. "Exactly. You understand a good flavor profile."

"Mmmhmm," she mumbled through her next bite.

"I know we have all your stuff set up in the living room, but is that okay for you? We can move it to the spare room so that can be your office and bedroom in one." He worried the couch wouldn't give her enough support to work through the day.

"It's fine for today. I got enough done last night that I can check in this morning, but then relax before I need to get to work. I was thinking about going to see the alpacas. They sound interesting."

"Interesting is certainly one way of describing them," Zach responded sardonically. "What time do you need to check in? Did one of your brothers say something about eight?"

Veronica's shoulders slumped forward. "Yeah. I'd like to think they'd expect me to be late after yesterday, but this firewall is important, so I need to get to it soon. Anyone who found the gap could take control of the bots and give them new commands. Leaving it without the patch would be lazy and a risk for the company."

It didn't sound like her words, and Zachary wondered if she was repeating something her brothers had told her. "I'm glad to hear you'll be taking a break to come meet the animals. I think you'll get a kick out of them. They keep me entertained when I'm not fighting the urge to kill them all," he joked.

"Ha, I can imagine. Once I finish up here, I'll go pop in and let Freddy know I'm around. Then I can come outside."

He wasn't sure if it was the right time to ask more about her work, but it was killing him not to fully understand. "What's the patch for? I don't mean to pry. I'm just curious to learn more about what you do."

Veronica heaved an exhausted sigh. "Freddy found that if someone was using Linux and opened the developer side of the bots' systems while signed in to an account on our website through Firefox, the propriety code was revealed. I was able to block that access, but in doing so, the microbots were blocked from communicating directly with the nanobots. That meant all communication had to go through the kilobots. Ninety percent of it has to anyway, but that extra ten percent slowed down their performance by about eight percent which is more than Patrick wants to allow."

She'd huffed it all out in a single breath and wasn't looking at him. Zach wasn't sure if he was understanding her right, but he decided to trust his gut. "Are you ashamed of your work on it?" he asked.

Veronica's head snapped up to look at him. "What?"

"I just," he started before closing his mouth to better consider his words. "I didn't understand most of what you just said, and I'm not a dumb guy. That makes you wicked smart, but instead of looking insanely proud of the way you can adapt your work to meet the company's needs, you're looking at the floor."

"Well, yeah. I failed to fix the problem," she said it like he was being stupid.

"How many people in your field use Linux?" Maybe a different approach would work better.

"Uh, a few. I mean, it's far from the most common operating system, but it's not unheard of."

"Quantify it for me," Zach prompted her.

"Say ten to twenty percent," she offered.

"Okay, and how many of those use Firefox?"

"Probably a third. Maybe half at most."

"And how many people have accounts through your website?" he asked.

"Not counting employees, twenty-six, though we expect that to double in the next couple of months." That answer sparked a gleam of pride on her face.

"So do the math. Let's go ahead and almost double it. Let's say fifty accounts for easy numbers. You said Linux is only used by a small percentage of them. Can we call it five people?" he waited to get her reaction.

She wobbled her head side-to-side to convey hesitant agreement.

It was good enough. "Say five people use Linux. Then one third to half of those use Firefox, so we're down to two or three people who have any chance of seeing the proprietary code. I'm not sure how developer stuff works, so help me out. How often would these people be using or opening that side of things?" This was the part that could blow up in his face, but he thought his point could withstand it.

"Never. I mean, they could, but there's nothing they need there." She'd cocked her head to the side while considering what he was saying, but it didn't look like she'd arrived at the conclusion he was going for yet.

"And right now, only half that number of people are in that position? We're saying there *might* be *one* person who *could* have seen the proprietary code before you patched it?"

"I guess?" She still wasn't seeing it.

"And that eight percent lag in processing speed or whatever. Tell me, in terms of time, how long we're talking about."

Her expression became more confident. "Freddy's last round of tests showed that big goals presented to the microbots would convert into action seen in the nanobots within eight seconds with a five percent variance."

This woman was going to force Zachary to use math he hadn't thought about in more than five years, but she was worth it. He debated pulling out his phone to help with the calculations, but before he could, Veronica interrupted his thoughts.

"Don't hurt yourself," she chuckled. "Eight percent slowed that time by zero point six four seconds." Then she froze.

And Zachary watched the light flicker on inside her head. He grinned. "Uh huh." Then he waited for her to finish the train of thought.

"My patch slowed the nanobots action initiation by about half a second considering the existing variance." She was smiling now, too, and it was the sexiest look Zach had ever seen. When this woman was able to step back and recognize just how amazing she was, the pride and joy made her glow like an angel atop the Rockefeller Center Christmas tree.

He stepped up, toe-to-toe with her, wrapped his arms around her shoulders, and kissed the top of her head. "Yeah," he agreed.

She relaxed into him for only a split second before going tense and stepping back. "But that does make a difference, and as the commands become more complex, it has the potential to increase at an exponential rate, which would be devastating and could endanger lives."

Zachary wondered what Veronica's father was like. Did her self-flagellation all come from her brothers, or did her dad have a hand in it? Hell, maybe it was her mom. Whoever had caused her to be so hard on herself deserved a swift punch in the eye, and Zach would be happy to deliver it.

That wouldn't help her right now, though. "Yeah, but you're still working on it." It was the best he could do.

"Speaking of which..." Veronica spun around like she was trying to decide where to go next.

"Go pop into work in the living room long enough to check in with Freddy. I'll clean up here. Then we'll both go outside, and I'll show you around. We'll move your set-up to the spare room this afternoon. I don't want you sitting on the couch all day and trashing your back."

Veronica smiled, but it quickly turned curious.

"What are you wondering about?" he asked.

"I can pet the alpacas, right?"

Ha! Zach couldn't stop his glee from showing, though it must have come with an evil glint based on the way she narrowed her eyes at him. "Yes, you can pet them. They love the attention, but they're also very smart and more than a little..." he tried to think of the right word. "I guess I'd say they like to investigate and test boundaries."

Veronica's brow furrowed.

"You'll see for yourself soon enough. Go check in with work." There were no words to explain the behavior of alpacas, and Zach swore his were more creative than most.

He finished cleaning up from their breakfast and stepped into his bedroom to dig out one of his old poopy suits for Veronica to borrow if she wanted. She didn't seem to be overly concerned about her appearance, and the coveralls would be big on her, but Zachary had been leaner when he was active duty.

He'd expected to return to the living room to find her waiting for him, but instead she was sprawled sideways on the couch with her wireless keyboard on her lap, clacking away like her life depended on it.

"Do you need to wait and come meet the animals later?" he asked her.

"Huh?" She looked surprised by his question. Her face contorted as realization dawned. "Oh shit. Um, I mean…" she sat up and looked longing out the front window. "I do really want to meet them, and I'm so curious about what the alpacas feel like." She jutted her jaw forward and rubbed her lower teeth back and forth across her upper lip.

Zach waited for her gaze to flit back and forth between her computer and the window twice more before he spoke up. "Did you check in with Freddy?"

"Yeah," Veronica sighed. "But he wants me to rewrite some of the code I put together last night before we send it to Wils. He thinks I can write it more efficiently."

As Veronica's lips pursed into a tight, flat line, Zachary's follow-up question came out more snarly than he'd prefer. "Can you, or is he asking the impossible?"

"I mean, we can always tighten up code," she hedged.

Zach strode over and sat on the coffee table in front of Veronica. "If someone showed you the code you wrote last night, would you ask them to rewrite it more efficiently?"

"No, but I'm not Freddy."

While Zach was thrilled to hear the sass return to her voice, he still hated the way her family made her doubt herself. "Is Freddy your boss?" he asked. He was pretty sure that wasn't the case.

Veronica's head reared back in offense. "Hell, no! He's younger than me, less experienced, graduated with a lower GPA, and is in charge of research and design."

"Hold up. Does Freddy even work with code?" He felt his body tighten like Batman's fancy cape wings did when they were charged with electricity.

"Yes. I mean, he has to as he designs how the bots should interact, connect, and work together, but he doesn't write code. He designs the user interface, tests everything from a user perspective, and then tells Wils and I what needs to change."

"So he doesn't actually know how to write code himself?" he checked.

"Eh, he can do some basic stuff, but it's not his specialty."

"I'm hearing that a colleague, who doesn't know how to do your job, is trying to boss you around and force you to do it his way, even though his way is based on no knowledge or experience. Is that a fair assessment?"

Veronica's jaw went slack, and she silently stammered before responding. "Yeah."

Zachary gave her a minute to consider the idea.

"Let's go meet your animals," Veronica said. "I'll send the code to Wils later and ask him if he needs me to adjust anything."

Damn, this woman was fire. When she stepped up and owned her confidence, it was hot enough to burn Zach's clothes off his body. He swallowed the thought and reminded himself that now was *not* the time to get naked. Instead, he shoved the navy-blue coveralls into her lap with a grunt.

"Uh, what's this?" she asked.

"An old poopy suit. It'll be too big, but it's the smallest thing I've got."

Veronica looked down at herself. "Is there something wrong with my clothes?"

"No, which is exactly why I'm offering you coveralls. There's always a chance of being hit with spit or shit, and I didn't know if you'd be happy to just wash your clothes after that or if you'd want to trash them or burn them." He wouldn't mind her wandering around naked, but he kept that to himself.

Her smirk suggested she might be aware of the effect she had on him. "I'm fine with my own clothes. Isn't it supposed to be strangely warm today? Like in the fifties?"

She was right, but that wasn't hot enough for her to break a sweat. "Can I at least give you a sweater?" he asked.

Veronica wiggled her eyebrows up and down like a cheesy cartoon character. "Only if it's one of your alpaca sweaters."

"I wouldn't dream of offering you anything less." He knew just the one, too. While Zachary hadn't invested in a spinning wheel yet, he knew a lady who'd offered to show him how. In exchanged for lessons, he'd taken all of Buttholes gorgeous rose gray wool to her last year. She'd spun enough to make him a hooded sweater, and he'd gifted the remaining fiber to her. He'd had to hire someone to do the knitting, but the soft gray color with just enough tinge of rose in it to create a shimmer effect when the light hit it right was unlike anything he'd seen in a store.

The way Veronica's jaw dropped, and her eyes bugged out as she tentatively reached out for it sent pride zinging through his body. He loved the fiber his animals produced, but impressing Veronica was a new level of satisfaction.

"Oh my gosh." She held it up to get a look at the whole thing before pulling it close and rubbing it against her cheek. "How is it scratchy and soft at the same time?" she asked.

"That's what most natural fibers are like." Zach had wondered the same thing the first time he'd felt it. Now, he loved sharing that experience with anyone interested.

"I can't wear this to work with the animals." Veronica started to pass it back to him. "You just said it gets messy. Is this even machine washable? No, I'll wear the coveralls."

Zach chuckled but didn't take back the sweater. "If you can't wear an alpaca sweater to take care of alpacas, when can you wear it?" he asked. "Besides, while it's always labeled as dry clean only, it's one of the easiest materials to care for. A quick water wash is all it takes. Then it dries overnight."

"Seriously?"

"Yep. Put it on." Zach wanted to see her in his clothes. He wanted it to be obvious to everyone that she was his, even though he knew she wasn't. *Not yet,* the voice in his head whispered.

"Are you sure?" she asked, while pulling it over her head.

"It looks good on you," he complimented her.

Veronica was running her hands down her chest to feel the texture. "Thank you."

"I don't have any work boots that will fit you. You should be okay in sneakers, but Snowball and Foxy both love to step on toes."

"Oh, I brought my boots over." As she sat down to put them on she asked, "Did you say you have an alpaca named Snowball, and another named Foxy?"

"Yep. Snowball's sweet, but Foxy's more curious than is healthy. We just confirmed her pregnancy, and I keep hoping she'll settle down a little."

"I take it that's not happening?" Veronica looked up before shifting her focus to her other boot.

"Last week, she found a brush pile along the tree line and stuck her nose right into a skunk's living room. I'm still not convinced I'll be able to sell her fiber."

"Hm," Veronica was giggling as they stepped out to the porch. "It sounds like I should be able to identify Foxy by smell, then?"

He stopped at the top of the steps and turned back to point at her. "That's a good idea. You can let me know if the smell has really faded, or if I've just become immune."

They both turned to silently survey the animals roaming around the yard for a few minutes. "Six alpacas in your... herd?"

"Yep."

"Butthole's the only male, right?"

"Uh huh." He could tell she was trying to match up the names she knew with the animals in front of her.

"This sweater was made from Butthole's wool, wasn't it?" she asked him with a sly grin.

"It was. He's only been shorn once so far."

For a second, they just stared at each other. It felt like they both understood the significance of him giving her that sweater, but neither was brave enough to say anything aloud.

Then Veronica blinked and turned her focus back to the animals. "The dark brown one has to be Foxy."

"How do you know?" Zach was horrified that she might still smell so bad, Veronica could identify her from over here.

"She just got pecked in the face by that white chicken, but instead of backing off, she snuffled her nose in the bird's feathers."

"Oh, yeah. That's a Foxy kind of thing to do."

# Chapter 12

As Veronica watched Bertha intervene between Foxy and the chicken, who was starting to squawk in protest, she wondered why no one was filming *this* for reality TV. It was a million times better than watching rich people spend money.

"Why does Butthole look so much crazier than the rest?" It was more than his behavior that made him stand out.

The question caught Zachary off guard, and Veronica enjoyed watching him fight to control his laughter enough to answer. "He's a different breed. The rest are Haucaya, which are more common. Butthole's a Suri."

"Oh."

"Are you brave enough to go pet them?" Zach challenged.

She smirked and gestured down the steps before them. "Lead the way."

For the next hour, the two of them played with partially inflated beach balls, rope toys designed for large dogs, and an old school bell. Zach had discovered the alpacas loved to pick it up by the handle and shake until the mountains echoed with the chime.

"I can't believe they play like that." Veronica hadn't stopped smiling the entire time. Her cheeks were red from the combination of chilly air and sweat she'd worked up. Fluffy had kept her distance, but the rest had been happy to engage with her.

"They're surprisingly smart. I try to give them enough enrichment to prevent boredom and keep them happy and healthy. I always felt like I was doing well until Butthole came along. I can't seem to keep him busy enough to stay out of trouble."

The animal in question nuzzled his nose into Veronica's face. He'd taken to her immediately and had been collecting beach balls for her to toss around and sitting down politely for her to rub his neck. Veronica was loving it.

"Oh, you're such a sweet boy, huh," she cooed at him.

"I just think he's trying to impress you. He's never given me kisses like that before." The jealous grumble under Zach's words was cute.

"Don't be mad." Veronica stepped away from the alpaca and turned her attention to Zach. "I'll give you kisses whenever you want," she teased.

They were standing close enough for her to feel his body go rigid, and she wished she could call back her words. Ducking her head, she hoped offering to help with his chores would end the awkwardness.

"You don't have to. There's not much to do today." He turned away from her, and Veronica's heart dropped into her stomach.

"Right, I'll just get out of your way then." She wanted to be useful, though, and everything had been so comfortable between them before. "Uh, what just happened? Why did it get weird?"

"Izzy would tease me like that when she wanted me to buy her something."

It took a minute for Veronica to shift gears and process what Zach had just blurted out. "Your ex-wife?" she asked.

"Yeah. I know you don't mean it like that. It just caught me off guard." He shrugged and dug around the dirt with the toes of his boots.

"Why did you care about her?" Veronica heard the words coming out of her mouth and grabbed for Zachary to keep his attention while she rephrased her question. "I know you told me about the tangible stuff like insurance, and you're obviously too nice for your own good. I'm just trying to understand why."

He didn't answer right away, and Veronica worried her question was too invasive. She was about to give up and go explore his kitchen when he finally spoke.

"Doc Ester, the vet, says I learned to be overly protective and caring because my parents expected me to be responsible for my sister."

"With Down Syndrome?" Veronica asked softly, hoping it would stop him from continuing to explain.

"Yeah. She never met my family or anything, but her niece, Amanda, and I served together for a few years. Amanda invited me to come out here with her once when we both had leave, and Doc kind of adopted me."

Veronica clenched her jaw as she fought through her jealousy. It hadn't bothered her at all when he'd talked about Izzy, but Amanda sounded like someone he cared for. She needed to let it go and get back to her work. This was stupid. His past wasn't her business. But one more question escaped her mouth before she could stop it. "Did she break your heart?"

"What?" Zach locked his gaze with hers and grabbed her shoulders. "No, it was never like that. *We* were never like that."

"Right. Sorry." Now would be a great time for the ground to crack open so Veronica could disappear into a fissure. She couldn't even turn and run because Zachary's hands held her firmly in place.

"Listen, Amanda..." He shook his head like he needed to clear his thoughts. "We were shipmates with the same rate. There were a couple more senior guys in our command who were always making comments and touching her."

Veronica stepped closer to him. She was afraid of where this was going.

"We both reported it to the command, but it wasn't anything *real*. The comments were brushed off, and the touches were considered innocent since they weren't technically inappropriate."

Veronica exhaled a soft, "Fuck."

Now Zach let out a sarcastic chuckle. "Yeah. They'd only touch her butt or chest when squeezing through a small space so they could say it was accidental."

"What happened?" Veronica didn't want to know, but Zachary wouldn't be sharing this if it didn't matter.

"They kept pushing the boundaries and eventually raped her. They beat the shit out of her, and then left her lying in a corner of the ship."

It shouldn't have been a surprise. Veronica wasn't naïve. She still gasped and covered her mouth with her hand as tears sprung to her eyes.

Zachary's color drained as he continued. "They proved they could get to her. They'd already proven the command didn't care. Those men did nothing to cover it up because they knew they didn't need to. She wouldn't tell anyone because she didn't have anyone to tell. At least, not anyone who would believe her or have the power to do anything about it."

"I'm so sorry." Veronica didn't know what else to say.

"Yeah, me too." They stood in silence for a minute before he continued. "I couldn't save my sister from the car accident that killed her, and I couldn't save Amanda from the men in our command. When I met Izzy and knew that I *could* help her, it felt like a form of atonement, and yes, I know how wrong that is now. But I didn't back then."

"Is that why you're helping me?" She had to know. If his feelings didn't match hers, she had to leave.

He cupped her cheek. "Look at me, Veronica."

Terrified of what she'd see on his face, she tilted her head up but kept her eyes closed.

Zach chuckled. "Open your eyes, please."

When she did, he was smiling at her.

"You are unlike anyone I've ever met before. I want to keep you close because you make me laugh and feel like home. I want to keep you talking because your voice sends sparks of electricity through me. I want to keep you safe because I'm selfish and want more time with you."

Veronica didn't have any words that could compare to that, so she wrapped her arms around his neck and pulled him down for a kiss that would show him how she felt. It must have worked, because he grabbed her by the ass and lifted her until she wrapped her legs around his waist.

Before he could carry her off to bed like she wanted, Foxy ambled over and tried shoving her head between them. Zachary side-stepped and kept them both upright, but it broke the moment enough for them to separate.

"Dammit, Foxy," he murmured.

"I think she felt left out," Veronica said while petting her. She was too cute and soft for anyone to stay mad, though she did still carry a hint of skunk.

"Her curiosity is going to be the death of her." Zach adjusted himself as he spoke, and Veronica couldn't resist checking him out. Based on the way he was filling his jeans, the man was very well endowed.

Her inspection must have been more obvious than she'd intended, since he snickered, "My eyes are up here."

"I think you have the biggest, most beautiful eyes I've ever seen," she answered with complete sincerity.

"As much as I love the way you admire my... eyes. You'll have to take a closer look later. I need to cruise through the barn and hunt down eggs. You're welcome to come help."

"Sure," Veronica agreed and followed him toward the barn. She didn't think anything of his word choice until he started pointing to random places while making comments about how often the chickens left eggs in each location.

"Why do they not have nests or whatever?" she asked. "I didn't think you meant you literally had to hunt around and find the eggs. This is like Easter gone wrong! Is there at least candy?"

"Nope. No candy. Sorry." The man did not sound sorry. "I do have nesting boxes. That's what's on that ledge over there." He pointed to a line of wooden cubbies with a mound of straw in each.

"Shouldn't the eggs be in there?"

"In theory, but mine do their own thing."

"Your animals are weird." Veronica didn't mean to sound rude, but his alpacas rang a brass bell and played with beach balls. Now she was learning his chickens laid eggs all willy-nilly.

"That's what I love about them," he said as he pointed her toward one corner of the barn while he headed to a different corner. "Go find eggs, and I'll explain why weird creatures are best."

Veronica walked around picking up eggs as she found them while he talked.

"In the Navy, we weren't allowed to be weird. Everyone looked the same, responded the same, followed the same rules, and colored within the lines, so to speak. It made sense in that context, but after twenty years, seeing unique differences is refreshing."

"I suppose, but this feels extreme." Veronica was debating picking up her next egg. It was covered in brown stuff that looked concernedly like bird shit.

Zach had his back to her and didn't notice as he continued, "Don't get me wrong, the people in the military are all different, but only within certain boundaries. These animals don't have that rigidity. They do what makes them happy."

The lightness in his voice had her turning to him. "Them being happy makes you happy?" she checked.

He thought about it before answering. "In a way. Ensuring they're happy feels like I'm doing something meaningful, like my life has a purpose." His gaze shifted to the bench where the gross egg still sat. "Something wrong with that one?" he asked.

"It's covered in something." Was there a polite way to ask someone if their egg was covered in shit? "It looks like it might be, uh, excrement?"

Zach tossed his head back as he laughed. Veronica's eyes traced from his strong jaw to his bobbing Adam's apple and down to his collarbone. She could see the ridges of his muscles flex as he shifted the eggs he'd carefully piled in his hands to the Tupperware sitting on a nearby workbench. "Yeah, chickens only have one back door. It gets used for releasing waste and laying eggs."

Veronica stifled her gag. She'd never eat an egg again. "That's so gross. I'll let you come collect this one." She stepped further from the offending orb.

"I wash them right before I cook them," Zach explained, like she should find the information comforting.

"But you put them in the fridge dirty?" she checked.

"It keeps the bloom on them. They stay fresher longer, and it decreases the risk of salmonella."

"But it's covered in *poop*." How was he okay with this?

"We can leave them on the counter, if you prefer. They don't need to be refrigerated."

"Contrary to what you seem to believe, that is *not* a better option. No poop should be in any kitchen, ever." This felt like a basic human rule.

"I'll tell you what. How about we feed that egg to the chickens instead of taking it inside? The rest don't look too bad, right?"

"You feed eggs to chickens?" What alternate universe was this? Wasn't that cannibalism? What the fuck?

"The shells are good for them, and they love it. I try not to do it too often, or they can get spoiled and start eating the eggs before I can collect them. Come on, I'll hunt for more eggs tomorrow. It won't hurt to leave a few behind today." Then he grabbed the plastic container of eggs with one hand while placing the other on the small of Veronica's back to guide her out of the barn.

Once they reached the middle of the yard and were surrounded by animals, Zach held out the egg. "Do you want to give it to them or should I?"

"I don't feel like either of us should be touching it," she said.

Zach laughed. "I promise I always wash my hands the minute I get inside, but you don't have to touch it if you don't want to.

Dropping it on the ground isn't the fun part. That comes from watching the chickens trip over each other trying to get to it."

They were facing each other with just enough space between them for Zach to drop the egg, but before he could Butthole came bounding over to see what the excitement was all about. If Veronica had known the way he'd slam into Zachary's back with all his might, she'd have warned him.

Unfortunately, he knocked Zach forward with enough force, that the man fell right into Veronica's arms, smashing the poopy egg between their bodies and sending yolk oozing down the beautiful sweater he'd lent her.

She stepped back as quick as she could, but her heel caught on a tuft of grass, throwing her off balance. Next thing she knew, she was flat on her back on the ground and covered in egg, with Zachary half on top of her. She wiggled and twisted to free herself to stand, but when she turned her face to the side, the top of her forehead collided with something wet and gooey.

Zach must have seen what it was and known how she'd react. Before she could even think the word poop, he'd rolled them both the opposite direction. Suddenly, she was on top of him as he used a hanky he must have pulled from one of his pockets to wipe her face clean.

"Hey, it's okay. I'm so sorry. No more poop." He was consoling her as he worked.

It wasn't until the first tear dropped from her eye to his shirt that Veronica realized she was crying. "It's not the poop," she tried to explain. "Not just the poop, anyway. I'm sorry. I don't know what's wrong. I just–" She wasn't kidding. The tears felt like they came from nowhere and everywhere all at once.

"It's okay. I've got you." Zach tossed his hanky to the side and sat them both up, but he kept her close and wrapped his arms around her again as soon as they were situated.

Veronica's tears had evolved into blubbers as she fought to understand what caused them. "I ruined your sweater." That was bad. Awful, even. He'd given it to her, and it was special, but it wasn't enough to make her cry. "My house isn't safe, and everything's a mess, and my date stood me up. I'm not even allowed to talk to Renner anymore."

Zachary kept rubbing her back while she let out everything she'd been trying to ignore. When she calmed down enough to catch her breath, she was still wrapped in his arms with her face tucked into the crook of his neck.

"Fuck, I'm sorry I fell apart on you." She lifted her head enough to wipe her tears, but she didn't want to pull out of his embrace. It was warm and safe and comfortable, despite sitting in the dirt while covered in egg.

Zachary's response surprised her. "Tell me who Renner is and what you meant about your date standing you up," he growled while keeping his touch gentle.

Veronica thumped her head against his chest. She couldn't believe she'd mentioned all of that, but she explained about Kurt not showing up for dinner. When she told Zach about her date with Brian Renner and the awkward questions he'd asked, Zach surprised her again. "Remind me to thank Patrick for getting that right, at least. If the man's going to be so disrespectful to discuss work while having dinner with someone as amazing as you, you shouldn't have to deal with him. It gives me a little hope for him to hear that even after six months he still kept Renner away from you at your Monday meetings."

"It has been nice not to have to talk to him after that," she confessed, but she needed to lighten the mood. "I guess you'll have to show me how magically easy it is to clean alpaca sweaters now," she suggested as she looked down and saw how filthy she was.

Thankfully, Zach accepted her nudge away from serious issues. "It will astound you," he promised before giving her a hand up and leading her into the house.

"I'm waiting with bated breath," Veronica said. "Will you be stripping off my sweater, or should I put on a show?"

# Chapter 13

"Will you be stripping off my sweater, or should I put on a show?" Veronica's sultry voice and word choice had Zachary tripping his way up his porch steps like a newborn alpaca.

There was no way he could just be friends with this woman when her body fit so perfectly in his arms, her needs aligned so perfectly with his desires, and her mouth enjoyed teasing him as much as it enjoyed eating the food he made for her.

He got them inside as fast as possible before spinning her around and pushing her against the door to finish closing it while he closed the distance between their lips.

She tasted like coffee and vanilla lip balm, but beneath those flavors was something uniquely her. Less than forty-eight hours ago, he'd told her they needed to wait for sex until they were sure they both wanted a relationship, but this was the second time since then he'd lost control. And he couldn't bring himself to stop.

Veronica parted her lips with a whimper.

Zach accepted her invitation and thrust his tongue between them to dance with hers. He slid his hands down to find the hem of her sweater and broke their connection just long enough to lift it over her head and off. They could clean it later.

Before he could resume their kiss, Veronica stopped him with a hand on his chest. "Your shirt's gross too," she whispered before helping him peel it off. The second it cleared his chest, she was nipping at his collarbone. Then she kissed and licked her way back to his mouth.

The sounds she made were enchanting. Zach forced himself to slow down and explore her jawline and neck. He wanted to find every erogenous spot she had and delighted in the shivers and moans she offered when he bit down on the junction of her shoulder and neck.

His hands got lost in her hair as he pulled her body flush against his, so she'd feel his throbbing erection as he returned his focus to her soft lips and inviting mouth. Veronica mewed her pleasure and dug her nails into his ass to pull him closer.

With great difficulty, he pried his lips away from her and flashed her an easy, lopsided smile.

"We should probably clean that sweater," he said.

Panting, she narrowed her eyes at him, as though he were a bug she needed to inspect before suggesting, "Maybe we should let it soak or something for an hour?"

"Perhaps," he said, bending to whisper in her ear and caressing her cheek. "What do you expect to do while we wait for it?"

"You," she breathed out, looking up at him with eyes so full of hope and life.

Zachary quirked an eyebrow as he let his hand wander down from her cheek to her neck, drawing small circles on her flushed skin, pressing down on her pulse point. A small moan escaped her lips.

He cupped her ass and picked her up so she'd wrap her legs around his waist the way she had earlier. She wasn't as prepared this time, but he secretly enjoyed the way she yelped and threw her arms around his neck. Veronica was wrapped around him. Clinging to him.

"Are you sure this is what you want?" he checked.

"Yes." There was no hesitation or uncertainty, but he needed to be clear.

"If we do this, you're mine. No cheating. I'm overbearing and might smother you. I'm possessive and jealous, but I promise I'll do everything I can to make you happy."

Her breath hitched in her throat. "I know you will, and if I can handle my brothers, I'm sure I can keep you in line," she said.

Zachary groaned, "I don't want to talk about your brothers right now, but you're welcome to punch me in the nuts if I don't listen when you try to tell me to back off."

"I can live with that." She tightened her grip on his hair and tilted his face back so she could kiss him again.

He carried her down the hall towards his bedroom, grinning like he'd won the lottery and squeezing her in his arms.

"Good," he replied simply.

He pushed open his bedroom door with his foot before striding across the room and throwing her on the bed. They let a few long, silent seconds pass as his eyes roved over her body.

Taking in the outline of her breasts, clearly visible beneath the t-shirt she'd worn under his sweater, he admired the perfect proportions with her waist and hips. Her long brown hair flowing across his forest green sheets made him think the universe had helped him choose the perfect color to complement a woman he hadn't met yet.

He must have stared too long. Veronica crossed her arms and grabbed the bottom of her tee before crunching her abs to raise up enough to pull it off. Zach took the hint.

With deft movements, he undid the button and zipper of his jeans before shoving them down his legs. Next, he removed his boxer briefs, revealing his painfully hard cock. Zachary was no fool. He knew he was well-equipped. Still, he reveled in the way her eyes widened and her mouth fell open when she saw him. She'd gotten a glimpse earlier, but he doubted she could tell his true size through his jeans. Grinning, he stepped out of his pants and closer to the bed so he could press his thumb to her lower lip.

"Ready for this?"

"Fuck, yes." It was all she managed to say.

"Mmmhmm, I love the easy way your mouth shifts from filthy to sassy to genius in the blink of an eye," he said as he climbed onto the bed beside her.

Patiently, he licked and teased his way down her body. He sucked along her collarbone and then nipped at each of her ribs while trailing his fingers down her abdomen, leaving goosebumps in his wake.

"Zachary," she whimpered. "Please."

"Patience, V," he said.

He slowed his progress even more as he discovered the way her back arched and she pleaded for more when he teased the skin over her hip bones between his teeth. Veronica shivered beneath his touch, the palpable heat radiating off her body egging him on.

Zach finished pushing down her pants and threw them off to the side of the room. He ran his hands with splayed fingers up her legs and thighs, slowly, teasingly, as his desire and unrestrained want heated her skin. When he ran his finger along the waistband of her panties, Veronica started squirming beneath him, trying to hurry him along.

"Shhh," he said. He kissed and licked her thigh. "Relax and enjoy. I don't want to rush this."

He shook his head and hooked the waistband of her panties to pull them down far enough to reveal her glistening center.

Veronica gasped, and he smirked up at her before winking in reply. At the same time, he dragged her underwear the rest of the way down before tossing them to the floor. He shifted to place himself between her thighs and threw her legs over his shoulders. With a small groan, he parted her folds, feasting his eyes on the swollen, pink flesh between her legs.

Zachary knew she must feel exposed, but he would never let her doubt his admiration for everything about her. And fuck, did he admire her all spread open for him, wet and wanting. Slowly, when her squirms had settled, Zach lowered his head and licked her slit, covering his tongue with the intoxicating taste and scent of her juices. He licked a second, longer stripe through her center and all the way up to her clit. Once there, he pressed a few kisses to it. Then, without warning, he took it in his mouth and sucked.

"Christ, Zachary!" Veronica cried out and clutched her fingers in his hair.

Smiling, Zach wrapped his tongue around her clit and alternated gentle nibbles with his teeth, slow licks, and firm suckling. One hand kept her lips parted for his access, while the other explored deeper. His first finger slid in easily, and he groaned against her feverish flesh.

Then he inserted his second finger and curled them to feel her inner walls. She was so tight, and her body was doing everything it could to provide the lubrication they would need. That thought had him aching and throbbing to claim her.

"Mine," he said, in between licking and sucking harder and more erratically. "You're all mine now." He knew how possessive he sounded, but he needed her to understand how much it would hurt if she ever betrayed him.

He drummed his fingers as if playing a piano or strumming a guitar as he returned his mouth to her pearl. Her breath came faster, and she clenched around his fingers.

"Fuck yes, Zachary!" she screamed, as her orgasm crashed through her.

As the wave crested, Zach didn't slow down. He fucked her with his fingers through her climax and kept going, still sucking and biting as though she was his favorite meal.

"Aah," Veronica moaned. "Too much. So much. Zach!"

"You can take it," he assured her, though he glanced up to confirm the uncomfortable pleasure he heard in her voice wasn't contradicted by the look on her face.

"Zachary..." she whimpered and grasped at his head.

"Easy," he said. "I've got you." Relentlessly, he continued. He was painfully hard and desperate to sink inside her, but he'd wait until he was sure she was ready for him.

It didn't take long before she was rocking her hips against his face again. She maintained her tight grip on his hair, holding him where she needed him while moaning his name.

Zach pressed a few kisses to her engorged clit as he plunged his fingers in and out of her tight, wet pussy. Then he took her clit in his mouth and worried it between his teeth, making her cry out in pleasure.

As her second climax overtook her, Zachary shifted up until he was holding himself above her, kissing her deeply and passionately, so she could taste herself on his tongue. Veronica broke the kiss and caressed his cheek. He'd love to get lost in her eyes, but his cock was demanding its turn. "Condom?" he asked.

"Oh, uh. I haven't been with anyone in," her eyes rolled back as she thought, "let's just call it a very long time. And I have an IUD."

Zachary groaned as her meaning clicked. "You'll let me in bare?"

She bit her lip but smiled.

"I got tested a while back and haven't been with anyone since," he assured her.

"Then I want to feel all of you."

His tip was notched at her entrance before she finished her sentence. Zach slid in slowly, but he still had to stop twice to catch his breath and back away from his climax before he filled her completely. He paused again and kissed Veronica to silence the sexy noises that would push him over the edge faster than he wanted.

Only once he was sure he had control over himself did he begin to slowly withdraw before sliding back in. Zach kept his pace steady and pushed up so he could see between them. The sight of him disappearing inside her was better than any porn he'd seen, and the military had exposed him to a lot of it.

"Fuck, that's hot," he groaned. Then he shifted his weight to one arm so he could massage her clit with his other thumb. He leaned forward for another kiss. "I want to see you come again. Give me one more, Veronica."

He sped up and felt her nails pierce the skin of his shoulders where she was clutching him as she lifted her hips to meet him thrust for thrust. "Zachary, oh! I'm so close. Oh fuck, don't stop!"

"That's right. Let me feel your pussy strangle my cock, V." He was getting so close, but he wanted to make her fly one more time. He wasn't sure he could last as his own whimper escaped. He latched his mouth to the flesh covering her collarbone and sucked.

"Zach!" she called as she peaked for the third time.

It was what he'd been waiting for. He let go of his control and slung his hips back and forth until everything in him clenched before exploding as he buried himself as deep inside her as he could get. "Mine," he whispered in her ear.

"Hmm, all yours," she agreed sleepily.

# Chapter 14

By the following morning, Veronica's movements and the ginger way she sat revealed how well-loved she was, and Zachary's cheeks hurt from grinning with pride. After their latest round, he'd kissed her forehead as she drifted back to sleep. He needed to handle morning chores, but then he'd make coffee and bring a mug back to her in bed.

Zach threw on work clothes and headed down the hall, only to shriek embarrassingly and clutch at his heart in alarm when he stepped around the corner to find a man sitting at his dining table cleaning a pistol.

"Jesus fuck, Ben," he scolded the man, who was dressed in the most boring blue business suit that must come free with every accountant certification. Ben had once called it his civilian costume, and Zach had filed the comment away as the single most honest thing the man had ever said.

"Zachary." Ben didn't glance up from the brush he was using to clear the barrel of his weapon. "It sounds like you've found happiness. And don't be so shocked. You knew I was coming." His tone was flat and devoid of emotion. Zachary had received robocalls that sounded more human than this man.

"No, I didn't. Your last text said you'd look into things. In fact, that was the only text I've received from you in almost a year, asshole." He released a sardonic chuckle as he felt his heart rhythm return to normal, or at least close enough that he'd remain among the living. When he'd sent Ben the message, he'd figured the odds were only about three to five the man was still alive.

"Hm well, I did, and what I found was interesting enough, I decided to come see for myself. Besides, it's the first time you've ever mentioned a woman, or another human for that matter, since you retired and escaped from Izzy."

"Five key strokes, man. That's all it takes. The letters "c" and "u" followed by the at symbol and a number for the time. What if I'd had a security system set up?"

Now Ben looked up at him, though the smirk he wore beneath a single raised eyebrow was his only reaction.

"Did you at least make coffee?" Zach asked.

Ben tsked at him. "Don't you know it's impolite to make yourself at home in another person's kitchen?"

Zach turned into the kitchen to get a pot brewing as he mumbled under his breath about people who are happy to break into homes and clean firearms on tables but draw the line at getting coffee started.

"I did bring you a present," Ben called after him.

"Shhh, Veronica's still asleep," he tossed a glare over his shoulder.

"No, I'm awake."

Zach glanced over his shoulder to see Veronica rubbing sleep from her eyes as she asked, "And who's the guy cleaning a gun in the kitchen?"

"As I'm sure Zachary loves to inform you, this is the dining room. His location is the kitchen."

Zach kept his back to them until he'd hit the start button. Then he turned around to find Veronica blinking, like she wasn't sure if this was real or a dream. He understood that feeling well. It tended to arrive and depart on the exact same schedule as Ben.

"I didn't know he was coming, or I'd have given you a heads up." He shrugged an apology toward her. "He says he brought a present, which could mean anything from a dead body in his trunk to a credit card receipt he thinks is interesting."

The way Veronica's mouth opened and closed as she tried to come up with a response drew Zach's attention to her lips. He wanted to spend the morning sitting on the porch with her, sipping coffee and stealing kisses. He did not want to help find an appropriate location to disappear a body and then dig the hole to bury it.

"It's good you're here, Veronica. My present is more for you than him, anyway." He finished reassembling the nine-millimeter before replacing it in the side holster under his suit jacket. Then he adjusted the glasses on his face before folding his hands neatly in his lap. "Perhaps we should have breakfast first?" He looked to Zach.

"No. Tell me what interesting stuff you found, show me the present, and then we'll talk about breakfast." Zach wasn't about to let this man spring something traumatic on the woman he was falling for.

"Hmm, I swear you used to be more adventurous." Then Ben turned his attention back to Veronica. "You should drag him out somewhere and force him to have some fun. Though perhaps it would be best to wait until we've resolved this little stalker issue you seem to have picked up."

"You know about what's going on?" Veronica glanced from Ben to Zach. "I don't even know your name," she prompted.

Ben stood from his seat and extended his hand to her. "I'm Lynch. Though Zachary here insists on calling me Ben."

Veronica glared at him without unfolding her hands from her chest. Then she shifted her eyes to Zach with a silent question about trusting Ben, or maybe touching him. Zach wasn't sure exactly what she was trying to ask, but it didn't matter. He shook his head *no* to every possibility.

"Oh fine," Ben huffed. "I'll go get the present while you two say good morning to each other, or whatever." Then he waved his hands as if shooing them away before striding out the front door.

Veronica shuffled over to him and stepped up close enough to rest her head against his chest. It was nice. Zach wrapped his arms around her and just stood there for a minute. He didn't think either of them were awake enough to properly deal with Ben Lynch.

"Who is he, really?" Veronica asked softly while still snuggled into him.

"Not a fucking clue," Zach confessed. "Remember how I told you about what happened during my first deployment? With Amanda?" He waited to feel her head bob up and down in confirmation before continuing. "Since I was transferred to a different command in the middle of deployment, I was left behind in Dubai when my former command left. There was supposed to be a two-day gap before my new command arrived and picked me up, but like most things in the military, shit got fucked up, and I ended up spending a little over a week there. That's when I met an American businessman named Lynch. Meeting someone from the State Department felt like my saving grace."

Ben had been younger back then, too. At the time, Zachary had thought the man was middle-aged. In reality, he was probably just a few years older than Zach. He was just more experienced and confident.

"Did he help you get what you needed?" Veronica asked, while rubbing her cheek against his soft cotton tee.

"Huh. Yeah, I guess, though it wasn't what I wanted or what I expected."

That was enough for Veronica to pull back and look up at him.

"Let's pour coffee, and I'll explain," he suggested.

By the time they were both seated at the table with hands wrapped around their mugs, there was still no sign of Ben returning. "Where did he go?" Veronica asked when Zach caught her staring at the door.

"I don't even try to guess."

"So back to Dubai," she prompted him to continue.

"Right, so he took me out to dinner and to a club where he got me drunk. In fairness, I may not have mentioned that I was only twenty and had never really indulged in alcohol before." Zach winced at the memory.

"Wait, isn't alcohol a big no-no there?" She was clearly more aware of the world than he had been back then.

"Yep, it sure is. Which is probably why Ben was so pissed by my drunken behavior. He dragged me to the tiny room he was renting. I don't remember everything about that night, but apparently, I told him about what Amanda was dealing with and why I was waiting for a different ship to pick me up. We ended up hanging out for most of the week, though he'd occasionally disappear for a few hours. On the sixth day there, he said he needed my help with something and asked me to go to the local market with him. When we got there, he made us sit in the car for almost an hour before he pointed out a well-dressed Emirati man and told me to go compliment his car. Since the man had just pulled up in an Aston Martin, I didn't think too much of it. I had no idea Ben was planning to sneak up behind him and stick a needle in the guy's neck while I distracted him.

"What the fuck?" Veronica breathed out the question in a whisper.

"Yeah, you're telling me." Zach could chuckle about it now. "I was completely freaked out. I still have no idea what I helped do that day, but Ben was more relaxed after that. He showed me around Dubai like a tourist for the next two days. He'd just show up at my hotel and drag me out. On my last day there, I woke up to find an envelope on the night table with my name on it. Ben had stuck a few hundred dollars in there with a note saying to be at the pier at 1pm to report to my new command."

"And that was twenty years ago?" Veronica checked.

"Just about." Zach stood up to check out the front window to see if Ben was out there or if he'd parked a car in the driveway, but there was nothing to see. Someday he wanted to learn to disappear the way Ben did. He sighed and turned back to Veronica. "It was two or three years later that I saw him next. We ran into each other at a pub in Norway, of all places."

"Wow."

Zach poured more coffee in each of their mugs and got a second pot brewing. If Ben said he'd be back with a present, Zach knew he'd return. It might take an hour, a week, or a decade, but the man had always followed through.

"Lynch asked about my friend that had been harassed, so I told him about what they did to her. He had me write their names down on a napkin before tucking it into his pocket. Then he changed the subject, and we argued over the integrity of the band Journey before I called it a night."

"Now tell her what happened next," Ben prompted as he closed the front door behind him and carried a shotgun over to the dining table.

Zach returned to the table and slid into the second chair across from Veronica before Ben could sit down. "You should get yourself a mug and some coffee." He tilted his chin toward the kitchen.

Ben nodded, almost let a smile crack his façade, and left the shotgun on the table. "This is for her," he said to Zach before striding directly toward the cabinet Zach kept the mugs in.

Of course, the man knew exactly where the mugs were. He made a point of *not* thinking too much about the stuff Ben knew and how he might know it. If he spent too long considering it, he'd end up paranoid, terrified, and likely locked up in a mental facility.

Instead, he turned back to Veronica. "The day we were pulling out of port, I found another note. This one was left on my rack, but it was a similar envelope with my name on it. The handwriting was the same, too. This one only had an Associated Press news bulletin inside."

Veronica frowned at him and asked the obvious. "What did it say?"

"Three sailors had been found dead. They were three of the four guys who'd assaulted Amanda."

He waited for Veronica's eyes to expand, adjust, and return close enough to normal for him to feel secure about dropping the last thing he'd learned. "At the next port, I stopped by an internet café and did a search for the fourth guy. CNN had reported him missing the same week the other three died. No one has seen or heard from him since."

"He'd gone on shore duty in fucking Kansas. It was better for him not to be connected to the other three," Ben added casually from the kitchen where he was sitting on the same counter Zach had been leaning against. His feet were swinging side-to-side just enough to give a strangely innocent look to the man confessing to killing someone in Kansas and hiding the body.

When Zach turned back to the table to check Veronica's reaction, he found her staring fiercely at Ben. "Good," she told him with a dip of her chin.

The tightness in his chest released. Zach had been worried Veronica would run screaming into the woods to get away from both of them. If he'd have thought Ben would show up in person, he'd have never texted the man.

"Good. That shotgun's designed for indoor use, so it's got a shorter barrel than most. It makes it easier to turn corners, and it's a hell of a lot more accurate and reliable than the redneck sawed-off variety. Have Zach teach you how to use it. Keep it loaded with something heavy and think of it like your third arm. I know you don't have any experience, but you don't need great aim to use a shotgun. If they've gotten close enough for you to need it, you'll be close enough to hit them. Be ready to run, though. You're more likely to hurt them and slow them down than kill them. If that's the case, we'll follow their blood trail and finish them off unless we're already dead."

Unlike Ben's bland delivery of information, Zach's next words were an emotionally driven outburst. "There's no fucking way anyone will get close enough to her for her to shoot them unless it's over my dead body."

In all the years of them popping in and out of each other's lives, seemingly at random, Zach had never seen Ben smile before. He did now, though it was a sad smile. "I'm glad you've found your person, Zachary." Then he finished his coffee, set the mug in the sink, and announced he needed to be on his way.

"Wait. I appreciate the shotgun, though I do have my own guns I was planning to share with her." A small lick of jealousy may have laced Zach's thanks. "But you haven't said if you found any useful information about the men or why they're interested in Veronica."

"Oh right. Mustn't forget this." Ben hopped down from the counter and extracted a manilla file folder from the back of his pants. He handed it to Zach before readjusting his suit coat to conceal his holster. "Further digging requires travel, and a few flags have popped up suggesting the state department may be interested in these individuals as well. I'll send along relevant information as I find it. You'll find the email information to access my updates in the folder."

Then he strode over to Veronica, bent down close to her ear and whispered something before standing back up and winking at Zach, who was trying to remind himself that punching Ben wouldn't be a good idea.

"It was a pleasure meeting you, Veronica. You appear to have exactly what it takes to keep this one on his toes. Lord knows, he needs someone to add a bit of excitement to his boring retirement. Try not to die sooner than nature intended." He was out the door and gone before either Zach or Veronica could respond.

Zach clenched his teeth and listened to the absence of an engine starting up. He didn't hear tires crunch down his gravel drive, either.

# Chapter 15

Veronica wanted nothing to do with the folder Zach was running his hands over. She was seriously concerned he'd want her to open it, read it, and talk about it, but Veronica wouldn't do it. That was a big ol' no from her. She'd seen folders like that before, and not just around the office. Those were different. They were crisp and clean, with sharp edges that gave the worst papercuts.

The folder being fondled by Zachary's large, calloused hands was soft, with frayed edges. It had obviously been folded in half at some point, and there were a few smudges ruining the consistency of the manila coloring. The only thing it was missing was a circular coffee stain. That detail was the only thing that allowed Veronica to stand up from the table, make a semi-coherent comment about work, and escape into the spare room they'd turned into her temporary office.

Once she'd shut the door behind herself, she took a few deep breaths and reminded herself that her father had retired. It wasn't his folder. He wouldn't open it and spend days mumbling to himself while drinking through every bottle in their cabinet. Her mother wasn't here to yell at him about it, nor did Veronica need to stay small and quiet to prevent making things worse.

Even knowing how this was different didn't change her ultimate source of comfort, though. When Veronica settled into the chair that wasn't hers, fear flickered inside. She wasn't in her place. But then she flipped on her computer and listened to its morning chime of greeting. She rested her fingertips upon the keyboard she'd used for so long, many of the letters had been rubbed away from the keys.

She opened the code she'd been working on the day before, but before she could escape into it, she pulled up her email just long enough to send a single message to Freddy.

*I'm working. Leave me alone.*

He'd ignore the part about leaving her alone, but that was why she turned her phone all the way off and closed her email program before diving into coding.

Eventually, a knock at the door, followed by Zach's gentle rumble requesting entrance, pulled her out of the zone. She was pretty sure she'd managed to isolate various groups of bots within the larger swarm so different humans could be given partial access to direct only a small aspect of any given project.

"Come on in," she tossed over her shoulder while checking some of the commands she'd used in her code. There was a loop in there somewhere. She could feel it, but she'd need to draw everything out on paper to find it.

"Are you okay?" Zach asked.

"Yeah, but I didn't bring my sketch pad. I might need to pop over to my place to grab it."

"Why don't we have dinner first?"

"I'm good, thanks. I'll eat later." She could grab her colored pens, too. If she drew out the different paths in different colors, it would be easier to spot the loop. Or maybe she should do each level in a different color to see the progression through the code?

"Veronica, you haven't eaten in almost twenty-four hours. Come join me for dinner."

She kept her face turned away from him so he wouldn't see her eye roll at his dramatics. She'd eaten last night, and it couldn't be later than noon. "I'll be out in a bit." She waved him away over her shoulder.

Instead of hearing the door close behind him, though, his footsteps brought him up right behind her.

Reluctantly, she twisted herself around to look at him. If she'd had her own chair, she could have just spun around, but this wooden one had four solid legs and no swivel. "What?" she snapped.

His soft smile aggravated her even more. "It's almost seven, Veronica. You've been working for almost twelve straight hours. Your eyes and body need a break. Will you come have dinner with me, please?" He spoke softer than she'd heard from him before, which was enough to fully pull her attention away from work. The long, orange shadows stretching across the room surprised her. She expected it to be coming up on lunch time, but a glance out the window revealed the sun dipping below the horizon.

Shaking herself and blinking to confirm what she saw, Veronica turned back to Zachary. "I'm sorry. I didn't mean to snap at you. Is it really that late?"

He held up his phone to show her the time. Damn, he hadn't been exaggerating. "Shit. Sorry. Um, do you want help making dinner?" she offered.

Zach's expression shifted from cautious and gentle to his genuine smile of joy. "Nah, it's already done. I thought comfort food sounded good, so I made meatloaf with mashed potatoes and fresh rolls."

"That's what I'm smelling." Until he said it, Veronica hadn't noticed the enticing aroma of bread baking that was wafting through the room. Then again, it might just now be reaching her since he left the door open. Either way, it alerted her stomach, and she made the choice to leave finding the loop until tomorrow.

This meal was just as amazing as the previous times he'd cooked for her, and when he responded to her moans of delight with flirtatious innuendoes, she exaggerated her enjoyment even more. By the time their plates were empty, her stomach was just as sore from laughing as it was from being delightfully stuffed.

"You cooked, so I clean," she declared with a wink before standing up with her own plate and grabbing his. She swished her hips and wiggled her ass as she walked away from him and into the kitchen.

He followed behind with the butter and other condiments from the table but didn't interrupt her rinsing the dishes and loading them into the dishwasher. Though, the way he leaned against the counter beside her with his arms crossed over his chest made it obvious he was watching her and waiting for her to finish.

"What?" she teased, flicking water at him to make him blink. She'd just finished with the dishes and was about to wipe down the counters. "You look way too serious right now." Veronica rubbed her body all over his as she reached around him to wipe behind where he was leaning. She didn't want him to move out of her way, but she did want to bring back his smile.

"Are you aware of your beauty?" he asked with the seriousness of someone asking if they knew the location of their child.

Compared to the playfulness she'd been feeling, his question was like a bucket of ice water. It didn't sound like he was being sarcastic. Maybe she went too far with the flirty and teasing.

His fingers wrapped around her waist with his thumbs in the front pointed toward her belly button. "Veronica?"

She forced herself to breathe. "What?"

Zach pulled her forward until their hips were against each other, and she was leaning back to keep her shoulders far enough away that she could look at his face.

"You are beautiful." He kissed her forehead. "And you are smart." His grin was back. "And it's so fucking sexy when you shake your ass at me."

Veronica felt his chest heave and braced herself for whatever he would say next.

The crinkles around his eyes smoothed back out as his face returned to a neutral expression. His fingers dug more tightly into her hips, making it impossible for her to turn away or escape as he finished what he needed to say. "But I need you to talk to me about some of the things Ben found."

Her litany of objections and excuses was cut off before she could say the first word as he leaned down to kiss her lips. Softly, he placed chaste kisses across her mouth, along her jaw, and back toward her ear.

Once there, he whispered, "I saw the way you ran from the folder as if it were a hellhound. Was it the folder or the contents or something else?" He pulled back enough to see her face, but his grip on her hips remained strong and solid.

Veronica focused on the way his lips had felt against her skin and channeled the strength of his hands into grounding herself enough to answer.

"My father had a folder just like it. It was the file investigating the death of his partner. When he pulled it out, we all knew."

Zach's hands slid around her waist and began a gentle rhythm of rubbing circles up and down her back.

"He'd start off determined, but when he failed to magically divine any new information, he'd get frustrated. He'd have a drink. And then another. He was never violent or anything like that. He'd just be distant mand unpredictable. Mom would send us outside or to friends' houses as much as possible until she could convince him to tuck the file back in a drawer." Veronica wasn't sure how to explain to Zach that her father was an amazing man. He'd built a company, raised five kids, and was a loyal husband. While she remembered the anxiety that came with that manila file, she also had memories of him taking her and Phee's side to wage a water gun fight against her brothers.

Zachary continued to hold her and rub her back, but eventually he asked, "Did he get angry?"

Veronica considered his question. She did think of him as angry during those times, but never in a way that was directed at anyone but himself. She thought back to her mom's behavior during those times, but no. Katrina had been worried, and now that Veronica was an adult herself, she could see the irritation in her mom's behavior.

*Everyone outside! I can't deal with all of you and him*, she remembered her mom saying as she shooed them out the door.

"I think he was angry at himself, maybe?" she told Zach.

"Can you tell me about it?"

She did pull away from him now. "It's not that interesting of a story. His original business partner died in a car accident the night he and Dad secured funding to expand the business into AI programming and government contracting instead of just being a normal tech company. AI was brand new back then. Anyway, Josh and Dad had driven separately, since Josh and his family lived in the city. Josh was on I-66 when he was run off the road and killed. They never found who did it." She shrugged.

"If I were to bring out a few papers with some information on them, could you help me understand them?" Zach asked.

Veronica rolled her eyes. "Yes, it's really not a big deal. The folder just reminded me it's better to be productive rather than in people's hair bothering them. I had work to do, and you had animals to take care of."

Zach hummed at her but dropped the subject. "Shall we sit at the table, or would you prefer the couch?"

"Couch. No offense, but your office desk chair sucks. I think it bruised my ass." She rubbed the offended body part with an exaggerated wince. It was sore. She hadn't noticed it while sitting there, but once she got up, she'd become very aware that she needed her own comfy, ergonomic, swivel chair that reclined and had adjustable arm rests.

"I bet I can help it feel better," Zach offered with a waggle of his eyebrows.

"You do, huh?" She stepped away from him, prepared to make a run for his bedroom to see who could get undressed faster.

"Right after we make sense of the information Ben gave us."

Damn it. That was so much less fun than her plans. "Fine," she agreed.

He sent her to the living room while he grabbed the papers and followed behind her.

She'd expected a stack of pages, but Zach only handed her four pieces of paper before sitting right up against her hip.

When she tossed him a side-eye, he smirked. "It'll be easier to look at them together if we're closer to each other."

"Right." She nodded and looked down at what she was holding. The first page looked like a financial document. It showed an account ledger of some sort, but she didn't recognize anything on it, and there was no heading to it. She passed it to Zach. "I have no idea what that is, beyond the obvious accounting of some kind."

The next page was a medical bill from a hospital in Haymarket. The patient's name was Joshua Baker. "That's my dad's partner," she told Zach. "He's the one who died, but this is dated 2020." She took a second to think through the math. "I was twelve when we went to that funeral, so he had to have passed in 2003 I think."

"So that can't be his medical bill. Was there a Joshua Junior?"

Veronica felt stupid for not thinking of him right away. Of course, this would be Josh's medical bill. "Yeah. He's two years younger than me, so I guess I still think of him as a little kid. Plus, he was always Josh or Joshie, while everyone called his dad Joshua."

"Okay, so we have a medical bill from the son of your dad's former business partner, who died mysteriously."

"There wasn't anything mysterious about it. Some asshole just ran him off the road. My dad just hated that the person was never caught."

Zach frowned as he thought, but Veronica wanted to collect more pieces before she started attempting to solve the puzzle. She passed the medical bill to Zach and looked at the third sheet of paper. This one was completely different, and it took her brain a minute to shift gears and catch up. "Why would Ben give us a copy of an email between some Asian guy and Brian Renner?"

"It's he the one you went on a date with?" Zach nudged his shoulder into hers as he teased her. "What does he do?"

"He's the liaison between our team and their's, but as far as practical, day-to-day responsibilities?" Veronica shrugged. "I have no idea."

Maybe we start by looking him up online?" Zach nudged his shoulder into hers. "I've got my iPad right here." He pulled it out and started searching.

"Point for you," Veronica conceded as she read over his shoulder. The results were all basic profile stuff, like his LinkedIn account and his old college profile, but they didn't provide any insight beyond listing his profession as a software developer. His LinkedIn profile listed Dynamic Solutions as his current employer, but that wasn't helpful either. "We need to check the company site," Veronica suggested.

Zach grunted an agreement and started pulling up Dynamic Solution's website. Once it loaded, he looked at her with concern. "Is this it? Isn't it a huge company?"

"It is, but they mostly work on defense contracts, so there's not much to be shared publicly. Our website's even worse. I had our developer set it up so you need some kind of login credentials to get beyond our first page, but even the one public-facing page is out-of-date and doesn't include any useful information."

"This doesn't help us at all, does it?" Zach's shoulders drooped.

"Oh no, this is a huge help. We just need to use my computer."

He turned to her with a nervous look. "I'm not sure hacking into their system is the best idea."

This time, Veronica got to be the one to laugh at him. "No hacking required. I have low-level access to a couple of their systems because of our contract with them."

"How does that work? Would he have a reason to be searching your house for something?"

Veronica sighed. "I want to say no, but he might. Basically, we don't want to mess with physically building the bots. It's a completely different skillset from what anyone at TI has and requires a ton of special equipment and tools. The manufacturing has to be done in a clean room, too. Instead of dealing with all of it, we teamed up with DS. They officially won the contract, but we got the software development piece of it while they're responsible for the manufacturing."

"So how would Renner benefit from any information you have?" Zach asked.

Thinking back to Patrick's point about the value of their proprietary code, Veronica wondered if Renner could be coming after that.

"Can I see the email again?" she asked.

"Sure, but I'm going to ask you to explain it to me as you read."

Once he passed it back to her, she squinted to read the tiny print. Someone had smashed a chain of three emails onto a single page to print. She could make out what it said, but just barely.

"Have you already read this?" she asked Zach.

"Yeah, but it may as well have been written in a foreign language for all I could understand." He was drawing shapes on her thigh as she read.

Veronica explained the gist of the email to him. "It's basically pointing out that Dynamic Solutions would operate more efficiently and significantly increase their profit if they were able to fulfill their contracts in-house."

Zach stopped scrolling and stared at her blankly. "Like by not working with you?" he asked.

"Right."

He continued to stare at her.

"Zach, this is why Patrick stresses so much about keeping our proprietary code secure. If DS had our code, they wouldn't need us. They could do exactly what's being suggested in this email." She watched his face shift in awe as his understanding grew. "I mean, it's a little more complicated than that."

"I'm guessing that contract is worth a lot of money?" he asked.

"Yeah, like millions, but it's not just one contract. We partner with DS on contracts with the Navy and NASA." Patrick and Greg handled all the contracts, so Veronica didn't know all the details. She was aware of how stressed Patrick got when contract renewal time came around, though. If Dynamic Solution's developers could program the bots themselves, Taylor Industries would cease to exist.

"Is it really that easy for them to steal from you?"

Veronica tossed the paper on top of the other two Zach had put on the coffee table in front of them. He was still holding the fourth page.

"I mean, no, but yes?" How could she explain their code was copyrighted, but that was more of a deterrent than something to stop theft? "It's like cartoon characters. It's copyrighted code, and we would go to court if someone popped up using it. But all they have to do is change enough of it to claim they wrote their own version. I mean, how many times have you seen a mouse with red shorts and black ears? The proportions and details may be off enough for the artist to say it's their own unique creation, but every five-year-old will call it by the same name."

Zach deflated. "Right. Yeah, I can see how that would go." He held out the last page, but before letting go of it, he looked at her and cautioned, "This one's upsetting." Then he stared at her as she took it from him to see what he meant.

There were four images on the page. Veronica's hand flew to her mouth in horror.

"Every single one of your worries, concerns, and fears is valid." Zach had twisted toward her and bent forward until his face was so close to hers, he appeared blurry. Or maybe that was the tears collecting in her eyes. "I'm not letting you out of my sight," he assured her.

"They took my picture." She hoped saying it aloud, even in a whisper, would make it feel more real, but it didn't. "How did they get this? I'd have seen them."

One photo was in gray scale, and the resolution was terrible. But the only way to get a picture of her climbing into her Jeep while it was parked right in front of her house would be from standing in her driveway, or maybe alongside her driveway. Either way, she'd have seen them. It wasn't like there were any other houses around or other vehicles coming and going. The second photo of her was in color and much clearer, but considering it showed her changing clothes in her bedroom, that made it worse. The window frame around the edge of the image made it clear the photo had been taken from outside, but that didn't lessen the violation.

Zach put his hand on her knee. "You're right. You'd have seen someone if they were by your driveway, so I'm betting they placed a camera. Looking at the quality, it's probably a basic game trail cam you can get at any sporting goods store."

"Do you think it's still there?"

He shook his head, and Veronica blinked away the pools of moisture before they could streak down her cheeks. If someone was stalking her, and that photo sure made that seem to be the case, she didn't have time to cry about it. She needed to figure out what the fuck was going on, what it had to do with work, and why Joshie's hospital visit would matter. "Did Ben say anything about why these are connected?"

"He's not sure they are. I asked him to look into you, and when he did, this is what he found. The common connection is you. Even Joshie's hospital bill, Ben found by searching for information about you."

That just confused Veronica more. Why would a bill like that show up connected to her. "I need to dig into why and how this relates to me," she told Zach.

He nodded his agreement. "I plan to confirm the cameras are gone and do another thorough sweep of your place first thing in the morning. Ben brought me a device I can use to scan for anything we might have missed. I'll hike over and check the whole area. It looks like whoever it was used a better camera, likely their phone, to take the other picture while standing outside your bedroom window. I'll see if they left anything behind that might help us figure out who it is."

"No, Zach. We need to call the sheriff or police or someone."

"I agree." There was a but coming. Veronica could see it on his face, so she waited for him to continue. "Veronica, will this be enough for Patrick to work with law enforcement?"

Shit. That was a big but. Patrick wouldn't let the local sheriff anywhere near anything related to their business. He'd been elected by the majority of local residents, but that didn't mean he gave a shit about law, order, or justice—at least not the way the outside world did. The man was related to half the people who voted for him. He'd won over the other half by promising not to give the wealthy invaders special treatment.

"I see your point," she agreed. "But then, what do we do?"

"Let's start with what we have. Can you tell me anything about the other two pictures?" Zach kept his hand on her knee. It felt like he was the only thing preventing her from floating up and away into nothingness. "Breathe for a minute," he suggested.

She inhaled through her nose before releasing the air slowly through her mouth. The floaty feeling subsided, and she focused on the other images in front of her, squinting to get a better look. One was grainy and gray scale, but it looked old instead of low quality. It showed a man slumped in the driver's seat of a jeep. He'd been shot in the temple. Between the low quality and the odd angle of the shot, it was hard to tell who it might be. "I'm not sure. I feel like he might be familiar, but he also looks like every other businessman on earth."

Veronica shifted her focus to the details around the man. "Does that look like a stick shift to you?" she asked Zach.

"Yeah, why?"

"Mr. Baker, Joshua, drove a jeep like this."

"He's the one who was your dad's partner?" Zach checked.

She nodded as she thought. "He had a soft-top, and I thought it was the most amazing thing. His was blue, but I can't tell in this photo what color this one is."

"You said he died in a car accident, right? Wasn't he run off the road?"

"Uh huh, so this can't be him." Even as she said it, Veronica didn't believe it. Mr. Baker's Jeep had sparked her lifelong obsession with them. It was why she had the one she drove and a classic that needed serious work stashed in her garage. Someday, she wanted to fix it up.

Zach grunted and took the paper from her gently. "What about the last image?"

Veronica couldn't stop the laugh from bubbling up and out. "That's HQ. The sign was our gift to Patrick when he took over. It was the ugliest one I could find, and he hates it, but we won't let him take it down."

"When did you put it up?" Zach asked.

"January 2021, or maybe February." She couldn't remember how long it had taken them to get it hung up.

"If the guy in the car really is Joshua Baker, when would it have been taken?"

"Twenty years ago," she suspected he already had a rough timeline, but now she could see what he was considering. "These photos were taken a long time apart. One in 2003-ish, one about three years ago, and the two of me were taken within the last two months. Ophelia gave me that scarf I'm wearing for Christmas this year."

Zach gathered up all four pages and frowned at her with worry.

"I'm going to start searching online and see if I can figure out how this connects to me," she offered instead of letting herself wallow in what a mess she was.

"Do you want a cup of tea or anything? I'll put this away and then bring drinks to you."

"Coffee would be great," Veronica answered.

"Nope. I'm out of decaf."

She grimaced at him. "Decaf is gross. I meant real coffee."

"Is this your gentle way of refusing to join me in bed tonight?" Zach's face was completely neutral except for a tiny twitch at the back of his jaw by his ear.

Veronica hadn't thought that far ahead. She usually worked until she was tired and then passed out. Repeating last night, both the mind-blowing sex and the incredible sleep that followed it, was a welcome thought. Surely, she could have coffee and join him in bed. It wasn't like chili that would make her fart or give her indigestion.

She was still puzzled by the question when Zach spoke again, though he was avoiding looking at her as he spoke. "Never mind. I'll make you coffee. See you in your office in a minute." Then he stood up and started to walk away with his shoulders hunched.

"Wait, Zach." She'd missed something. When her brain wasn't focused on work, keeping up with the world around her wasn't too hard, but when Veronica allowed the puzzles of her job to take center stage, her human interaction skills went out the window.

"Yeah?" He paused but didn't turn back around to face her.

"I did kind of expect to sleep with you again tonight, especially after last night, but I also want coffee. I don't understand the connection between the two."

That was enough for him to turn around, though he looked hesitant. "Won't it keep you awake?"

Well, that explained the decaf comment. "I typically drink three pots of coffee a day. I've only had three or four cups today, so another cup now is more likely to relieve my headache than prevent me from sleeping."

"Oh. I can get you some painkillers, too."

This man was the sweetest she'd ever met. "I appreciate that, but I've got some in my bag. I was going to take two while looking for connections." Her cheeks felt like they could cramp up from how big she was smiling. He'd been disappointed when he thought they wouldn't share his bed again tonight. Damn, that made her feel good.

Zachary grinned back at her. "I'll be there with your coffee in just a minute."

She bobbed her head in agreement and stood up to hit the restroom on her way to the spare bedroom slash office.

# Chapter 16

Zachary had to remind himself to breathe. He'd been terrified she'd say it was just a one-time thing with them. After doing all he could to ensure she understood what he wanted and expected, at the end of the day, her agreement was just words. Izzy had proven those didn't mean shit. He'd respect her right to change her mind, but there was no way he could imagine sleeping by himself with her in the other room. The way they'd connected the night before had been too powerful for him to ignore.

He got her coffee quickly before tucking the papers from Ben under his arm and hurrying into the spare room to see what she'd found.

"Thank you." She accepted the mug and blew on it before taking a sip.

Her screen was the boring home screen Zachary associated with most computers, but he held back from asking if she'd started searching yet.

"I don't get any results when I search for him," Veronica shared. "It's a dead end for now, but I bet Patrick knows a hell of a lot more. Then again, if Lynch got these files, other people have probably seen them, too. Patrick would want to report it to Dynamic Solutions, and I worry that might just give them more reason to come after me."

"Thank fuck!" Zachary was glad he'd set his tea down on the desk already. He hadn't meant to say that aloud and quickly held out his hands in apology. "I just meant, I'm glad you're considering your safety."

"It's okay, Zachary. It's kind of nice having someone worry about me. It's weird, but in a good way, I think."

"Yeah?" She'd been looking down into her mug, so he wasn't sure if she really meant it.

When Veronica looked up at him with a soft smile, he was relieved. Then she took it a step further. "I don't feel like I'm all alone when you're around."

It should sound pathetic, but Zach understood exactly what she meant. When it was just him and the animals, he struggled to remember why anything mattered. With Veronica around, she mattered. He wanted to be there for her. It made him feel like he had a purpose again. That probably sounded just as idiotic as saying she made him feel less lonely. Hell, they might even mean roughly the same thing.

"You can stay forever," he blurted out.

"Huh?"

"I meant to say I like having you around, too."

"Right." Her smirk made it clear she'd understood what he'd said the first time, but she was letting it go. Zachary appreciated that.

"What time is it?" she asked.

"Almost ten. How late do you usually stay up?" He wanted to curl up in bed with her. Wearing her out with orgasms before wrapping his arms around her would give him the comfort of knowing exactly where she was, and that she was safe. Unfortunately, sleeping in wasn't something alpacas understood.

When Veronica sighed and set down her coffee, he braced himself for her to say she'd be working for a few hours yet.

"You should kidnap me and drag me away with you."

It wasn't anywhere on his list of anticipated responses, but he could work with it. Well, if she were serious, which she probably wasn't. He'd thrown Izzy over his shoulder and carted her off to bed once. She'd been so mad, he'd been concerned for his family jewels. Even the memory made him cringe.

"I didn't mean kidnap me in a bad way," Veronica rushed to add. "I just meant I don't want to work, but I should." She sounded so tired. Was she really expected to work this late into the night, or had she taken too much time off during the day? She'd spent time with him yesterday, but she'd worked straight through today.

"What would happen if you stopped work and came to bed with me?" he asked.

She tilted her nose down, so she was peering up at him through her eyelashes. "I'd feel guilty as shit."

"If I pick you up and haul you away from your computer for the night, will you be upset with me?" If she said yes, he might still do it, but he'd put on a cup first. The more he considered how long she'd already worked that day, the more confident he became that she needed someone to tell her it was enough.

"If you throw out your back trying to lift me, I'll be livid."

Zachary rolled his eyes at that thought. The woman barely remembered to eat and spent her life in front of a computer screen. She couldn't weigh more than one-twenty. "I didn't hear any concern when I carried you to bed yesterday," he reminded her.

"That was different. I was distracted." She shifted nervously as he began stalking toward her.

He moved slowly to give her time to warn him off.

"Zachary?" she asked with concern.

"I'll stop if you ask me to." Amanda flashed into his memory. "That will always be true for everything with us. If you say stop, I will no matter what."

Veronica's shoulders shook with her soft chuckle. "I have no doubt that you would, but the predatory look in your eyes makes me think I'll like what you have in mind."

He was standing close enough to bend down, scoop her up, and toss her over his shoulder, so he didn't bother with further commentary.

Sure enough, she yelped and smacked his ass before grabbing onto his belt to steady herself as he banded his arm tightly around her thighs to keep her balanced on his shoulder. Then he turned to carry her to his room and add to the marks he'd left along her collarbone the night before.

The second he lowered her onto the bed, Veronica pulled off her shirt and began shoving her pants and underwear down her legs. Zachary wasn't about to interrupt her and used the opportunity to strip himself.

He was faster than her and engulfed her nipple with his mouth before she expected it. Her moan made it clear she appreciated the way his teeth bit down and teased the tip, but he didn't linger there. She had so many spots that garnered even better reactions. Zach's hand had already moved between her legs, and his finger had slipped into her easily.

He wasn't surprised to find her wet, but there was enough moisture for him to wonder if she'd been thinking about this for more than the past few minutes. He bit and kissed at her neck while enjoying her moans as he shifted further onto the bed until he was braced above her.

Zach slid down her body with gentle nips and sweet kisses. This woman deserved bliss and joy and love, and Zach wanted to be the man to give it to her. Parting the swollen lips of her pussy, his tongue teased at her clit before lapping at it like it was an ice cream cone. He pulled back just enough for his teeth to nibble the pearl while he basked in her whimpers and hitched breathing.

Veronica's legs spread even further apart, and Zach accepted the invitation to fully savor her sweet center. His tongue moved in little circles around and over her clit before diving deep into her core. It had been years since he'd enjoyed this level of intimacy, but Veronica's responses were so easy for him to read. Like last night, his confidence didn't falter. He slid his finger into her tight hole and relished the way her body writhed and shook as he stroked deep inside. Zachary wrapped his mouth back around her clit and sucked while teasing his tongue along the bundle of nerves.

She exploded with so much intensity, his free hand clutched at her hips to prevent her from bucking away from him. Part of him worried his grip was too tight. There'd certainly be bruises, but when her hands came down and clutched his head to hold it to her apex, he knew she was enjoying it just as much as he was.

As Veronica came down from the rush, Zach could feel her entire body shaking and quivering. Her breath was stuttering enough for her words to be halted as she flexed and clenched her fingers after releasing her grip on his hair. "Need. You. Fuck. Please. Zach. More. Need you."

"You've got me," he assured her. "I'm here, and I'm yours."

He adjusted his position to align their hips while he teased the skin along her jaw with his teeth. Then he kissed down her neck until he found the spot on her collarbone that made her whimper with need. She was grasping at the sheets on either side of her head.

"You okay?" he checked in.

"Tingly," she said breathily. "Don't stop." Her breathing was unsteady still. "Zachary."

He couldn't resist the way she begged with his name. Still, he kissed his way up to her ear and whispered, "Deep breaths, beautiful. You gotta keep breathing. That's why you're tingly." Then he pushed up with his arms to look into her eyes.

"I like it." Her eyes sparkled, and those three words had come out with enough clarity and smooth breath to reassure him she wasn't about to pass out.

"Good."

Before he could say anything more, one of those tingly hands wrapped around his cock and squeezed at the root before dragging the pressure up to his tip as if she were trying to milk the cum out of him. He shouted with pleasure but grabbed her hand and pulled it back to the bed, holding it there while he closed his eyes and recited state capitals to regain control.

He blinked and couldn't ignore the proud smirk she wore. "You're evil," he told her.

"And you love it."

"Hell yes, I do." Already positioned perfectly, he slid his entire length into her with one slow, steady thrust as he said it. Then he ground deeper into her and reveled in the way her eyes glossed over as she moaned with delight.

When he pulled back, he set a steady rhythm, never fully withdrawing from her, but giving her short, deep thrusts that kept driving her pleasure without throwing either of them over the edge. Her breathing became choppy again, and Zach was fighting his need to drive into her hard and fast. He wanted the extended pleasure this would bring too much for him to give in, though. At least not yet.

He could see her stomach ripple as she curled her hips up to meet his thrusts. Veronica's hands had shifted to clutch the ends of the pillow her head rested on, but he wanted to feel her nails scrape his back. Zachary wanted to wear her stripes just as much as he wanted her to carry the bruises from his mouth below her neck.

"Hold on to me, V." Her face was pinched with pleasure, so he wasn't certain she understood until her hands slid around his neck to clutch at his shoulder blades. "That's it. Sink your claws into me while you cum for me." He drove in as deep as he could and ground his hips side-to-side.

"Ugh. Need." She was close.

Zach bit down on her shoulder, and she exploded in his arms, screaming his name and carving her marks across his back.

"Fuck, yes," he praised her. "So fucking perfect.  Beautiful." There was no more control behind his movements, and he let his hips pull back before driving the full length into her again and again until any rhythm there might have been reached a chaotic crescendo of pleasure.

Zach's brain was fried, but he managed to lean to the side to avoid crushing Veronica as his shaking arms gave up, and he collapsed to the bed. He was still half on top of her, but her continued soft whimpers assured him she could breathe.

Once his heart rate calmed and at least some blood had returned to his brain, he wrapped his arms tight around Veronica's trembling body.

"You okay?" he asked softly.

"Uh, huh. Intense." She was still flexing and clenching her hands, so he shifted enough to massage her forearms while keeping her tucked close against him.

Between kisses along the back of her neck and shoulders, he whispered to her. "You're gorgeous. So beautiful. But you gotta remember to breathe. Though the way your entire body responds to me is so fucking sexy. I love causing such a big reaction. I want you to love it, too." He didn't expect a response. If anything, her need for attention and care post-sex was like a drug to Zachary's system. Sure, he loved the way it stroked his ego, but this felt like she needed him. That reliance lit him up with purpose and pleasure.

"I'm okay now," she assured him as the worst of her trembles subsided. "And I need to pee." She wiggled, and he gave her space to slide from his embrace.

As Veronica strode back into Zach's bedroom, he celebrated the February chill as her nipples peaked and her slender form jiggled to stay warm.

She leapt back under the covers and pressed her cold skin against him. "Brrr."

"You turned into an ice cube," he teased her while pulling her back into the warmth of his arms.

"It's fucking cold out. I should put clothes on," she rubbed the frozen tip of her nose into the dip in his collarbone just below his Adam's apple.

"Never. I won't allow it, and I don't appreciate the threat."

Her giggle assured him that she was enjoying their playfulness as much as he was.

# Chapter 17

"No more," Veronica begged. "My legs feel like jello." After working so long on Friday, Zachary had insisted she use Saturday for other things, like learning about guns and practicing some basic self-defense moves.

"Earlier, you said they felt like someone had shoved rocks inside your muscles, making it hard to move them?" Zach's deep, rumbled laugh made Veronica smile despite her misery. "Which one is it?"

"Both." He should be able to understand that. It was now Sunday, and she was forcing her already sore muscles to do things they didn't like. "It's like those jello molds with fruit in them. The fruit is the worst, but even the jello isn't great."

"I suppose now's a good time to break for chores and getting dinner started."

Veronica accepted Zach's outstretched hand to pull her up from where she sat in the dirt, but he didn't stop pulling once she was standing. She was dragged up and forward until she was pressed up against his chest with his arms wrapped around her.

The temperature had been dropping throughout the day, so they'd started with target practice. Zachary had her fire his pistol several times, but most of her *firearms training*, as he called it, was spent with her new shotgun. She'd unloaded and reloaded it over and over again. He'd had her put the safety on and take it off and fire and put the safety back on as if they were playing a deadly game of Simon Says.

Eventually, she'd zoned out and been following his direction on autopilot. That was when he'd stopped her and had them shift to practicing the self-defense moves he'd shown her. She appreciated that he didn't expect her to know something forever just because he'd told or shown her once. After going through this same routine two days in a row, she'd felt confident that she'd remember how to do it again tomorrow. Except tomorrow was Monday, and that meant spending the day at HQ instead of practicing with Zach while the chickens and alpacas observed. It also reminded her of the niggling worries she'd been ignoring for the past few days.

Being here with Zachary was amazing, but it wasn't real life. At least, it wasn't *her* real life. She couldn't stay here forever but going home sounded scary and lonely. The longer she was away from it, the more anxiety she felt about returning. As much as Veronica wanted to ignore the world and stay in this bubble, the experienced adult in her knew that delaying the inevitable would just make going home harder.

She'd tried to pour as much focus into the physical movements he'd taught her as she did with shooting, but the thought of her morning meeting being just a single sleep away kept tugging at her. Her activity should have offered some escape, or at least distraction, from the decreasing temperatures, but with her focus already divided, the cold air became one more thing pulling at her. Add in her sore muscles and physical exhaustion, and it was hopeless.

"What's going on in here?" Zach asked her while gently tapping her temple without letting her escape the warmth of his embrace.

It was hard to believe she'd met him less than a week ago. If it was already this scary to think about going home, how much worse would it be in another week, or even another day? "I'm sorry. I don't mean to seem ungrateful, really. I appreciate everything you've done this past week."

Zachary frowned down at her for a minute before responding. "Let's go in and warm up while we talk. I'll even make another pot of coffee."

The man did get bonus points for knowing her weakness. Once inside, with the coffeepot hissing and burbling, Zach turned back to her and asked again. "You had something on your mind all day today. I could tell."

They were both in the kitchen, though he was leaning casually against a counter with his arms crossed over his chest while she stood in the middle of the floor scratching at her nails and fighting the urge to run away from him. She shrugged.

He reached out and pulled her closer to him. He didn't wrap his arms around her, but he spread his feet so hers fit between them and held her hands in his own. "Tell me about your dream?"

Not the question she'd expected. She didn't want to relive it, but since her nightmare had woken him almost an hour before he normally got up, it was fair for him to ask. Describing the dream would also be easier than explaining how she felt like there were fifteen cords tied to different parts of her body, all pulling in different directions and trying to rip her apart like a stuffed dog toy used for tug-of-war.

It only took a second for her to decide where to start. "It was about us, but not like now. We were a couple and lived together. Butthole lived with us, but he was a dog in the dream." She squinted and thought back. "Except sometimes he was a rooster?" Dreams were weird.

Zach chuckled and rubbed his thumbs over the back of her hands.

"We were miserable. We lived in an apartment in the city, but you couldn't leave. It was like there was a forcefield or something. I don't know, but you were trapped in the apartment. You hated it and were always frustrated and disappointed and unhappy. There was something coming at work. I don't know what it was, but it felt like a big meteor we knew would kill us all. It was never named, really, but there was always this feeling of needing to hurry up before it gets us. Patrick was there sometimes. He'd scream about it almost being too late, and I needed to work harder if I wanted... something?"

She couldn't remember what. There'd been something in the dream that she wanted. She'd only get it if she did her work on time, though.

Zach hummed and squeezed her hands just enough to encourage her to keep talking.

"Uh, Freddy was there sometimes, but he never looked at me or talked to me. He'd just tell Patrick that I was going to fuck them over. It's all fuzzy now, but it was like I couldn't do it all. If I did what I needed to do for work, you were left alone and hated me. If I spent my time with you, I'd cease to exist along with the rest of my family. I know that doesn't make sense." She had no idea how to explain it. The whole thing was just one of those weird, scary dreams that forced you to bolt awake in a nervous sweat.

"Most dreams don't make much literal sense." Zach used his hold on her hands to pull her close enough to press a chaste kiss to her forehead.

It was perfect.

Which was why Veronica was able to make her decision. She felt the tears crawl up through her throat, but she wouldn't let them out. She could do this. As the day had gone on, the answer had become clearer. Veronica couldn't do it all and continuing to try would mean failing everyone. Part of her wanted to choose Zachary and everything he'd promised her. But she wasn't stupid enough to let a man pull her away from her work and family. The way Taylor Industries blended those two aspects of her life was so much bigger and older than her relationship with Zach. She couldn't fail them, even if she often felt like the tiniest cog in their gigantic machine.

"I think I need to go home tonight," she said without looking at Zachary's face.

"Tomorrow you have to go in and work at the office where your brother lives, right?"

"Yeah."

"We can go pick up the stuff you need tonight. That way, you don't have to rush around in the morning." Zachary was so calm about it. He didn't understand what she meant.

"Zach. I." Fuck, she didn't want to do this, but eventually he'd get tired of her always running late, getting lost in her work, and generally being bad at relationships. Then she'd lose him, anyway. It was better to make the break now. "I need to go to my home alone and sleep there. It's been great spending the week here, but I can't just cower behind you forever. I need to live my life and do my work. Besides, I think it's clear the threat is against the company more than me. Even with me as the common connection, there haven't been any issues this week."

"Are you saying you were only here because you didn't feel safe at home? I thought we both had real feelings here. Was I wrong?" His grip on her hands shifted from a gentle caress to a desperate clench.

She wiggled her hands, and he relaxed his grip with an apologetic look. "No. I mean, I just don't think this will work for us like this. Lasting relationships don't start with a stalker coming after one of them. You should be able to enjoy your retirement without me sucking you into some kind of investigation or whatever you and Lynch are doing. It's not fair. It's not right." She focused all her brain power on Zach's mind and telepathically tried to help him understand.

"That's not how this works. Remember when I said you were mine? Remember me telling you that I don't do casual?

You accepted those terms. You don't get to run away now just because you had some stupid dream. You're stronger than that."

The fuck she was. And of course, she remembered his words, but this was different. "I agreed when I thought the stalker thing was just me being crazy. But it's real now. We have that file, and I don't know what it means, but I need to find out. That means doing that work in addition to my regular work. I need to keep my focus there, and we both know that means I'll get sucked in and be terrible for you. Just look at the other day when I snapped at you for pointing out that I'd worked through the day without noticing. It wasn't a stupid dream, either," she added while scowling.

"All of that is why you need to stay with me so I can watch your back while you figure it out." His voice took on a pleading tone.

Veronica shook her head. "No. Everything in me is screaming to leave you out of this mess, whatever it is. I need to go and deal with my shit. My family needs me fully focused on them and work, and I don't want to ruin us because I can't do both at the same time." She pulled her hands out of his and stepped back.

"Veronica, no. If you need to be in your own space, I'll come with you. I can come back here to take care of the animals but sleep at your place."

She needed to be alone. She needed to turtle her head into herself, so the world couldn't get to her. Zachary wouldn't let her do that. He'd keep pulling her out and reminding her about the world around them. How was she supposed to explain that? It was too much.

He must have seen the resolution in her face. "Stay for dinner. I'll send the leftovers home with you, so you have hot food tomorrow."

Now that she'd decided, the urge for home was scratching away at her insides, but she'd need time to pack up her stuff. If Zach happened to have dinner ready before she was ready to go, grabbing a quick bite wouldn't hurt. The man was a very good cook. "What time will dinner be ready?" she checked.

"An hour?" His eyes darted across her face as he studied her reaction. "How about thirty minutes? I'll make meat sauce instead of meatballs with the pasta."

"I'll go pack up my stuff and load my Jeep. I should be done about the same time you finish cooking, but then I need to leave."

"Fair enough." He didn't look happy about it, but there was a glimmer of hope in his eyes that Veronica hated. She didn't want to smash something so beautiful, but what choice did she have? "You're taking the shotgun and the pistol with you."

She turned away to gather her things without bothering to argue. She'd take the shotgun. Zach had one of his own, though his had a longer barrel. Lynch had given the short barrel to her, and she'd already accepted it. The pistol didn't belong to her. She wouldn't take it away from where it belonged.

True to his word, Zachary was scooping pasta onto plates as she came back inside after carrying the last of her things to her vehicle. "Come eat," he called to her.

"How is it still getting colder?" she asked, to avoid an awkward silence as they both sat at the table.

"It's supposed to be a big storm. They're calling for some snow and ice mixed, but the real concern is the wind. We're supposed to be ready for power outages that may take them a few days to fix." Zachary's eyes stayed focused on the cheese he was grating onto his plate while he spoke.

Veronica may not have the most efficient code, and she wasn't the fastest worker, but she wasn't too stupid to see where he was going with this. "Thank goodness I always have storm stuff prepped at my place, though we usually all end up staying at HQ and working through storms there, since the place has a big generator. I should eat fast and get going before it gets worse."

She knew she'd hit the nail on the head when Zach's face fell and his shoulders slumped forward.

"Just stay here. Stay through the storm. I'll buy a fucking generator. You agreed we were together. You can't take that back when things feel hard."

The hurt in his voice ripped at Veronica's insides, but she refused to give in. She needed her home. She needed to deal with her shit. And she would not drag him along. It would ruin him. It would ruin them, and she'd rather have the memories of this past week with the possibility of a future someday than light it on fire and be forced to watch it burn through her own fault.

She would go home, give herself over to her work completely, and work the problem until she solved it. It was how she did things. She might not eat or sleep much for a few days, but she'd figure out the connections and find the core issue. Then she could solve it. Veronica knew the world would disappear for her during that time. That world included Zach, and that wasn't fair to him.

There was one thing she could offer him without any reservation, though. "I won't be giving myself to anyone else, Zach. I can still be yours, but I just need some time and space."

He huffed a defeated grunt. "Yeah, I get it. You don't need me, and you're better off without me. But sure, you do you and come back whenever. I'll certainly still be here."

It was the bitterness that tripped her sadness and changed it to anger. "You're only here because you chose to be, so don't put that on me. Early forties is hardly late in life. You don't like it, change it." She pointed her fork at him as she spoke.

He glared at her before pushing back from the table and standing up to turn toward the kitchen. Veronica resumed eating while ignoring whatever he deemed more important than their conversation.

"Here." He set a stack of three individual pasta portions in plastic containers on the table before her. "I'll still be here because I love it here. I just loved it more having you here with me. I thought you needed me and wanted me to fill in your picture or whatever bullshit metaphor you want to use to describe letting me love you and take care of you. Obviously, I was wrong, so at least get out of here before the weather gets worse." He was standing a half step behind her chair while he spoke, so Veronica couldn't see his face. She wasn't sure if that was a blessing or a curse, but he was right about her needing to go. They were starting to hear the first gusts of wind whipping through the woods. Soon it would whistle around the cabin and shake the windows.

She finished chewing her final bite, wiped her mouth with her napkin, and stood up to face him. "You're right. It's time for me to leave. And if all I am is some pitiful creature that you take care of to make yourself feel better, maybe I shouldn't come back." Even as she said it, she didn't think she really meant it.

Veronica scooped up the three containers and stared at Zach.

He stared back until she blinked and walked past him toward the front door.

Silence followed her across the living room. The click of the door latch as she pulled it closed behind her was the only thing to break it.

At least she'd be home before the storm got bad. There were snowflakes swirling in circles through the air, but the roads were still mostly dry. She was still careful, but it didn't take any longer than usual for her to pull up to her dark house.

Veronica left the headlights on and aimed at her porch while she carried the first load of stuff up to the door. She used the spare key she kept inside the fake rock that was buried under a mixture of old mulch and dead leaves to unlock the door. Usually, she'd have left a light on for herself, and there was one she kept on a timer that should be on by now, but maybe it was earlier than it felt. Either way, she needed to cross the room to get to the switch that turned on the living room lights.

She'd only taken a few steps forward when she stumbled over something in her path. Righting herself, she took a closer look at the shadows and realized something was off. The couch was facing her instead of the TV, and when she bent to place her bag and CPU on it so she could pull out her phone, she found it was too close to the ground and angled funny.

With no better options, Veronica put down her things, anyway. She had no interest in breaking an ankle trying to turn on a light when her phone had a perfectly good flashlight. Actually, maybe that was why the house was dark. Sure, the storm was only getting started, but it was already windy enough to take down a tree that would knock out her power.

It was enough for her to relax and breathe normally while she grabbed her phone. But the second she flipped on the flashlight app, any sense of calm she felt disappeared as she took in the state of her house.

The couch had been tipped over backward, so the back was on the ground with feet pointing to the TV. That explained why it was so low to the ground, but it got so much worse as she looked closer. The cushions had been slashed, and the stuffing pulled out. Everything had been swiped from her shelves and left scattered across the floor. Even her kitchen cabinets had been opened, and the dishes were strewn in shattered bits.

Veronica's breath caught and stuck in her throat as she rushed for her office. Part of her knew what she'd find, but that did nothing to lessen the stab she felt deep in her gut when she opened the door to find all of her drawers pulled out, her belongings tossed around, and her futon shredded. Instead of stepping inside and facing the mess, she continued down the hall to her bedroom. It was equally destroyed. Even her pillows had been sliced through.

Amidst the chaos, a black and white greeting card congratulating a new graduate was standing up in the center of her bed. As much as Veronica didn't want to touch it, she had to know what it said inside. The card itself wasn't new and pulled at a memory that wouldn't quite surface. Wavy and warped, it had been wet at some point, and the ink inside had bled to blur the words. But she didn't need to read the words. She had them memorized. Her mother had made her write graduation cards for every member of her class. She'd made all the kids do it. Veronica had written the exact same thing on everyone.

***Best wishes for your future! – Veronica***

There should have been fear. Or maybe she should be angry. Scared would also be a reasonable reaction, but Veronica felt none of them. She felt nothing but exhaustion, and she knew she needed to finish unloading and pull her Jeep under the carport before the snow and ice got worse.

Feeling numb wasn't so bad. It made going out into the cold to unload as easy as going out in fair weather. After parking her car, Veronica put the leftover pasta in the fridge. She noticed it hadn't been destroyed, though it held nothing but condiments, anyway. None of it felt like it touched her, though. She took her bag to her room and dropped it on the bed. Trying to put clothes away in the midst of the disaster zone was pointless, so she didn't bother.

Veronica returned to the living room and waited, but nothing changed. There was no anger or fear. It was just another mess. Calling her brothers wouldn't change anything, and there was no point in freaking out her parents. She would have to clean up eventually, but not tonight. While she flipped the bolt to lock the door, she felt a flicker of laughter huff from her mouth. It was comically pointless to lock her door when someone had obviously made it inside without needing to break in. That glimmer of feeling disappeared in as little time as it took her to turn back to the living room.

She collected her CPU, all the cords, her laptop, and her workbag and retreated to her office. The place where her CPU went was covered with pens, scissors, calculators, and sticky notes that had been dumped from the drawers of her desk. That was when her feelings returned.

Water pooled in her eyes, forcing her to reach through the blur to move everything out of the way enough to put down the computer. She sniffled while reconnecting cords and placing her favorite keyboard where she liked it. By the time she was gathering papers, she was fighting to brush the moisture from her face faster than it could drip and smear her printouts.

After learning to shoot and fight, dealing with her inner turmoil, arguing with Zachary, stressing about the storm, and coming home to this, Veronica was out of fucks to give about nonsense like sorting her favorite gel pens into the right portion of the right drawer. She'd buy new ones. Or not. It didn't matter. Everything was shoved into the trashcan from her kitchen before she put it back in front of the stove. Whoever had been here had dumped it across the floor and left it on its side. While she did leave it standing this time, she didn't bother trying to pick up anything else. There just weren't any fucks left.

She was still sniffling, and fear had begun to weave through the grief, which was the only word even close to appropriate to describe how she felt. So, she turned to the cabinet where she stored her glasses, saw the open door and empty shelves, and rerouted herself through the laundry room. The cabinets in there were also open and empty, but she had a case of mason jars that hadn't been touched. It would do just fine.

Veronica sucked in one last sniffle and pulled her shit together. She returned to her office with the mason jars, a plan, and a fresh attitude.

The room wasn't back to usual. The futon was destroyed, but she'd done enough to make it feel like her office again. She refused to embarrass herself by calling her brothers or Zachary to drag them out in a storm because she was afraid. Veronica was not the incompetent mess everyone thought. She could handle this herself. She set down the mason jars and made one last quick trip to the kitchen to grab a wooden dining chair. No one would be out to get her in this weather, but she needed something tangible to ease her mind. Stacking the glass jars like a pyramid in the hallway would provide early warning if anyone came down the hall.

She pulled the final two jars into the office with her and the chair. Wedging the chair under the door and placing the final two classes under it to shatter if the chair fell from under the knob was the icing on her security system cake. She checked that the shotgun was loaded and placed it on the desk beside her computer. Then she settled in her chair and got to work.

Zachary had left the pages of research from Lynch with her, so she started by digging into the financial statement. There was no way she would be able to sleep tonight, so she might as well learn as much as she could to share with her brothers in the morning.

Sometime in the wee hours, her need for the restroom was great enough for her to dismantle her early warning system. Her eyes were burning from working so late and staring at the screen for so long, and she considered making coffee. But that would require going into the kitchen, and it just wasn't worth it. Instead, she took care of business, returned to the office, re-stacked the jars, replaced the chair, and returned to work.

Not too long after that, she had enough puzzle pieces to feel like some of them should fit together, but she couldn't figure out how. Knowing her eyes needed a break from the screen, she moved to where she'd thrown a blanket over the futon and sat down to think.

Staind blared from her phone, jolting her awake. She had no interest in speaking to Patrick this early in the morning, but he was also her boss.

"What?" she answered his call.

"Where the fuck are you? I get that time doesn't mean shit to you, but you usually show up. I highly doubt the storm turned out to be any worse on your side of the mountain than it was here. So again, where the fuck are you and why are you not here?"

"What time is it?" Normally, she'd look at a clock instead of giving him the satisfaction, but she didn't have one handy.

"It's after nine!" There was so much emotion behind his screamed announcement that Veronica made a mental note to get someone to convince Patrick to get a stress test done so they didn't need to worry about him keeling over from a heart attack in the middle of a meeting.

"Fuck. Right. I had a rough night. Don't be a jackass. I'll be there soon." As she pulled the device away from her face, she could hear him shouting again, but there was no reason to listen to it now. Veronica was out of fucks to give. Her mason jars were unbroken, so she moved them out of her way. She grabbed her work bag. The Monday folder was already in there since she'd taken it to Zachary's with her, but even if it weren't, she couldn't muster up the energy to care.

Veronica stopped to pee but didn't bother with anything else. So what if she wore the same clothes? Who would care if her breath or pits smelled bad? None of it mattered.

# Chapter 18

The wind had howled through the night, but the snow didn't accumulate as predicted. The foot plus with ice mixed in turned out to be no more than an inch or two. There was ice involved, but it wasn't much. It should have reassured Zachary that Veronica likely had a smooth drive home, but it didn't. He couldn't stop the visions of her sliding off the road and spending the night stuck or injured.

Their fight kept replaying in his mind. He could have handled it differently, and he should have. Instead, he'd just kept making it worse. He'd pushed her to turn *I can still be yours, but I need time and space* into *maybe I shouldn't come back, ever*. Zachary had spent some extra time with Butthole in the barn. He seemed to understand Veronica better than Zachary did, so maybe he could help Zach figure out what to do. Butthole didn't magically learn to speak English but petting him provided some of the calm that Zach needed to clear his thinking and consider real options.

By the time he'd crawled into bed, he hadn't worked any miracles, but he did have some plans. He'd start by giving Veronica the time and space she needed while still caring for her. Food seemed to be a basic need she struggled with, and her appreciation when he provided it never faltered. Even when she'd been walking out the door, she'd taken the time to eat his spaghetti. Hell, she'd even taken more home with her.

Taking food over for her dinner on Tuesday night was his starting point. He knew she'd likely eat dinner at work with her brothers tomorrow, and she could have pasta for lunch on Tuesday. His confidence that she'd remember to eat lunch Tuesday was low, but that's why he'd show up with dinner around seven that evening.

While lying in bed and listening to the wind howl, Zach considered his provisions and planned out dinners for the week. Between jotting notes on his phone, he'd flip back to see if he'd gotten a text from Veronica letting him know she'd arrived home safely, but no text ever arrived. Fucking idiot that he was, he hadn't asked her to text him, so he couldn't even get mad about it.

As the clock struck midnight, Zachary was still tossing and turning. He seriously considered hiking through the storm over to her place to check that she arrived okay. It would be smarter to drive, but then she'd know he was checking on her. As overprotective as he was, he knew Veronica had the right to walk away. He didn't understand where things had gone wrong, but he'd respect her request for space. He'd doze off only to wake up and decide to text Veronica to ease his worries, then delete the text and return to tossing and turning until he drifted off for another short while. At four-thirty, he gave up and turned off his alarm. At least he'd have extra time to work.

Morning chores were done before Zachary was awake enough to notice how little snow they'd gotten, and he'd pulled down two mugs for coffee instead of just one. Apparently, it only took a couple of days for him to adapt to having another person in his life. That was when he'd caved and sent a text to Veronica. It was just past seven, so she should be getting ready for work.

For the next ten minutes, he stared at his phone, waiting for it to show she'd read his message. It was ridiculous. Zachary was not going to spend his day staring at his phone pining for a woman who'd been gone for less than twenty-four hours. The alpacas probably needed some of his time, anyway. He shoved his phone into his back pocket and finished his coffee.

It turned out to be a good thing he had the extra time. When he returned to the yard, Fluffy had claimed an area near the barn and wouldn't let anyone else near her. She was pacing and refused any treats Zach tried to offer her. Those were all signs of labor, and it was as close to on-time as anyone could expect nature to be. Having a newborn cria would be a great excuse to drag Veronica back over here.

Zach played with the other alpacas for a while before Fluffy's discomfort had her terrorizing the chickens. He shooed them back into the barn. It was probably too cold for their feet to be out too long, anyway. The other alpacas were enjoying the fresh air and goofing around with Zach and each other, but he wasn't sure if he should leave them out as Fluffy's labor progressed. It was moving along slowly enough that he didn't have to make a decision right away, so he decided to call Doc Ester and get her advice. He should probably let her know about the impending birth, anyway. She'd been here to deliver Butthole herself, and she'd shown him what to do beyond all the studying he'd done. They both agreed he could probably handle Fluffy himself, though Doc had encouraged him to keep her in the loop in case her help was needed.

"Is this an emergency?" she asked as a greeting when he called. She was out of breath and sounded stressed.

"No. Fluffy's in labor, but I've got it." He still wanted her to know what was going on, but there was no need to pull her away from whatever she was doing.

"Good. Her timing sucks. The Jensons had a tree come down on top of their horse barn and two are trapped."

"Shit, do you need help?" With Fluffy in labor, he couldn't be gone long, but if they needed him, he could help for a little while.

"I need you to help Fluffy. The Jensons are out past Fisherville. There's no way I'll be able to make it to you. If things go to shit, you'll need to take her to Wildwood. They have no experience with alpacas, but it'll be your best bet." She was talking fast, and Zach could hear a commotion in the background.

"I've got this. You take care of those horses."

"Text me updates," she told him before signing off.

Only then did he realize he'd forgotten to even ask about moving the others away from her. "Well Butthole, it looks like we're on our own for this one." The animal leaned his head into Zach. Compared to the biting and spitting he was used to, Zach took it as a peace offering to let him focus on all the other shit he was dealing with.

Speaking of which, Zach checked his messages again, but there was still nothing from Veronica.

"Alright, buddy. Let's move everyone into the barn and out of the cold and the wind. You've had enough play time. You should be okay, and it might be easier for me to help Fluffy in a stall."

The alpaca offered no response, but when Zach led the animals inside, he didn't run off or cause any issues. Fluffy was reluctant to leave the space she'd claimed, but the day had shifted to late afternoon, and Zachary wanted to get her inside. Assisting with a birth in the dark and bitter cold was not on his bucket list. It took some cajoling and some dragging, but he got her settled in the largest stall with a bunch of fresh straw.

This birth was going much slower than Butthole's had, but everything looked okay so far. Zach checked all her vitals and decided to get himself a quick dinner while things were slow and stable. Of course, he checked his messages. This time, his message was showing as read, but there still wasn't a response. It was only a little after four in the afternoon, so Veronica would still be in meetings or whatever. At least he knew she'd gotten his message. Hopefully, she'd reply when she could. He cleaned up his plate and headed back out to the barn.

The screaming reached his ears before he even opened the door. Bertha had complained during active labor, but it never sounded like this. Zach ran to Fluffy, but nothing was obviously wrong. She was still standing, though she was twisting her head back to her right. He checked her, but nothing was visible. Knowing there must be something wrong inside, he ran back to the house to grab his book about alpaca births while cursing himself for not bringing it out with him the first time. He'd been inside for less than forty minutes, but so much had changed.

He flipped open the book to the page that showed the most common issues with the way the cria could be situated. Doc Ester had told him that more than ninety percent of issues at this stage of labor were related to leg positioning. She'd been very clear that fixing legs might feel like he was hurting both animals, but it would ultimately save them.

She'd reached in to twist Butthole's leg as a demonstration, and Zachary had been shocked by the intensity with which her muscles flexed as she pulled force from her entire body to adjust the cria. Now it would be his turn. He shoved his hands into gloves that went up to his shoulder and checked that he could clearly see the book while standing behind Fluffy.

If any of his Navy buddies had tried to tell him he'd be fisting an alpaca after twenty years of service, he'd have laughed them off the ship. He could handle this. At least that's what he told himself before shaping his fingers like a cone and inserting them to try to identify different parts of the cria.

He was only in up to his forearm when he found the problem. Doc Ester had warned him that legs and noses could feel strangely similar when you were elbow deep and going by feel alone, but he could tell right away that he was feeling a leg first. It was too long and skinny to be the face, especially when he slid a little deeper and felt the face behind the leg, which was not where it was supposed to be.

Butthole had come out ass-backward, in the most literal way. Doc Ester had been able to position his head and neck to line everything up, but there was no way for her to turn him around. She'd grabbed him by his tail and pulled before getting a better grip on his hips and pulling harder.

At least this cria had its head pointing in the right direction. Once Zachary was sure he understood the issue, he got a good grip on the front leg and pushed it back under the chin before plunging in with his second hand to try getting a grip on the head. No matter how he tried, there was no way for him to grab the head and help pull it out without risking the baby's spine, though.

He returned to the book, read a few paragraphs, and decided it was still too early in the labor to do anything more. Adjusting the leg seemed to help, though. Fluffy stopped screaming. She was grunting and obviously uncomfortable, but she was moving her head around more freely and the pain appeared more manageable and appropriate.

It didn't take long for Zach to spot the rhythm of her contractions. They were increasing quickly, and before long, he could see something trying to make its way out into the world. He put on fresh gloves and checked to ensure it was the nose, but it wasn't. The leg had shifted back to the front again. This time, he didn't even have to go as deep as his wrist to shove it back under the cria's chin, and he could feel the second leg right there along the baby's neck.

He timed his movements with Fluffy's contractions and let the next push shove out his hand along with the head of the soon-to-be-born. Everything sped up from there, and Zach was soon watching Fluffy bond with her baby boy. Both appeared healthy and happy, if exhausted. For his part, Zachary felt like he was ten feet tall. He'd never been so proud of anything in all his life. Being able to help bring a new life into the world was magical.

Doc Ester got the first text. She replied right away to congratulate him and promise to stop by in the morning to check out the little one. They'd freed one of the horses, but the other had been injured and couldn't be saved. Doc had asked if he needed her to stop by before heading home, but it was a few minutes after six already. Fluffy and the cria were doing well, so he urged her to go home and relax unless she needed to see a newborn to counter her loss. She assured him that would be just as effective for her in the morning as it would tonight.

Between texts with the doc, Zach had checked his message thread with Veronica, but there was nothing there. Knowing she should be finishing up and about to enjoy dinner, he sent her another message. He didn't want to bother her when she obviously didn't want to talk to him, but he couldn't hold back the birth announcement. It delivered, but didn't show as read, so he went inside to clean up and distract himself.

Part of Zach was terrified he'd miss Veronica's response. He knew it was dramatic, but just this once, he allowed himself to take his phone into the bathroom with him while he showered.

He was glad he did when he heard it ringing as he finished rinsing off. There was no way to hide his joy when he saw Veronica's name on the screen.

"Veronica, I'm sorry," he said before he'd even wrapped a towel around himself.

"Me too. It's okay." She sounded so tired. "Cria, or whatever you called Fluffy's new baby sounds great, though." He could hear how hard she was trying to sound upbeat and excited, and it took everything in him not to ask where she was so he could come get her.

"Cria's the term for all baby alpacas. I haven't picked a name yet. Nothing's coming to mind or feeling right. Are you back at home?" Hopefully starting with alpaca talk would make his question sound less intrusive.

"Not yet. I'm pulled over at the top of the spur road where there's that big pull off VDOT uses sometimes." Zach knew exactly where she was talking about. It was one of the few places that offered consistent and reliable cell service.

He wanted to invite her to come back to his place, but that might not go over well. Instead he asked, "How was your day?" At least then he could hear more of her voice. Maybe her answer would help him figure out their next steps, too.

Veronica's sigh crackled though the phone. "Long. I am sorry about last night, and I should probably tell you something, but I don't want you to get all worked up about it."

Well, fuck. That didn't sound good. And how was he supposed to *not get worked up about it*? "I promise I won't scream or be mean or anything like that, but I can't promise I won't feel upset if something happened that hurt you." It was the best he could offer and still might be more than he could deliver. If Patrick was an asshole to her, he would be screaming and mean; it just wouldn't be directed at Veronica.

She sighed again. "Someone broke into my house."

Zach clenched his jaw as tight as he could to prevent anything from escaping his mouth until he had control of himself. "Tell me what happened," he prompted once he could speak without swearing.

"You're growling," Veronica told him.

"It's the best I can do right now, and I'm working very hard at limiting myself to just that, so please fill in the details for me. Maybe start by telling me if you're okay?"

Her voice was significantly more relaxed when she spoke again. "I'm fine. I would have called you if I weren't, even though we're fighting."

"We're not fighting anymore. I apologized." That was his stance, and it was a hill he was willing to die on.

"Right. Anyway, my place was trashed when I got home. Someone went through everything, but they were gone by the time I arrived. They even locked the door behind themselves. At least, I think they did. I guess I didn't check it before I put the key in, so maybe not."

Zach reminded himself to keep his grip on the phone loose enough that it wouldn't shatter. "Veronica, what happened?" he asked again.

"That was it. Oh and they left one of my old high school graduation cards on my bed. I don't know if it's one I mailed out, or one of the extras, but I need to look into it. I cleaned up the office already, but I'm kind of dreading getting home and having to deal with the rest of it tonight. It's been a long day."

It was the perfect opening. "Come here. You can see the baby, and we'll watch a movie. I'd love to have you sleeping beside me, but you can always crash in the guest room if you're more comfortable there." He held his breath waiting for her response. If she said no, he'd call Patrick. The hell with his pride, he just needed to know Veronica was safe.

She sighed, and he braced himself for her to decline. "I know I should go back to my place and clean."

There was a *but* coming. He knew it. It would all be okay. Zachary let his lungs resume their usual rhythm.

"Shit," she interrupted herself. "Someone's pulling in behind me. They're probably checking to see if I need help."

"Veronica–"

"I'll be there in a few minutes, Zachary. See you soon."

He hated the idea of a stranger approaching her alone on the side of the road. But he reminded himself, it wasn't likely to be a stranger out here. She'd probably recognize the person or at least have heard of them. And she was right to figure they'd be checking on her to see if she needed help. She'd be coming to him afterward, and he'd be able to see for himself that she was fine. He'd get her some dinner, too. If she'd already left HQ, it meant she probably didn't stay for dinner.

It was okay. Veronica was okay. Zachary forced himself to focus on what a good day it had been. The cria was born healthy, Veronica was coming home to him. It was all okay.

So why did he feel like someone tightened a vice clamp around his heart?

# Chapter 19

Veronica dropped her phone into the space in the console where she always kept it and popped open her door just as she heard the slam of a car door come from behind her.

"Hi," she called, while waving as she stood in the open doorway of her car. "I'm fine." The car's headlights were still on, and they were blinding her. "I appreciate you stopping, but I don't need any help." She squinted to try to see who was there and if they were approaching her.

Right as her eyes adjusted enough for her to see there was no one, an arm grabbed her from behind and yanked her away from the door. Whoever it was had circled around her car. Spinning to face the darkness after letting her eyes adjust to the light left her blind again. She squeezed her eyes shut to help them adjust faster and tried to focus on her other senses. Someone was rummaging through her car.

"Where's your purse?" they demanded.

She opened her eyes enough to see the man was larger than her, but not by much.

"Your purse!" he shouted again while wiggling the gun in his hand to make his threat obvious. She knew that voice.

A week ago, Veronica would have frozen. Or maybe sat down and cried. But the last week had changed her. At the very least, Zach had forced her to practice enough that she stomped on his foot and raised her knee to his groin without thought. "I. Don't. Have One." she yelled as she attacked and then ran while trying to place where she'd know him from.

Veronica darted into the woods. It was darker and harder to make progress, but it would be easier to hide. Considering the darkness and the weather, it was probably safer than the road, too. A gunshot came from behind her, and she added *makes aiming difficult* to her list of pros for the forest. Still, she cursed every time a branch caught her in the face, or a root tried to send her flying. The footsteps behind her were loud and getting closer. The guy might be leaner and lankier than bulky and muscular, but that just meant he had a runner's build and was using it to gain on her.

There was no way to tell where she was or where she was going, not that she'd have known even if it were daylight in the summer and there was a trail marker beside her. It just felt worse in the dark. He'd gotten too close, too fast for her to hide. Short of climbing a tree faster than a monkey, she was screwed.

Just as she realized her fate, he slammed into her and knocked her to the ground.

"Give it to me," the guy was snarling.

"Kurt?"

"You were such a stuck-up bitch in high school, but this time it's my turn to win."

"Get off me!" Veronica didn't waste time wondering what he was talking about. She wouldn't go down without a fight.

"Where's the drive, you stupid–" he was reaching into the pocket of her leggings, and that was not okay.

Veronica rolled both of them with more force than she knew she had. Then she smashed her fist into his throat. Zach had taught to her slam her palm into his nose, but she wasn't at the right angle. A throat-punch would have to do.

She took full advantage of the second he let go of her and took off again. The scuffle had turned her around enough that she didn't know if she was heading away from her car or back to it, but right then, it didn't matter. Veronica just needed to get away from him.

Her punch must not have done much damage since she heard his feet pounding behind her again after no more than a few seconds. Breathing was more important than crying, so she shoved down the tears trying to escape and did her best to look around. What options did she have?

Panic was catching up faster than her attacker, but then she popped out of the trees to a clearing with a great view thanks to the serious drop off of the rock ledge in front of her. Veronica had no idea how she stopped herself before flying right over the cliff. It didn't matter, though. She needed to ensure Kurt wasn't as lucky.

Veronica got down on her hands and knees and listened to him getting closer. She fought through her jagged breathing to inhale and exhale slowly and quietly through her nose. It wasn't nearly enough oxygen, but if Kurt noticed she'd stopped, he might slow down. That would foil her flimsy plan, and it was the only one she had. Thank goodness for her childhood love of the Roadrunner. Hopefully, it would be more successful in real life.

"You're going to make me shoot you, huh?" he yelled as he got closer.

There was just enough moonlight through the partly cloudy sky for Veronica to see his form emerge from the trees. He was headed right for her.

She rolled from her knees to her toes but kept herself crouched as low as possible until his body connected with hers. The second she felt contact, she roared like the angriest mama bear she could envision and shoved upward, throwing the guy over her back. The plan had been for him to fly off the ledge and crash down the rocky cliff, but she'd been just a little too far away for it to work.

The guy landed with half his body still on the rocks, though he was disoriented and moaning instead of shouting. Before she could make it over to check on him, or maybe smash her foot down onto his face, he regained enough sense to aim his gun in her direction, though he was far from steady. "You stupid bitch," he slurred.

Before she knew what she was doing, Veronica's foot connected with his head rolling him toward the ledge. He was close enough to go over this time. The abrupt end of his scream as he crashed to the forest floor would haunt Veronica's nightmares for a long time to come.

She stood and stared, trying to piece it all together. She'd been shot at and chased through the woods. Checking her pockets, she ignored the tears pouring down her cheeks. Her phone was missing, it was cold and dark, and she had no idea how to get back to her car. Collapsing to the ground and curling tightly into a ball, Veronica's mind spiraled.

# Chapter 20

Zachary paced his house, but there wasn't enough space. Everything in him was screaming for him to go to Veronica, but there was no reason to. She was on her way here. He just had to hang on for a few minutes, and he'd see her and hold her. Yanking open the front door, he moved to the porch. He'd see her headlights sooner this way, and the fresh air would help him clear his mind and relax. Maybe this was the drop of adrenaline after helping Fluffy with the birth.

Seconds after closing the door behind him, a gunshot rang through the hollow. The mountains became an echo chamber that made determining the direction it came from impossible, but Zach's eyes darted around, anyway.

When nothing but silence followed, he forced his heart to slow down enough for his brain to pick through the landmarks he could make out in the limited moonlight and pinpoint where Veronica would be pulled over. He'd stopped at that spot before. It really was one of very few places with solid cell reception around here. That reception came with a great view that included the small clearing where his farm was located. There were a few rock ledges between the two as that part of the road was almost a thousand feet higher in elevation that his property, but there were a series of animal trails that made their way around the rock faces. Zachary had explored it before and been surprised to discover the pull off was less than a mile from him as the crow flies. Hiking it was a little longer, but nowhere near the almost five miles of road between the two points.

He cursed himself for not having a pair of binoculars handy. There was an old set packed away somewhere, but now was not the time to go digging for them. They probably wouldn't do much good in the dark, anyway. Zachary felt a splinter slide into the flesh of his pointer finger and forced his hands to relax their grip on the porch railing. He'd been staring intently toward the place he knew Veronica had called from, but there was nothing to see. Then he heard the scream.

It was too faint to echo the way the gunshot had, but that also made it impossible to tell if it was male or female, if any words were shouted, or if any other sounds came with it. Zachary couldn't just stand there anymore.

Pulling his phone from his back pocket, he ran back inside to grab his hiking pack and stuff mixed nuts and a couple of bottles of water in with the first aid and wilderness supplies he kept in it. He hit the button to connect a call to Patrick on his landline while zipping up the pack and thanking the stars he'd gotten HQ's number from Veronica.

"Taylor Industries. This is Patrick."

"It's Veronica's neighbor, Zach. She needs help. There was a gunshot and a scream. I'm going to hike to her, but you need to drive and check the road along the way."

"Woah. Slow down."

Zach needed to move. Veronica needed him. What if that had been her scream, and she was lying somewhere hurt? "We need to go find her. Now."

"Okay. I hear you, but I need more info. She just left here maybe fifteen or twenty minutes ago, so it's not unreasonable for her to not be home yet."

Fuck. He wasn't listening. Zach raked his hand through his hair and forced himself to back up and start from closer to the beginning. "Listen to me. She stayed with me this week, but last night we argued. She went home. I didn't hear from her again, but I texted her this morning and again this evening. Apparently, she got my second message on her way home. She pulled over at the place at the top of the spur and called me. Patrick, someone broke into her place last night and left one of her old graduation cards on her bed." He was ashamed of how long it took him to put together how personal that made this.

"What the fuck?" At least Patrick was listening now.

"Someone pulled up behind her. She hung up before I could ask her anything else about it, but she promised to be here in a few minutes. Except she's not here, and there was a gunshot and then a scream. You check the road, and I'll hike through the woods. It's only about a mile, so I'll meet you at the pull off in about half an hour. Take a whistle with you. Do you have a whistle?"

"A whistle?" Patrick sounded shellshocked. Under any other circumstances, Zachary would have completely understood his reaction, but right now he didn't have the patience for it.

"Yes, a whistle so we can find each other. Your sister is out there somewhere with someone shooting at her."

"Okay. Greg left shortly after her, so there's a good chance he's the one who pulled over to check on her. It's probably nothing, but I can hear your worry. Freddy and I will meet you there, but Zach, she may have just chatted with Greg and then stopped by her place to grab clean clothes."

He still wasn't getting it, but he'd agreed to drive to the pull off. That was the important part. Once he was there and saw Veronica's car, maybe he'd get how serious it was. "I'll see you at the pull off. Wait for me there." He hung up before Patrick could argue.

Zachary debated leaving his phone at home the way he usually would. He had a satellite GPS unit with an SOS button in his pack, but with how close they were likely to be to the pull-off, a phone call might make more sense. Plus, he'd mapped the route using All Trails the first time he'd hiked it, so the path he needed to follow should still be on the map he'd downloaded. After double-checking it was still there, he slid the phone back into his pants pocket, slung his pack over his shoulder, and left to find Veronica.

Parts of his route were steep and avoiding rocks and roots that tried to knock him down required paying close attention, but Zachary kept moving forward as fast as he could. His headlamp was bright enough to provide a good field of vision, and he kept it focused on the ground in front of him.

Because of the way it avoided the tall rock outcroppings, Zachary knew he'd pop out from the side of the pull-off, after hiking the last ten yards almost parallel to the road. He heard a passing car and knew he was close. There was one more steep climb, but Zach ignored the burning in his legs and pushed on with quick steps.

He made his way around a final bend and could see the open space where the road was just ahead, but he was still too low to see if any cars were parked there. He could hear voices, though. It was enough to push himself to jog the final few yards until he could see a black Nissan Titan parked at an odd angle. Veronica's jeep was behind it, and there was a gray sedan behind that. It was once he was walking up to greet Patrick, Freddy, and the third man standing with them that Zach could see the fourth car behind the gray sedan. It was a dark colored Subaru.

"No sign of her?" Zach asked.

"No, but I think I found which way she went." The man who spoke was the one Zachary hadn't met before.

"Are you, uh, Greg?"

"Yeah, I left HQ shortly after Veronica. She's the only red Jeep I know of around here, so I turned around and pulled in here when I saw it and this other car."

"She wasn't here?" Zach forced his feet to stay planted. Running back out into the woods wouldn't do any good. He glanced back at the gray sedan and tried to reassure himself with the knowledge that she hadn't been taken away. It had only been an hour since he'd spoken with her, so she couldn't be far.

"No one was here." Greg shrugged.

"But you found her trail?" Zachary looked Greg up and down while trying to see past his tailored gray suit. Looking like a stuffy businessman didn't mean someone didn't have wilderness or hunting skills. His loafers might make him look like a city playboy, but he could be an expert tracker underneath all that.

"Sort of." Greg put one hand on his hip and rubbed the back of his neck with the other hand. "See by that brush?" He pointed to the edge of the pull-off.

"The shiny thing?" Zach checked.

"Yeah, it's a shell casing. I didn't want to touch it, but I went past it and looked around. It's further back, but there's a place that's tramped down with stuff scattered around."

Thank fuck! Zachary could work with that. "Show me," he demanded.

"Easy." Patrick made calming motions with his hands as he spoke. "We're all trying to find her, and it will be better if we work together. Greg, please lead us to that spot you found."

Greg nodded and walked off toward the shell casing he'd pointed out while Patrick, Freddy, and Zach followed behind like ducklings following their mother. By the time Zach reached any given point, the other three had already tromped through. He'd never be able to spot what was from Veronica through their movements.

"Stop. Please." He added the second word with the hope it would encourage them to listen. "I've been out here before and have some experience, but I can't tell if things are disturbed because of us or from Veronica when I'm back here. It would be better if I could lead, while Greg points me in the right direction from behind." It wasn't a question, but he managed to avoid barking out the order.

Freddy and Patrick both stepped to the side to let him pass them. Greg looked nervous, but also let him pass. "I'm not sure exactly where it was, but I know I went this way."

"That's a good start." Despite the terror gripping his chest, Zach was grateful Greg had stopped and found as much as he had. He continued the way Greg pointed and quickly picked up the trail. Now that he could take in the forest in front of him, the path of destruction was obvious. Veronica had run through here. He could see broken branches where she darted between trees, and when he angled his headlamp toward the ground, overturned rocks revealing darker soil beneath them marked each time she'd stubbed a toe, turned an ankle, or tripped.

It wasn't even fifty yards further that he spotted the place Greg mentioned. It looked similar to a nest where a deer would bunk down for the night, except there were two random twigs sticking up at different points in the otherwise flattened space. Zachary slowed his steps. "Hang back. I want to check this area without disturbing it. Did you walk through it, Greg?"

"I mean, I was more worried about Veronica than trying to preserve the crime scene or whatever."

"Zach," Patrick called his attention. "We're all on the same team here. Stop snarling and barking at us."

"You–" he stopped himself before pointing out that Patrick wouldn't even be out here if Zach hadn't called him and pushed him to come check it out. That argument would waste time that should be spent finding Veronica. "You and Freddy can go call 911 from up by the cars." *Be nice*, he chided himself before adding, "If you want. You don't have to."

Freddy coughed to cover his laugh, but Zach still heard it. "I'm trying, but the woman I love has been missing for a full hour now and finding her is my top priority."

"You love her?" Patrick asked. "How can you love her when you've only known her a week? Never mind. It doesn't even matter right now. Just find her. Freddy and I will call out the rescue squad." He turned and stomped back toward the vehicles.

Before Freddy turned to follow his brother, he cocked his head at Zach and asked. "Do you really love her?"

Stupidly, Zach had assumed Veronica would be the first one to hear he loved her. This situation didn't change his feelings, and he wouldn't deny how much it would break him to lose her. "Yeah. I do." He braced himself for Freddy's reaction.

"She needs someone to love her first. If you ever cheat on her or break her heart, I'll hunt you down, but if you make her happy..." he trailed off without finishing.

"That's all I want. Just her to be happy."

Freddy nodded at him and started to turn away.

"Freddy," Zach called and waited for him to look over his shoulder. "She doesn't know, and I'd like to be the one to tell her."

It was enough to make Freddy chuckle. "Yeah, man. No way I'm telling my sister that her neighbor fell in love with her. That's all you." Then he continued back toward the vehicles.

Zachary turned back to the trampled area and found Greg standing in the middle of it. "The whole thing about not disturbing the area went right over your head, didn't it?" His rage felt like lava rolling through his veins. If this fucker made it harder to find Veronica, Zach would kill him.

"Huh?" Greg looked up. "No, I was careful to step in the same places I did when I walked through before. This is where I stood before when I was looking around to see where she went next, so it's where my footsteps stop."

It was still not what Zach wanted, but it was better than he'd feared. "Don't move."

The man clicked his tongue and flashed Zachary a thumbs up.

Greg had been right about stuff being strewn around, though. Zach pulled out his phone and took pictures before investigating each thing he found. There was a gas receipt from the only gas station in the area. It was dated that morning. Next, he found a gun tucked under a low shrub. The dirt was smeared like it had slid across the ground to land there. Zach took a picture of it but didn't pick it up. A ball of lint sat atop a leaf. It would blow away with the slightest breeze, and its white color wouldn't last long out here, so it had to be fresh. Then he came across Veronica's keychain, and it took everything he had not to lose his shit and collapse to the ground in a mournful mess.

Veronica needed him, and there was no way he'd let her down. He scanned the surrounding undergrowth, looking for a clue about the direction she'd run from there. With his headlamp on its brightest setting, Zach spotted a single indentation where it looked like a large animal had torn through a group of ferns.

"Stay here," he commanded Greg.

"I was actually thinking I'd head back to the cars?"

"Fine." Zach honestly didn't care what he did, so long as he left Zach alone and didn't fuck up any more evidence. He made his way toward the indentation he'd spotted. There was nothing there, but Zach could see another broken branch just ahead, so he kept going.

The woods had fallen silent. The events of the evening had sent all the insects, birds, and other creatures scrambling to hide in safety. It was eerie but made it easier to listen for any human noises. If the second car hadn't still been there, Zach would be blowing his whistle and screaming Veronica's name, but with an unknown person in the mix, he couldn't do that. If this was the stalker who'd been breaking into Veronica's home, messing with her stuff, planting listening devices, and terrorizing her, he wanted to hold on to the surprise advantage he had. So, he listened, hoping to hear voices or fighting or anything to give him hope that he wasn't too late.

Instead, he caught the faint sound of someone crying. It would be Veronica. It had to be. He could fix crying. Whatever caused her tears, he'd fix it. It didn't matter. Crying meant alive, and alive meant he could figure it out. Disturbing the area didn't matter as much as getting to Veronica as quickly as he could.

Zachary recognized the view as soon as he emerged from the trees, but he didn't see Veronica. He was at the top of one of the rock ledges between his house and the road. Had she gone over the edge? Depending on how she landed, he didn't think the drop was enough to be fatal, but it would certainly do some serious damage. Was she crying from pain?

He was moving across the rocks and toward the edge when he recognized the lump off to his right. She was wearing Butthole's hoodie. Zach rushed to her side and kneeled down to check on her.

"Veronica? Hey, it's me. It's Zach. It's going to be okay. I'm here. I've got you. Are you hurt? Is there bleeding?" He spoke softly to avoid startling her and was relieved when she turned her face to look at him. The light of the moon shimmered off the streaks of her tears, but he didn't see any blood. He adjusted his headlamp to keep it out of her eyes while trying to check over the rest of her.

"Are you really here?" she asked.

Zach wrapped his arms around her and pulled her into his chest as he plopped back on his ass. The rock beneath him was colder than Siberia, but he didn't care.

Veronica shifted with him until she was sitting on his lap with her legs pulled up on top of his thighs so that none of her would feel the chill of the ground. She faced him and quickly tucked her frozen nose into his neck, making him shiver.

"Hang on." He pushed her back just enough to unzip his coat and tuck her arms inside it so he could pull it as far around her as it would reach. It was the puffy coat he always kept in his pack, so it offered great insulation but only worked with existing body heat. He'd put it on while Greg explained his arrival on the side of the road. Once they were settled again, he asked, "Can you tell me what happened?"

Her head rubbed up and down against his chest when she nodded.

"The guy that had pulled up behind me left his headlights on so I couldn't see. He must have gone around my car on the other side, because he came up behind me. I did the foot stomp, knee in the groin combo you taught me and broke free to run, but I didn't know where to go." She sniffled and choked back a sob.

Zach rubbed her back and whispered into her hair. "I'm so proud of you for surviving. You did great."

Veronica shook her head in disagreement before continuing. "He caught me. He shot at me, too. I got shot at." It sounded like a revelation. Having never been shot at, Zach couldn't relate, but he imagined it would fuck with a person.

"Did he hit you?" He wanted to inspect every inch of her for injury but wasn't willing to untuck her from his chest. She was clutching the back of his t-shirt with enough force for him to feel it stretching across his front.

"No. It was when I first ran."

"Before he caught you?" It hurt to say those words, but she was here. He could feel her breath against the bare skin above his shirt collar.

"Yeah. I could hear him behind me. I knew he was going to catch up, but I didn't know what to do." There were tears beneath her words, but Veronica was controlling them enough to keep speaking clearly. Zachary was so fucking impressed.

"It was Kurt. He tackled me. I don't know how I got away. I just remembered you saying not to hold anything back and to fight as mean and dirty as possible. Then I kept going and thought maybe it would be okay, but it wasn't. I could hear him chasing me. I didn't know what to do." She took a moment to work through her hiccupping sobs. Zach wanted to offer her water from his pack, but that would mean letting go. He couldn't do that yet.

Instead, he nuzzled the top of her head, kept his arms tight around her, and waited for her to continue.

"I used to love Wiley Coyote and the Roadrunner when I was little. When I saw the cliff, I thought of all the ways he'd try to capture Roadrunner. I know it's a cartoon, but Kurt's footsteps were right behind me. He was going to catch me again. What if he'd pushed me over the edge?"

"He didn't. What you did was perfect because it kept you alive and safe so I could find you," Zach assured her.

"I squatted down and waited for him. As soon as he ran into me, I pushed up to throw... him..." Her words were punctuated by sobs. "Over."

"That's genius, Veronica."

"But it didn't work," she puffed out before letting her tears take over.

Zach didn't understand. If he didn't go over the edge, was he still around somewhere? Had Zachary fucked up by sending the others back to the car? He looked around but couldn't see anything. With his headlamp, the two of them were an illuminated target, so he reached up and shut off the light. Zach had found Kurt's gun back where they must have fought. Did the man have a second firearm? Veronica was small and light enough that Zachary could carry her back to the cars, but if his arms were full of her, he wouldn't be able to do much against anyone attacking them.

"Beautiful, I need you to tell me what else happened. Where is the guy now? Please. It's important." It should have been the first thing he asked. He kicked himself for not starting with that.

"Dead. He's dead. I killed him."

Well, at least that meant he could relax and keep his attention focused on Veronica.

"Tell me what happened, beautiful."

She sniffled, but explained, "I was too far from the edge, so he just landed on the rock. Well, he was partway on the rock. He was reaching for his gun and called me a stupid bitch. I didn't even think about it. I just hauled back and kicked him, right in the face. It must have been too much. I just wanted him to stop, but I kicked him over the edge. He screamed, but I couldn't do anything. I'd already kicked him too hard and then his scream just…"

Even in the shadowy light of the moon, Zach could see the fear, relief, and guilt on her face. "It was self-defense. You didn't have a choice, and you did exactly what you needed to survive. We'll sort everything else out." He rubbed her back and gave her time to settle a little more.

Once her breathing was steady, he asked, "You said it was Kurt, but did he say anything about why?"

Her face rubbed against his chest as she shook her head. "Just something about me being stuck up in high school, but now he was going to win."

Zach fought to remember what she'd told him about Kurt. They'd had a date planned, but he'd stood her up. Was that the same night Zach caught the men breaking into Veronica's house? Had this been planned?

Shaking himself from those thoughts, he placed a chaste but heartfelt kiss on the top of her head. There'd be time for those questions later. "We need to head back to the road. Your brothers are there, along with Greg. The police should be there by now, too." He had no idea how long they'd been sitting there, but he wanted her to be prepared for flashing lights if emergency services arrived before they returned.

Veronica nodded her agreement and climbed off his lap before offering him a hand up. Zach took it but was careful to use his legs to hoist himself without pulling on her. "Here, you take my coat. You know I run hot, anyway." He didn't wait for her to respond before helping her fit her arms into the sleeves and zipping it up to her chin.

"I don't know which way it is," Veronica confessed.

"I do. It's okay." Zach hadn't even considered the possibility of Veronica getting turned around while running for her life, but it made sense. He held out his hand to her and waited until she entwined their fingers together before stepping back into the woods to make their way toward their cars. It might have been faster or easier to keep their hands to themselves, but Zachary needed the connection with her to reassure him she was there and alive. Hopefully, it would give her some reassurance as well.

# Chapter 21

Veronica was struggling to get her mind to keep up with the events of the evening. She'd felt so bad about everything with Zach, but his text and news about the baby alpaca was so happy. When she'd called him and accepted his invite to come stay the night with him again, she'd thought she was getting her happy ending. But then she was shot at, chased through the forest, and attacked.

Surviving felt amazing, but having killed a man, she fully expected her life to be over. It didn't seem to matter if she died on that rock ledge because she was lost or if she died in prison for being a killer. Then Zachary had appeared and wrapped her in his arms. Between the warmth of his body, the safety of his presence, and the loving caress of his words, she'd regained some clarity. The jury would understand it was self-defense.

When he reached out to clasp hands and kept ahold of her the entire hike back, she focused on his warmth and strength. Now, as the first pulses of red and blue illuminated the surrounding trees, she braced for the reality of being handcuffed and arrested while they worked through the investigation. Veronica shoved back the despair clutching at her chest and allowed her exhaustion to consume her. If she slept through most of her time in jail, it would be like it didn't happen. She'd wake up in time for them to tell her they knew she didn't want to kill Kurt and let her go back to Zach.

She was jostled as Zachary shook their clasped hands to pull her attention.

"How are you doing?" he asked.

How was she supposed to answer that? "I'm alive." That felt important even through her desire to sleep for the next millennia. "They'll have a bed, right?" Sleeping on a concrete bench would suck. Maybe she could deal with it if they gave her a pillow and blanket. If they didn't, it would feel just like the rock Zach had found her on.

"What?" Zach stopped and pulled her around to face him. "What do you mean? A bed where?"

Veronica looked around at the colorful lights bouncing off the trees and leaves around her. "When they arrest me. There will have to be a bed, right? Not just a hard bench?"

Zachary stepped close enough for her to smell his deodorant. Over the last week, she'd learned it was the only scented thing he wore. Even his shampoo didn't have anything more than a simple, clean smell. Now, his Old Spice deodorant smelled like comfort, safety, and home.

"Veronica, listen to me." He used his free hand to lift her chin until she was looking into his face. "They aren't going to arrest you."

"How do you know? Why wouldn't they?"

"He attacked you. He pulled over behind you and shot at you. What you did was self-defense."

It was sweet that he was trying to reassure her, but she knew real life was never that simple. "I know, but the sheriff here campaigned on not giving my family a free pass for anything." She fought back the tears clogging her throat again. If she was strong enough to face it all, maybe Zach would wait for her.

He must have heard the hiccup that slipped out. Zachary's lips brushed her forehead before the weight of his skull came to rest atop her head. "It's over now, and we're both okay. I'm not going to let them arrest you. We'll do whatever is necessary tonight but push as much back to tomorrow as possible. Then we'll go check on the newborn alpaca. You'll be amazed by the texture of their fur."

Thinking about the baby animal was exactly the distraction Veronica needed. Who knew when or if she'd ever get to see it, but she could dream about it. Focusing on that required more details, though. "Is it a boy or a girl?" she asked.

Her insides still quivered, but no more tears flowed. She shoved aside dehydration as a problem for later. Right now, Veronica wanted to speculate on the texture of baby alpaca fur and what they should name the new little one.

The hum Zachary emitted before responding sizzled through her like a live current resetting her body's rhythms. "It's a boy." His voice revealed his delight. "If he's even one tenth as obnoxious as Butthole, I'm selling him to the first person who expresses interest."

The way the threat faded into a chuckle assured Veronica neither of the male alpacas would be sold anytime soon. They may be cursed multiple times per day, but they were part of Zach's family. He'd care for them, protect them, and love them *because* of their unique brand of crazy. Maybe he could feel the same way about her.

"What are you thinking for a name?" If she did convince Zachary to keep her, she didn't want to be shouting something insane like *Dickwad* every time the new addition got into trouble. Yelling at Butthole was bad enough.

"Oh, no. You get to figure that out. Why do you think I want to introduce you tonight? I figure you might want time to think about it, and if you name him while he's still cute and sleepy from just being born, he's got a better shot at receiving a nice moniker."

The confident hope in his voice ignited the bile in Veronica's stomach. She wouldn't be meeting the little one tonight, but she could play along. Maybe it would even help. Letting her fingers tap and swirl on Zach's chest, she asked, "Do you really want me to name him?"

He sighed and shifted his hands to her shoulders to push her off his chest. Then he moved them up to cup her face as he bent forward enough to look her right in the eyes. "Veronica, I was kind of thinking he'd be as much yours as mine. It's still early, and a day like today is not the time to make big decisions, but I was hoping you would stay with me while everything gets sorted out. Then maybe you can stay even longer?"

Holy shit! Was he asking her to move in with him? And back on the emotional rollercoaster she went. Before she could freak out even more, she reminded herself that Zach was right about tonight not being a good time to make any big decisions and refocused on their newest alpaca. "Naming him's not too big a decision. Maybe we should call him Lucky? Or Monster? Oh, Nick is a good name for an alpaca, right?"

"Any of those are great, but we need to get home first."

Veronica didn't believe that was how the night would unfold but didn't have the heart to crush their dream. She'd face whatever came so she could get back to him. "Yeah," she agreed before taking Zach by the hand and moving both of them back toward the cars.

The first responders must have seen Zach's headlamp shining through the trees, because the two of them were met by an entire EMT crew before they made it beyond the tree line. A sheriff's SUV was parked half on the road and half on the pull-off, and a state trooper car was pulling up to the front of the parking area. Between all the vehicles connected to Veronica, in one way or another, and the first responders with their cars, ambulance, and firetruck, the extra-wide shoulder was jam-packed.

She tried to assure the EMTs that she was fine, but Zachary insisted they check her over. They cleaned some scrapes and scratches and applied a few band-aids before assuring her she'd be fine. Sheriff Carter had been hanging back, but he came over as soon as the EMT gave him space.

"Ms. Taylor," he rumbled.

"Sheriff." She couldn't bring herself to look at him. Fuck. She didn't want to be taken away. Just as the dam holding back more tears cracked, Zachary's arm wrapped around her shoulders and a different voice spoke up.

"Ms. Taylor, I'm Trooper Manion. I'm working with the Sheriff's Department and the Forestry Department on your case."

Sheriff Carter huffed, but Trooper Manion kept speaking. "It's obvious there was a chase and a struggle. We've got the gun and will check it for prints. We'll also need a statement from you, but given what we have so far–"

"–Is there a problem, Sheriff?" Zachary's interruption shocked Veronica into looking up at the men around her. Sheriff Carter was sneering at her.

Resting her hand on Zach's thigh and leaning into him even more, she was relieved when the trooper offered a kind smile before taking charge again.

"The Sheriff and his department are an important part of the team, but I'm coordinating the investigation. In fact," he turned to the man beside him, "you can go help search Kurt's car, Sheriff. I can see this kind of conversation isn't your favorite part of the job, and I'm happy to handle it for you."

Sheriff Carter's jaw clenched, and Veronica swore she heard him comment under his breath. But she couldn't tell what he said, and the State Trooper didn't seem bothered.

Once he'd stepped away, Trooper Manion continued, "I'll need to interview you first thing tomorrow, but we can do that at your house. I'll be there collecting evidence from the most recent break-in."

"We can be there at eight," Zach promised.

Veronica wanted to object to the early hour, but if it meant sleeping in a bed instead of a cell tonight, she'd get up early.

"Good. Ms. Taylor?" Trooper Manion waited until she looked up at him.

"Yes?"

"It's best to report home invasions immediately. I understand you're in an *interesting* situation." The way he glanced over his shoulder at Sheriff Carter made it clear he understood exactly what the *situation* was. Then he pulled a card from his pocket and held it out to her. "You can always file a report with State Troopers. It sounds like there was a second person involved who we haven't identified yet. Take my card. I expect to hear about anything else that happens the minute it happens."

His glare hammered home his order.

"Yes, sir," Veronica agreed.

"Good. I'll see you both in the morning at Veronica's address of record."

Zach answered for both of them, "Of course, and thank you."

Veronica held back her questions just long enough for Trooper Manion to be out of earshot. "What second guy?" she asked. Was it not over yet? She couldn't take much more.

"I saw two men at your house that night, remember?" Once she nodded, Zach continued, "The car is Kurt's, but they found a wire transfer receipt suggesting someone hired him to come after you. It makes it clear you were the one attacked, which is why Trooper Manion could overrule the Sheriff's demand to arrest you. You weren't kidding about him not liking your family, either."

"So, it wasn't a threat against the company?" Veronica remembered Kurt demanding to know where the drive was. "He was looking for something. Kurt wanted my purse, and when he caught me in the woods, he tried digging into my pockets while asking me about a drive. Why would Kurt want any of my work stuff, though?"

Zachary's arm tightened around her shoulders. "You're safe now. Hopefully we'll learn more in the morning after they've had a chance to search Kurt's home. Right now, I want to take you home and get to bed."

"Because you agreed we'd meet them at eight," Veronica grumbled. Now that she knew she wasn't being arrested, she could complain about the early hour. If getting attacked didn't earn the chance to sleep in, what did?

"I'll make you breakfast." Damn, Zach knew exactly how to bribe her.

"As in that stuffed French toast you've told me about but never made?" she checked.

Zachary's eyes rolled up as he thought. Veronica noticed he always looked to the sky for his answers, even though he ultimately ended up pulling them from his gut. "Yeah, I think I have everything to make it."

"Deal. You make me stuffed French toast, and I'll be ready to go before eight."

"Works for me. I hiked here to check the woods along the way. Any chance you'd be kind enough to give me a lift?" he asked.

Veronica shook her head. "I don't think me driving anyone anywhere is a great idea right now."

Zachary ran his fingers through her hair. "It has been a long day, hasn't it?"

"Yeah."

After a minute of just standing there together, Zach hollered across the pull-off, "Patrick, any chance you and Freddy can help us out? Could Freddy drive her and me to my place in her Jeep and then catch a ride back with you?"

Veronica couldn't see Patrick, but he must have nodded or something. Freddy appeared beside her and leaned in to ask, "Did you get a concussion?"

His hands were shoved as deep into the front pocket of his jeans as possible, and he was shifting his weight while staring at his shoes. It almost looked like he was worried about her.

"No. It's just been a long day. I only slept a couple of hours last night." No need to explain that she was oscillating between hysterical joy, complete numbness, and heart-wrenching despair.

"Hm. Smart not to drive, then," her younger brother agreed before turning his attention to Zachary.

"I would drive us," Zach explained, "but between helping Fluffy give birth and hiking a few miles after a long day of work, I'm toast.

Freddy gave him a side-eyed look and agreed sarcastically, "Right. You're too tired to drive. It has nothing to do with wanting to keep your hands all over my sister."

Zach just winked at Freddy, but Veronica could feel the way his hands and arms trembled every time he put his muscles to work.

Thinking about climbing into bed and curling up with Zach's arms holding her sounded like heaven.

"Do we need to check with anyone else or do anything before we go?" she asked.

Zach assured her they were good, but Freddy turned to Patrick to check. "You're good to come get me, right?"

He was huddled with the state trooper to look at the papers they'd found in Kurt's car. "I want to look through these papers for a few more minutes, but then I'll be right behind you."

Freddy huffed and yelled back, "I'm not sitting out in the cold waiting for your ass, so you better not be more than sixty seconds behind us."

While her brothers argued, Veronica leaned into Zachary and asked a question she should have asked when he first found her. She felt stupid for just now thinking of it.

"Zach?"

"Yeah?" He focused completely on her.

"Did anyone, um, I mean Kurt, do we know for sure? Has anyone checked the body or whatever?" She should have done that. Instead of sitting on the rock and crying about her own problems, she should have gone down and checked to see if he was already gone or just injured. Why had it taken her this long to even think about it?

Zach massaged the lobe of her ear between his index finger and thumb. "That's not our responsibility to worry about, Veronica. It's not *your* responsibility. Your job was to survive, and you did. My job was to find you, and I did."

"But are they just leaving him?" Even in death, the worst people didn't deserve to be abandoned in the cold wilderness overnight.

"No, the forest service is using an old access road to get to him from below, but they could tell right away that his neck was broken. There's nothing anyone could do for him, and his body is being recovered." Zachary's arm came around her shoulders, and he leaned into her to kiss the top of her head. "Please don't give him anymore of your care or concern. He doesn't deserve it."

She appreciated Zach's words, especially since he said them with kindness and compassion rather than anger. Veronica just didn't know if she could let it go that easily. She could try, though. Maybe sleep would help. Maybe returning to her ransacked home in the morning would help. For now, she nodded and turned back to where her brothers were arguing.

"Freddy," she shouted, "are we going?"

"Yeah. Get in," he barked before snarling a final threat at Patrick. "If it takes you more than three minutes to pull up behind me, I'm calling Mom."

Once she and Zachary were buckled into the back seat, with her in the center of the bench so Zach could keep his arm around her, he nuzzled her neck. "Your family is going to be fun, isn't it?" he asked softly enough for only her to hear.

"You haven't even met Gabe, Ophelia, or my parents," Veronica laughed.

Zachary groaned but smiled at her. "You'll let me hide behind you, right?"

"Do you really want to meet them?" Veronica genuinely asked.

"Well, unless you're planning to break up with me again," he glared at her without dropping his smile, "I figure meeting them is inevitable." Then he dropped all teasing and light-heartedness from his tone. "But you need to understand that if they undermine your confidence, belittle your intelligence or your work, or are disrespectful to you, I don't care how much you love them, I will put them in their place. You can stand up for yourself, or I'll do it for you, but there will be no more letting your brothers treat you like you're an idiot."

Zachary maintained eye contact with her until she nodded that she understood.

"Can you two not wait the last three minutes until you've got a room?" Freddy grumbled from the front seat. "At the very least, break it up long enough to let me know when we're getting close to your driveway."

Veronica was disappointed when Zachary pulled back enough to look out the window and update how far to his turn, but he placed a hand on her knee and traced an infinity symbol on her thigh the entire time he chatted with Freddy. It was reassuring. And relaxing. It had been such a long day. Veronica let her head fall to Zach's shoulder and pushed everything from her mind except for the feel of Zach beside her and the voices of the man she loved and the brother she'd grown up with.

By the time Freddy parked her Jeep in front of Zach's cabin, she was feeling relaxed and sleepy. If she were at her own home, she'd be walking in the door and collapsing directly onto the bed. Except that her house was trashed, and her bed had been shredded. Veronica frowned at the thought.

"What has you looking so disgruntled?" Zach asked as he released his seatbelt and opened the car door.

"I want to crawl into bed immediately, but I'm gross and need to shower." It was a corollary to the truth.

Zachary extended his hand to help her slide out of the Jeep as well, but before she cleared the door, he stopped her. "How about we share the shower to keep each other awake and make it go faster?"

She'd be happy to suds up Zach from head to toe, but only so he'd smell nice when she used his chest as her pillow. Veronica didn't have the energy for anything more, but how was she supposed to tell him that? She chewed on her lip and tried not to cry. Fuck, not feeling horny shouldn't cause tears. What was wrong with her?

"Are you about to cry again?" Zach didn't sound judgmental or annoyed, but his question just made Veronica more emotional.

"Damn, she really is tired," Freddy added.

In a firmer voice than he'd used with her, Zach asked, "Is there something I need to know?"

Patrick's headlights lit up the barn as he pulled in behind Veronica's Jeep.

"It's a fucking miracle," Freddy murmured before responding to Zach. "Not really, she just cries anytime she doesn't know what else to do. Like, I used her good make-up for a prank with my friends once, and she was so mad she went from screaming to crying in, like, two seconds. She also cried at the end of every day we spent at an amusement park like Busch Gardens. Mom and Dad always said it was because she was too tired to hide her feelings and her body got confused about how to express them right." Then he shrugged and climbed into Patrick's passenger seat.

By the time Zach turned back to her, Veronica had mostly stopped the flow of tears and was wiping her face. "I'm sorry. I'm a mess. I don't mean to be."

The furrow that appeared in Zach's brow surprised her. "Inside, bathroom, shower, now. I'm going to pass through the barn just long enough to check that Fluffy and the cria are good. I expect to find you stepping under the spray of hot water by the time I join you, and I will be joining you." He stared at her for a second before adding, "There will be no sex tonight, but I want to help get all the sticks and leaves out of your hair. I'll feel better when I can see for myself that none of your scrapes are too bad either. Then we'll tuck ourselves into bed together and sleep."

"Okay." It was so much more than that. His hands soothing her after this nightmare of a day sounded like heaven.

# Chapter 22

Zachary woke at his usual pre-dawn time, but the warm body beside him made it harder to remember why he needed to get up. Then, an image of the new cria flashed through his mind, and he remembered they were expected to meet sheriffs and state troopers at Veronica's house in a few hours. He tossed on clothes, set up the coffeepot, and got to work on his morning chores.

His phone assured him it wasn't even seven as he finished his rounds and stopped by to spend a few minutes with Fluffy and her baby. Some new moms were protective and would spit on anyone who got too close, but Fluffy didn't mind Zach joining them in the stall. She lifted her head and perked her ears when the barn door opened and closed but returned to eating when Veronica walked up to the stall.

"Morning," she greeted.

"I was going to wake you with stuffed French toast and coffee." Zachary flopped out his bottom lip in a false pout that made Veronica chuckle.

"I didn't get to see this little one last night and couldn't wait to meet him. Have you given him a name?"

"You can come in and pet him. Fluffy's pretty chill, just be sure the stall door latches behind you. I haven't named him yet. Part of me is terrified he's going to be just like Butthole. I'm not sure I can handle two of them."

Veronica joined them and ran her fingers through the newborn's fiber. "He's so soft." She looked at Zachary in awe.

"Yeah, it's incredible, isn't it?"

"I heard you had a rocky start," she cooed while rubbing his neck. "But that just means you'll be a strong as granite and as brave as an underdog boxer, huh?"

"Maybe that's what we should call him," Zach suggested.

"What?"

"Rocky. We could name him Rocky."

Veronica thought about it before turning back to the little guy and asking him, "Are you Rocky? Is that who you want to be? Strong and brave."

Aware of the time, Zachary stood up and dusted the straw from his knees. "Rocky it is. I'm going to go get cleaned up and make breakfast."

"Don't worry, Rocky. We'll come back and see you again later," Veronica whispered before turning to Fluffy. "You did good, Fluffy. You're going to be a great mom." Then she stood to follow Zach.

As he closed up the barn, he fought with himself trying to muster up the courage to ask what he needed to know. He didn't want to ask. It was too soon after everything last night, and they still didn't know why someone was coming after Veronica. Hell, with the evidence he'd been paid, they didn't even know *who* was behind it all. But Zach was all in with this woman. She held his heart in her hands, and if she planned to slide it up and down a cheese grater to season her life, he'd prefer to know sooner than later. He turned to face her and braced himself for rejection. "Does this mean you're staying for real?"

Veronica clasped her hand in his. "I'm scared I'll be too much, and you'll get tired of my long work hours and craziness. I don't keep a clean house and rarely have real groceries. I never think to do laundry until I'm completely out of underwear." It was a soft confession.

"What makes you think any of that matters to our relationship? I mean, except for the long work hours, which we'll talk about together and agree to set some healthy boundaries around."

"Me staying here would mean my mess being here in your space."

Zach turned to face her and used his knuckle to nudge her chin up so she'd look at him. "You still don't get it, do you?"

She shrugged.

"Feeling needed is what makes me happy. It's why I chose to farm alpacas. They are one of the most needy and particular animals out there. Knowing that they'll get parasites or become ill without devoted care and attention from me is what makes me feel… loved. Most farmers choose easier animals, so I feel special for being the one who's there for them."

"I'm not sure I like being compared to an animal, even though they're amazing." Veronica had stepped closer to him as he spoke.

Zachary needed to explain it in a different way. He wasn't sure how, but he'd keep trying until she understood. "I don't need someone to do laundry or clean or cook or any of that bullshit, Veronica. I've been taking care of myself for a long time now. I need someone whose life is better with me in it. I need to know that you eat better because I cook for you. Letting me pull you away from work to give your life some balance is what makes me happy. It makes me feel special. And it shows you trust me like no one else."

"That doesn't feel real. I mean, the world's come a long way, so I'd never be with a guy who expected me to be his housekeeper, but this almost feels like the opposite extreme."

"I suppose it kind of is," Zach allowed. "But isn't the whole point that it doesn't matter so long as the people involved are happy, respected, and getting their needs met?"

He watched her consider what he said.

"I have one condition," she proposed.

"What's that?"

"You have to promise to tell me when you want me to do something. Like if my laundry is on the floor, and you want me to put it in a basket or something, you can't just get mad or try to ignore it. You have to tell me." The way she sucked her bottom lip into her mouth and chewed on it had Zach doing the math to see if they had time to go back to bed before meeting everyone at her place.

They didn't, so he'd wait, but her request fit exactly the kind of relationship he dreamed of. "You know that goes both ways, right? I want us to have those conversations, too. But that means you have to promise to talk to me when you need extra time at work for a project or something."

"I can do that," Veronica agreed.

"Then I promise I'll always talk to you as soon as something feels off or I need something to change." Then he leaned down to seal it with a kiss that couldn't last nearly as long as he wanted it to. "We need to hurry, or we'll be late."

Veronica checked the time on her phone. "Yeah, can we have French toast later? I'd rather sit and enjoy it instead of shoveling it in as fast as possible."

"Sounds good to me. I'll shower while you get coffee and make two of something, so you can share with me."

"Uh, I'm not sure what. I don't know what you have or what you like."

Her panic was cute, but not what Zachary wanted. "Relax, I have bagels and cream cheese, or you could make eggs, or you can just pop a couple pieces of toast for us to butter. It doesn't need to be anything more than that."

"Do you like bagel, egg, and cheese sandwiches?" she asked.

"I love them." It was one of the things he'd had in mind but didn't want to overwhelm her by suggesting something she might consider complicated.

"I'll make one for each of us."

"Getting cleaned up shouldn't take more than fifteen or twenty minutes, and then I'll meet you in the kitchen." He kissed her once more before darting out of the barn to shower, put on clean clothes, and get ready for the day as fast as possible.

# Chapter 23

Veronica focused on the weight of Zach's hand at the small of her back as she braced herself to enter her home. The place that used to feel safe and welcome now felt like a trap waiting to fall shut and destroy her, but she wasn't alone anymore. The man standing beside her combined his strength with her own. Maybe he was right about them both being better for it.

"The place is clear," the state trooper assured her. He'd introduced himself the night before, but she didn't remember his name and asking for it would require admitting that.

"Thanks." She took one more deep breath and crossed the threshold.

"We just need a list of anything missing. The rest we can process for evidence, though it looks like you cleaned up the office. Did you touch anything in the kitchen?"

"No," she assured him.

"Make coffee?"

She thought back to what felt like a lifetime ago. "No, I took the trashcan to clean up in the office and then put it back out here. It had been laying down. I left it standing. I also grabbed one of the dining chairs and dragged it to my office." She didn't see it back out here by the table. "I think I probably left it in the office."

A deputy approached the trooper. "She did. There's a chair in there, along with a bunch of computer equipment and a futon that's been shredded. The closet looks like it stores a bunch of records. Can you tell us more about them?" He turned toward Veronica as he asked the last question.

"Oh, I keep my old tax returns in there. There's a box for each year of college with records of each class, and I think six of the boxes are Christmas decorations. One box is cards people send me. I never know what to do with them. Throwing them away feels like I don't care, so I keep them all." She leaned into Zach more to stop her rambling.

"But they're all the same banker's boxes?" the deputy checked.

"Yeah, we buy cases of them for the business. I bring some home when I need them." Her fear that they'd tell her that was wrong or bad must have shown on her face.

The trooper immediately jumped in. "We just need to know so we can help point out if there's something you say should be there, but it isn't."

"Okay," she agreed.

Zachary spoke up with his own questions then. "What about everything from last night? Have you learned anything more?"

"Kurt Wright was disturbingly taken with you, but it looks like his obsession just started a few months ago. He's got a hefty rap sheet, but it's all theft and mugging level stuff. The papers we found in his car, along with what we found in his home, make it clear he was hired to get information about Taylor Industries. We did track down the other man who'd come here with him. He's still being questioned, but I don't think he has much more to tell us. He said Kurt was bragging about getting paid to get revenge on you from high school but haven't found any information about who paid him yet."

"What will happen to his friend?" Zach's protective streak was weirdly comforting. It was nice knowing someone cared about her so much.

"He just moved to the area about two years ago and has no idea who Veronica is." Trooper Manion turned to her. "You can press charges for trespassing, but I can't promise it will do any good without evidence of him being here."

Zach gritted his teeth but softened his words when Veronica gently kissed his jawline. "That fucker needs to be locked up."

She slid a hand into one of his back pockets and cupped his ass to encourage him to play nice.

"Do I need to worry?" she asked the trooper.

He thought before answering. "I'd stay alert until we know who hired Kurt, but it looks like his connection to you from high school was the only personal aspect of the case. I've talked to Patrick about the threats against your company."

Trooper Manion sighed, and the exhaustion behind his professional mask peeked through.

Zach must have seen it too. "I'm sorry for my earlier comment," he offered. "But I need to know if Kurt's friend will go after Veronica as revenge for Kurt's death."

The trooper's surprise made Veronica wonder just how much bullshit the guy was used to dealing with. "No, I don't have any worries about that. The night you saw both of them was the only time he was involved. As they drove away, Kurt apparently rambled threats and nonsense that freaked him out. That was when Kurt made the comment about getting paid for revenge. His buddy hasn't seen or spoken to him since that night, and he wasn't heartbroken to hear Kurt died."

That was reassuring.

"Did you find any contacts on Kurt's phone?" Zach asked.

The trooper gave him a funny look. "That's the strange part. We can't find his phone. It wasn't on him, and we've searched where he and Veronica fought along with the rock ledge. We're guessing he chucked it away somewhere. Neither of you have seen any sign of it, have you?"

Zach tensed again beside and snapped, "No, we were both much more focused on ensuring Veronica was alive and okay."

She squeezed his butt again and pressed her full body weight against him. "It's okay, Zach. He's trying to help. How do you know he had a phone?" she asked.

"Most people do. When we don't find one, we reach out to cell carriers and ask if there's an account in the person's name. Wright had an account with Verizon and had just paid his bill two weeks ago."

Zach's jaw twitched. "What are we supposed to do from here?"

"We need to figure out if he accomplished whatever he was hired to do…" The apologetic look from the trooper didn't make Veronica feel better.

"He demanded I tell him where the drive was," she remembered.

"Do you know what he was talking about?" Trooper Manion asked.

"No, but we use thumb drives to store our work." The thought of picking through all the broken pieces of her home made sleeping in a jail cell sound peaceful.

Luckily, both Zachary and the trooper agreed.

"That's why we're asking you to take the time to sort through things today." Trooper Manion gave her a kind smile. "You don't need to worry about every broken dish or spoon, but if you could look at the business stuff and see if there are notes missing or if files have been messed with, it would help. We could also use any information you might have about someone accessing your system when they shouldn't or compromised passwords. Patrick said you'd be the one to ask."

Veronica looked at Zach and tried to figure out how to ask him how much she should share. He leaned down to whisper in her ear, "What's up, V? We can step outside to talk if you want."

She considered the uniforms digging through the heap of rubble most of her home had been reduced to. "Just don't be upset with me," she whispered back.

"I can't promise to feel or not feel anything, but I won't take it out on you." It was similar to what he'd told her before, and that had worked out okay.

Veronica turned back to the officer. "I was here Sunday night, but I couldn't sleep after finding all this." She gestured to the mess.

"I went into my office and started digging around to see if I could learn anything. We already thought everything was work related. There were no firewall breaches, nor did the system detect any abnormal access."

The trooper stopped her there. "Can you explain what you mean by that?"

"One of the ways we protect ourselves is by monitoring traffic patterns within our system to spot any anomalies. For example, my brother is a morning person, so his accounts are often accessed at five am. I'm a night owl, so activity in my accounts at one and two am is normal, but someone accessing one of them at six would be a red flag. Same thing if someone were in one of Patrick's accounts at two, since he can never stay awake much past midnight."

"Makes sense," the trooper agreed. "None of that happened, though?"

"Right. There were no anomalies. There was a huge uptick in visitors to our website a few months ago, but it was when the news was covering those astronauts being stuck and talking about how our technology was involved in bringing them home safe."

"So more site visitors would make sense," the trooper finished for her.

"Exactly."

"Gotcha. Are any of your thumb drives or hard drives missing?"

Veronica frowned. "I'm not sure." She was wearing the same pants as yesterday. Collecting some clothes and stuff like that was part of their plan for coming over here. Veronica had always hated carrying a purse, so she either used a backpack or her pockets for everything. With her house such a mess, she'd stuck her Monday folder on top of her laptop, shoved her thumb drive into her front pants pocket and left everything else in her office. Patrick had copied the drive to give the code to Wils, and she'd tucked her drive back into her pocket.

She looked up at Zach as she felt her pockets. "It should be in my pocket, but it's not. Do you think it fell out at your place?"

"No, I picked up the bedroom while I was getting ready and didn't see it anywhere. You went straight to sleep, so there are not many places it could be. Could it have fallen out in your Jeep?"

The trooper was giving them his full attention, now.

"I doubt it, but we can check," she offered, glad they'd driven her vehicle over here, so it was already parked outside.

An hour later, they admitted defeat, and the trooper put the thumb drive on the list of missing things. It was right below Kurt Wright's cell phone. Veronica was going to have to let Patrick know they had firewall configurations and some beta testing reports floating around the world somewhere. If they were lucky, the drive was destroyed by mud, rocks, and mother nature. If not... well, at least she didn't have any of their actual code on the drive.

"That's all we need from you for now. We'll call if we have additional questions. If you think of anything, here's my card. I really don't think you need to worry about your safety, Veronica, but don't hesitate to call me if anything happens or if you think of something that could be helpful."

Zach had already collected as much of her stuff from her room as possible, and the techs wouldn't let her touch her computer. "Let's go make that French toast," Zach suggested.

Without her thumb drive or her big computer, she didn't have much else to do. She could work on her laptop, but she'd need a new big screen at the very least. The deputy in her office told her it could be months before they released hers. "Yeah, that sounds good," she agreed without enthusiasm.

"We'll take it one step at a time, but you're safe now. That's the most important thing. You can keep using the TV as your big screen until we either get a new TV or replace your monitor." His hand traced reassuring circles on her back as he spoke.

"I love that you get my computer stuff is more important to me than stupid decorations or clothes or whatever."

"Of course. You good with me driving us back?" He already had the keys since he'd driven them there, but Veronica appreciated that he didn't assume.

"Yeah, let's go."

She'd fully intended to spend most of the day moping. It felt like she'd earned that, but when they pulled up to Zach's, there was another truck in his driveway.

"Damnit, I completely forgot about Doc Ester," he swore.

Veronica turned to look at him as a woman a few years older than him stepped out of the barn.

"I'm glad you get to meet her, but I wouldn't have sprung this on you today if I'd remembered. There was an emergency she had to take care of yesterday, so she's stopping by to look at Rocky this morning," he explained.

"Morning, Zachary," the vet called out.

"Good morning, Doc. Though, it's almost afternoon now. I'm so sorry I wasn't here."

"Don't worry about it. I've got an easy day today, and spending some time with your cria was just the cuteness I needed."

Veronica had gotten out of the Jeep at the same time as Zach and grabbed his hand as soon as she stepped up beside him. He introduced them, but she couldn't tell if Doc Ester's grin was welcoming or threatening. There was an unhinged quality to it that made her nervous.

"You're it, huh? You hurt this boy, and you'll have to deal with me," Doc threatened without dropping her smile.

"Doc! She was attacked and shot at last night. Plus, I'm not a boy. Please be nice." Zach's words wiped every wrinkle of distaste from the vet's face as her entire demeanor shifted.

"I'm so sorry. Zach's like a son to me. If you make him happy, I'm all for it."

"It's okay," Veronica didn't have the energy to argue. "What about the baby? Is he healthy?" she asked Doc Ester.

"He's perfect. Have you two named him?"

Zach grinned at Veronica while answering Doc, "Rocky. Veronica pointed out his rocky start and suggested he'll likely be strong and brave, so the name seemed appropriate."

"It certainly is," Doc Ester agreed. "I left the vaccines you'll need, along with my notes on the bench outside Fluffy and Rocky's stall. I'm going to head out. Give me a call with any questions."

"We will," Zach assured her before climbing into her truck and driving away with a wave.

Just as Veronica opened her mouth to suggest they get French toast going, her phone trilled with Patrick's ring tone. Her suggestion morphed into a groan as she answered. "What, Patrick?"

"Yeesh, you don't have to sound so grumpy. I was just calling to check that you were okay."

"Thank you, but I need to tell you my thumb drive is missing. The police know, but we have documents floating around somewhere," she braced herself for him to yell at her.

"Give Zach the phone," he said instead.

She handed it over without hesitation, but she still listened as they spoke. The volume was loud enough for her to hear both sides.

"She's staying with you?" Patrick asked.

"Yes, and I don't see that changing."

"Sometimes she doesn't like to sleep. It's okay for one night, but if it happens twice in a row, she gets emotional and has a hard time functioning."

"I don't expect that to be an issue going forward. She'll use PTO when she needs to put her health first."

"I need you to find out exactly what she had on that thumb drive. She's only supposed to have one drive with her at any time, but I know my sister well enough to ask you to check on that."

Zachary wrapped an arm around her to pull her into his side and asked, "Why are you talking to me instead of her, Patrick?"

The phone was silent long enough, Veronica wondered if her brother had hung up. "I don't want to yell at her. She could have died last night. She almost did. A guy shot at her. That's so much bigger than business, but if that information falls into the wrong hands or we don't handle it properly, it's not just our company at risk. Space Force and the US Navy both use that code."

"Uh huh," Zach acknowledged.

"Look, I need to do damage control this week. I don't have the time or energy to deal with Veronica, and I get that makes me an asshole. My choices are to be a dick to my sister or fuck over two branches of our military. You obviously love her and put her first, which she deserves. I'm talking to you with the hope you can maybe make me look less like a cold-hearted asshole while I deal with everything else. If nothing else, I'm talking to you because she should be able to focus on what she needs without worrying about the company right now, and I can't give her that. I know you can, and I believe you will."

"Fair enough, but I think she needs some time off."

Veronica poked Zachary's side. What was he saying? She never took time off.

He looked her in the eye as he continued speaking to Patrick, "She needs to set up her new office, get comfortable in her new home, and process everything that happened. We just had a new cria birth, too. Having a little extra time with him would also be good."

"What the fuck is a cria?" Patrick's patience was wearing thin. Veronica knew he progressed from talking to swearing to grunting and stuttering before he started throwing things and punching people, though she had to admit, he hadn't punched anyone in at least five years now.

"It's a baby alpaca, and you're welcome to come visit him too. It's impossible to stay angry with him around. I could bring him to your place to visit sometime if you'd like," Zach offered.

Veronica pictured her brother in his bespoke suit sitting on the floor with Rocky and had to cover her mouth to hide her laughter.

"Whatever, just tell her to be back at work next Monday for our Monday meetings. Oh, and get me that information about what was on the thumb drive sometime tomorrow. Now give the phone back to Veronica." Her brother was even bossier than her boyfriend. Boyfriend. Zach was her boyfriend. It sounded weird, but not in a bad way.

She took back the phone. "Yeah?"

"I'm glad you're alive." It wasn't what Veronica expected him to say.

"Thanks, Patrick."

He grunted. "Yeah, I gotta go deal with this mess now."

The call disconnected before she could say anything else.

"I think that was the nicest conversation I've had with my brother in years," she said to Zach.

"Good. He better be nice to you. Now let's go get food. I would suggest we eat it in bed, but syrup is messy." He frowned.

"Food first; then bed?"

"I'll cook fast."

Veronica laughed. Things were still a mess, but at least she'd be well fed and well loved. Having alpacas to pet and a serious incentive to go to bed at a reasonable time made the future look even brighter.

# Epilogue

## March 12, 2024

*A brutal roadside attack in Rockinghurst County has left one dead this morning as State Police work with local law enforcement to understand how a high school crush could go so wrong almost two decades later.*

I ground my teeth in disgust as I clicked off the news. That idiot. I should never have trusted him to get me that thumb drive. If I could get past TI's firewalls, I could pull their code and sell it. Taylor Industries would be destroyed, I'd get the life I deserved, and maybe I'd even find the proof I needed to reveal their murderous intent.

Instead, the dumbass became so enthralled with Veronica Taylor, he lost all sense and got himself killed. After he shared their history from high school and his embarrassment over being puked on, I thought for sure his desire for revenge would keep him focused on the real goal. Now I'm back to square one.

Thumping my head down on my table, I tried to compile a mental list of options for my next move. Before I could get far, my phone chimed with a new text.

Loverboy: I think I have what you're looking for.

Matchmaker: I find that hard to believe considering you're dead.

Loverboy: That's what happens when you hire a boy.

Matchmaker: Cut the bullshit. What is it you think you have?

Loverboy: A thumb drive. How much are you offering?

Matchmaker: This isn't about money, and I'm sure as hell not paying you for shit. Who is this?

Loverboy: We don't need to know each other for this to work for both of us. Everybody's got a dream. What's yours?

Matchmaker: For the world to know the truth while I live in peace.

Loverboy: Peace costs money, doesn't it?

Matchmaker: Oh, I fully intend to collect what I'm due. Just don't mistake it for my primary focus. The truth must come out.

Loverboy: What truth is it you think you know?

Matchmaker: Taylor Industries only exists because their founder is comfortable with murder.

Loverboy: I need to consider my options. I'll be in touch.

Who picked up Loverboy's phone and what really happened to Joshua Baker? Keep reading in Taylor Industries #2, Encrypted Hearts.

# Also by Maria

**Romantic Suspense Fiction**

## Taylor Industries:

Rural romantic suspense with international intrigue
Linked Hearts
Encrypted Hearts
Tracking Hearts
Guarded Hearts
Auditing Hearts
Hacking Hearts

## Twisted Willow:

Small town romantic suspense full of action & adventure
Gloria's Gumption
According to Cora
Beth's Absolution
Letting in Liz

## On-Trail Love Adventure:

Romantic suspense on the Appalachian Trail
Alongside Lucy
Standing by Stephanie
Crossing with Kiara

## Nonfiction

The Truly Successful Author
The Truly Successful Writer

# About the Author

*Selfie of the author in the wild.*

Follow me on Instagram for behind-the-scenes sneak peeks and hints at what's to come.

Subscribe to my newsletter to be the first to hear about new releases, get special discount offers, and access bonus material including Hailey's Heart for free!

Maria lives in the woods and loves hiking, reading, and writing. Her first completed work was a play about her family's crazy holiday adventures. It was written in pencil on wide-ruled paper. Maria was 8. Since then, she's worked in restaurants, gone to college, taught middle school, published some stuff, written scary amounts of online content, and hiked sections of the Appalachian Trail.

When she can't go enjoy an adventure, she writes one down on paper. They usually involve the woods and hot, loving men who support strong women. She's lucky enough to be married to a man willing to cook dinner and care for the dogs when Maria gets too sucked into the story in her head to remember the world around her.

# Connect with Me

Scan me to connect!

# Acknowledgements

Writing a book is hard. Publishing it is even harder. There's no way I could have done this without Angel, Mary, and LeAnn listening to me prattle on about imaginary events for months before I even started writing.

Susan Barnes has been a HUGE help with ensuring the story reads well and says everything I imagine in my head. Her editing, ideas, and support have made this story stronger!

Jasmine C. Caldwell is a critique partner unlike any other. Not only does she point out where things fall apart, she shares creative and awesome ideas about how to improve it. If you like my books, you may want to check out hers, too!

Elijah created custom characters for the cover and nailed them!

Carrie Anne is an unmatched proofreader. As an avid reader herself, she catches many of the typos the rest of us miss.

Despite all that these amazing people do, none of them are the key to my work as an author. That honor goes to you, Reader! YOU are the most valuable people for any author's career. **Thank you for reading Linked Hearts!** I'd love it if you clicked on some Amazon stars to help others find this book. You don't even need to write a review; a quick rating helps a lot. Click or scan this QR code using the camera on your phone to discover all the wonderful ways I LOVE connecting with readers (including access to a FREE short story):

9 781961 330115